Freder

An Ev

In the early 1800s, London was the largest city in Europe, with the population of well over one million people including many foreign-born citizens from the Continent and further afield.

Frederica had been born and brought up in the rural county of Herefordshire, close to the border with Wales, whereas Alver, the Marquis, had lived in London for most of his life, except when he was away at school and at university.

During the first year of their marriage, Alver introduces Frederica to the many interesting places and entertainments in London; those entertainments were all available in 1818 and 1819.

There are many (true) stories included in this novel, including:

the aristocrat who bet £3,000 on the speed of a raindrop;

the private zoo with a bad-tempered tiger;

why the first shopping arcade was built because of discarded oyster shells;

the mathematical genius who supported his family at the age of 13;

how a river was diverted to re-enact a famous battle;

how to illuminate thousands of lamps at the same time;

and why Lord Jersey never fought a duel to protect his wife's reputation.

Meanwhile, Frederica and Alver adjust to their new life together, during a very eventful year.

Books by Janet Aylmer

Darcy's Story

The new Illustrated Darcy's Story

Walking with Jane Austen through Bath to Widcombe & Lyncombe

Julia & the Master of Morancourt

Sophie's Salvation

Dialogue with Darcy

Frederica and Alver: An Eventful Year

Frederica and Alver

An Eventful Year

by

Janet Aylmer

Author of the bestselling "Darcy's Story"

Copperfield Books

First published in Great Britain in 2024
by Copperfield Books

Copyright © Janet Aylmer 2024

The right of Janet Aylmer to be identified
as the author of this work
has been asserted by her
in accordance with the
Copyright, Designs and Patents Act 1988.

This is a work of fiction, and
the members of the Merriville and Dauntry families
and their employees and associates are products of
the author's imagination, and their resemblance to
actual persons living or dead is purely coincidental.

All rights reserved.
No part of this publication may be reproduced,
stored in a retrieval system, or transmitted,
in any form or by any means, electronic, mechanical,
photocopying, recording or otherwise,
without the prior permission of the copyright owner.

ISBN 978-0-952-82107-6

A CIP catalogue record for this book is available
from the British Library.

For the Gang of Four

and with thanks to Miss Heyer

Chapter 1

The Marquis was generally agreed to be a paradox – an enigma. Named Vernon by his mother, but always called Alver by his father, he was an only son born after three elder sisters. Alver had been raised by servants, and he rarely saw his parents. His sisters often said that his wealth had allowed him to indulge himself without any restraint.

The Marquis soon became tired of being pursued by ambitious mothers, and of being bored by debutantes without a sensible idea in their heads. Instead, he patronised those 'barques of frailty' whose charms were for sale, as well as favouring some high-born ladies who were willing to stray from their marital beds. To his close friends, the Marquis was generous without wishing to be thanked, but that fact was not widely known.

In 1818, and still a bachelor at the age of 37, he had been approached by a distant relative, Frederica Merriville, who wanted her beautiful sister Charis to be introduced to the Ton. He agreed to arrange a come-out ball for reasons of his own, and his boredom soon vanished when he became involved in Frederica's life and the escapades of her brothers Jessamy and Felix.

The determination of her family to repay him for any outlay that he had made on their behalf was a refreshing change from the grasping attitudes of some of his own relatives. Frederica's lively sense of humour had never bored him, and the Marquis had eventually realised that life for him in the future without her by his side would not be worth living.

Happily, he had been able to persuade her to accept his offer of marriage.

At the Merrivilles' rented house in Upper Wimpole Street, the Marquis viewed the 12-year-old boy in front of him with a jaded cynicism, whilst reluctantly admiring his persistence.

"Felix, if you wish to accompany us to my country estate next week, your priority must be to make excellent progress in your studies with your tutor, Septimus Trevor. Your sister wants you to go to Eton in September, and the school will not accept you unless you can prove that you are an able and committed student. Isn't that right, Frederica?"

"Exactly so! Cousin Alverstoke is quite correct!"

To reinforce his remark, the Marquis added, "I shall certainly not be allowing you to use a workshop at Alver Park for your experiments if you do not work hard at your studies! You are a devilish brat, and only too practised in getting your own way. However, in this instance, young man, that is not going to happen, I can assure you."

Apparently, Felix had sufficient reason to think that the Marquis would carry out his threat. So he did not attempt to pursue the matter any further, and he followed his brother Jessamy out of the drawing room.

With peace restored, Alverstoke turned to the much more agreeable task of putting his arm around Frederica. He could not recall having ever felt so happy in his life, embracing the only woman who he had ever loved, and with their wedding to look forward very soon.

Then he realised that Frederica was laughing.

"What are you amused about, Frederica?"

"Do you realise, love, that you have your eyes shut?"

He thought about her remark. Then Alverstoke realised that she was correct. He opened his eyes and smiled at her.

"Why were you doing that? I have never seen you with your eyes shut."

"I suppose ... that I am just feeling so content being here with you, having you in my arms, and having so much to look forward to in my future with you."

Frederica squeezed his hands in hers and then kissed his cheek, to which he was quick to respond.

"Now, my dear, we have a great deal to do today. However much I would love to stay here 'cuddling' you, as your brother Felix would say, we really must make good use of the next few hours."

Frederica Merriville had never expected to become betrothed or to be married, so she had no idea what major changes her new status might make to her life. Until yesterday, she had been looking forward to the prospect of several weeks at leisure, staying at Alver Park with three of her siblings whilst Felix recovered from his rheumatic fever, with nothing to organise, and every opportunity to enjoy the countryside around.

Now it was quite unsettling, however personally delightful, to adjust to Lord Alverstoke being not only a trusted friend of her family, but also her own betrothed, with a wedding to plan. She would be changing from the prudent manager of her family and their finances to becoming the future partner of one of the wealthiest men in London society.

"Frederica, please fetch your pelisse and your hat, and come outside to my carriage. Curry is patiently waiting for us. First, we must go to Child's Bank in the Strand. I have my account there, and we need to arrange for separate facilities for you."

For a person who had never had the independent control of any personal money, Frederica viewed this prospect with some delight. Although she had been responsible for managing her family's estate in Herefordshire for more than five years, first on behalf of her father when he had been unwell, and then, after his death, on behalf of her eldest brother Harry until he reached his majority at 21, none of that money had been her own. Even now, she dealt with the finances for the Merriville family with the assistance of their lawyer Mr Salcombe, since Harry was not really interested in matters of detail.

"I suggest," he said, "that we leave the house before either Felix, or Jessamy, tries to distract us again. We have a great deal to arrange before we leave for Alver Park next week. What I intend", said Lord Alverstoke, "is to deposit a significant sum today in your new bank account, for you to buy gowns and any other personal items in advance of our wedding. What I will also do thereafter is to give you a monthly allowance - pin money - for your everyday needs. You may, of course, decide in the future to become involved in various charitable enterprises or interests. I will be very happy to discuss that, and I would make suitable extra payments."

Alver regarded her rather surprised expression with some amusement.

"What is the matter, my love? Do you see a problem?"

"No, not a problem. It is just that I have never had an account of my own, and that all sounds very generous. Are those arrangements normal for the wives of the peerage? I don't think that my mother ever had a personal monthly allowance. I know nothing about such matters."

"I care nothing for what other members of the Ton may do, Frederica. What matters is how we deal with money between the two of us."

Frederica lifted her hand to his cheek, and gently caressed it.

Alverstoke thought, not for the first time, what a lucky man he was to have Frederica in his life.

During the journey, Frederica turned to him and said, "What am I to call you, love? I cannot keep saying 'Cousin Alverstoke'."

"My father very much disliked the name Vernon. My mother had chosen to name me after her own father. Papa always called me 'Alver' – that was what my grandfather George had called him, as a 'diminutive' for Alverstoke. I should prefer you to call me 'Alver'."

"I would be happy to do that, love!"

"One topic that we must decide upon quite soon is where we are to be married. Have you ever been to St George's Church in Hanover Square?"

"Not to a wedding. But my sister Charis and I were walking in that area one day and came upon the church. We had been told that it is a very popular location for a fashionable wedding. So, we decided to go inside and look around."

"And what did you think?"

"The interior was simple and pleasing, but rather large. The Rector, a Mr Robert Hodgson, was walking down the nave and introduced himself to us. He apologised for not stopping to show us around the church, but he said he was on his way to a meeting."

"Some people call it the parish church of Mayfair, because so many residents of the area are married there. Is that what you would like to do, Frederica?"

She paused before answering him.

"Not really. I suppose that I would like a smaller occasion, with just family and close friends present. What is your preference, love?"

"I have no desire to provide an entertainment 'event' for members of the Ton. I agree with you, my dear. Since your brother's property in Herefordshire is let to Mr Porth for several months yet, why don't we consider using the local village church near Alver Park? We can visit that location together next week before making our final decision."

When they reached Child's Bank, Alver presented his card to the clerk at the entrance. They were rapidly transferred to a much more senior person, with a very deferential attitude towards the Marquis. Alver explained what he wanted to arrange for Frederica, and the senior person took them to an imposing office where the manager of the bank himself welcomed them, who was delighted to be introduced to the future Marchioness of Alverstoke.

No more than 15 minutes later, their business had been concluded, and they were conducted to the door of the bank by the manager himself.

"Do you always get such excellent service?" asked Frederica, mischievously. The sparkle of laughter in her eyes reminded him how much he loved Frederica's charm, wit and good humour, her common sense and independent mind.

"Why not? I have always had a large amount of money in my account with Child's Bank, and my father taught me to pay my bills on time. I am not one of those aristocrats who is seeking credit and is always in debt!"

Then he realised that she was teasing him and added, "Minx! In any case, I have a personal connection with Child's Bank, as my sister Eliza is a great friend of Lady Jersey. Sally Jersey inherited the bank from her grandfather Robert Child, and she is the senior and managing partner.

Now. we must drive to the City of London for you to meet Mr Muirhead, my lawyer. I hope that you will like him; he is not a dour Scotsman, as he has a very pleasant sense of humour. I can rely on him to tell me the truth about any situation, rather than to say what he thinks that I want to hear! You will need to give him the particulars for your lawyer, Mr Salcombe, for our marriage contract."

"What would those details be?" said Frederica.

Alver's eyes danced with amusement.

"It is normal to make provision for all the future children, and sometimes grandchildren, as well as to secure an income for you in the event of my death."

"That last point," said Frederica, "sounds rather serious."

"All of us, my dear, will die sooner or later. It is best to plan for the worst, and to hope for the best!"

Frederica favoured him with her sunniest smile, and her most wicked expression.

"You mean that I might one day become a wealthy widow after your demise, especially as you are so many years older than I am!"

"Exactly, my dear. However, I hope that unhappy prospect lies many years in the future, for both our sakes!"

The lawyer's office, rather similar in style to the one in Herefordshire where Frederica had often met her family's lawyer, was on the first floor of the building. The lawyer, a man of about 45 years with a strong Scottish accent, was introduced to her, with Alver disclosing the details of their betrothal.

"Miss Merriville, I am very delighted to meet you. May I offer you both my congratulations? When and where are you planning to marry?"

Alver answered for them both.

"Muirhead, we have already decided that we do not wish to be married at St George's Church in Hanover Square. Frederica's youngest brother, Felix, has been unwell, and we need to take him into the country next week to recuperate at Alver Park. Frederica's eldest brother, Harry, has let their family home in Herefordshire for 12 months, and that lease does not expire for some time. So, subject to Frederica's approval once she has seen the village church near Alver Park, we plan to marry there.

You will understand," continued Alver, "that we need to draft the terms of the marriage contract quickly, and send them to the Merriville's lawyer, Mr Salcombe, in Herefordshire. Can you do that for me today?"

"Of course, my lord," he said. "When are you leaving for Alver Park?"

"Next Wednesday morning, I hope, so any correspondence after Tuesday should be sent to us in Wiltshire. My secretary, Charles Trevor, will be coming down every few days to visit us there."

In the coach during their return journey, Alver said, "I should like to take you to my house in Berkeley Square, my dear, before returning you to your brothers in Upper Wimpole Street. There are several things that I need to discuss with my secretary, and you should be there. Will that be acceptable to you?"

Frederica regarded him with some amusement. "What would happen," she said, "if I replied No?"

Alver always delighted in her ability to challenge his habit of controlling his world.

"I suppose," he said smiling at her, "that I would need to persuade you. You are really saying that I am much too used to having my own way on everything? From now on, I expect you to challenge that on every conceivable opportunity!"

On arriving at Berkeley Square, they were greeted at the door by the butler.

Addressing the head of his household, Alver said, "We have good news for you, Wicken."

"Sir?"

"I am the most fortunate man alive, Wicken, for today Miss Merriville has agreed to become my wife!"

Wicken's normally imperturbable expression slowly changed to a wide smile before he replied, "That is wonderful news, Lord Alverstoke, Miss Merriville. May I congratulate both of you?"

Frederica walked forward and held out her hand to him. "That is very kind of you, Wicken. I look forward to our becoming much better acquainted."

Alver, regarding this exchange with some amusement, began to realise that, from now on, Frederica would be charming every one of his staff, and that he might well find himself being the second in line for their attention.

"Do you know where Charles is, Wicken?" he said.

"I believe that Mr Trevor has returned from his visit to Somerset House, and he is in his office going through today's correspondence to make it ready for your attention."

Frederica and Alver made their way to the room where the secretary was indeed busily occupied with a pile of papers. Alver confirmed their happy news, and he then explained to Mr Trevor where they had been during the afternoon.

"We all have a great deal to do before next Wednesday, Charles. Frederica will need to visit a modiste to order some new dresses. Hopefully, some can be completed before the end of Tuesday. Once we leave for Alver Park, you will probably need to travel to Wiltshire twice a week, to bring me any urgent correspondence, and return here with any instructions that I may wish you to carry out."

Charles Trevor, with his usual calm efficiency, took all this information in his stride, smiling at Frederica as he did so.

Alver continued, "We have opened an account at Child's Bank for Frederica. Then we went on to the City to introduce her to Muirhead, and to arrange for him to send the draft marriage contract to Mr Salcombe, the Merriville's lawyer in Herefordshire."

"It seems, sir, that you have left me very little to do!" said Charles.

"Don't worry," said Alver, "I shall soon think of something! Now, is there anything in that pile of papers that I need to attend to urgently, Charles, before I take Miss Merriville back to Upper Wimpole Street?"

"No, sir, everything can wait either until you return here later today or, if needs be, until tomorrow morning."

Then they walked together to the library, and Alver shut the door behind him before he turned to face her.

"I owe you a sincere apology, Frederica."

"For what?"

"For behaving like an entitled rake, a few hours ago!

You are a lady, who is entitled to be offered a formal proposal of marriage, not to be seized in a fierce embrace without any choice in the matter. Please will you allow me to propose to you properly, Frederica, on bended knee?"

He looked at her and was quiet for several moments. Then the Marquis knelt and gently took her hands in his.

"Miss Merriville, I have lived too many years of my life indulging my own preferences and pleasures. I am in serious need of someone who will challenge me at every turn, and who will laugh at me when I become insufferable. Will you marry me, my darling Frederica, if I promise to leave my rakish ways behind me?"

She looked down at him, smiling into his eyes.

"Yes, I will. Alver, please rise. I have grown to love you as you are, so please do not try to change too much!"

The Marquis rose to his feet and took Frederica into a long and fervent embrace.

Then he released her and walked across the library to a bookcase on the wall beside the window. There, he seemed to release a catch, for a section of the books swung forward, revealing the door to a small safe.

"Before my father died ten years ago, he asked me to share my mother's jewellery between my three sisters, Augusta, Louisa and Eliza. I asked Augusta to choose which pieces went to each of them. But my father had asked me to retain the items that had been worn by my paternal grandmother, Caroline. He wanted them to go to my future bride."

As he spoke, Alver unlocked the safe, and took out a metal box, which he carried across the room and put on the top of his desk. Then he opened it, and Frederica could see several items, each carefully wrapped in blue velvet. There was also a small red leather box, and Alver picked that up and opened the lid.

"This is my grandmother Caroline's betrothal ring, which she wore every day of her marriage to my grandfather George. I hope that you like it, and that you will want to wear the ring for me?"

As he held out the palm of his hand, she saw there an emerald ring, the very large central stone being surrounded by small diamonds mounted in gold, sparkling in the light from the window.

"Oh! Alver, what a absolutely beautiful ring! Of course, I would be delighted to wear that for you."

The Marquis slid the ring onto the third finger of her left hand, where it settled as though made for her.

They smiled at each other before he said, "Frederica, on Saturday evening I have been invited to attend a ball at my godfather's home in Mayfair. Lord Ormond was my father's best friend, and my second name – Edward – was chosen because of him. Edward's son, James, is two years younger than I am. He married Marietta five years ago, and he and his wife now have young children. If I ask Charles Trevor to send a note to Edward and Susan Ormond, are you willing to go with me to their ball? James and Marietta should be there."

"I should be delighted to meet them, Alver. Will the ball at the Ormond's' home be a very grand affair?"

"No, and not a very large guest list, I assume, but there will be some interesting people for you to meet, my dear. Why do you ask?"

"I need to know what dress I should choose to wear, Alver."

"Ah! Perhaps the dress that you used for the ball in my house, three months' ago now? The dress was a most charming design. I remember it fondly!"

"Very well, if that is what you would prefer." She paused, and then added, "Tell me, Alver, why you have never ever danced with me, either at your ball here, or anywhere else?"

He paused for several seconds, and then replied, "To begin with, I did not wish to be seen to favour either you or your sister at public events, since I had such a longstanding reputation as a rake. I was very careful to dance only with ladies with whom I was already acquainted. Then people began to notice that I was attending more balls and soirées when that had not been my usual habit. I began to realise that I was becoming very fond of you, of the way that you smiled and teased me, your care for your sister and brothers, and your refusal to be beholden to me for anything without allowing me to pay even small debts that I had incurred on your behalf."

"I knew that those of my friends who were in love with their wives could not conceal that fact when they were dancing with them. That is why I realised that I could not dance with you in public, because it would soon become obvious that I was not indifferent. Is that an adequate answer to your question?",

"I suppose so. How very flattering you are!"

"Frederica, would you like to dance with me now?"

"Here, in the library?"

"No, love, in the ballroom, if you will come with me?"

He took her across the hall, and then they walked along the corridor to the empty space, which she had not seen since the evening of the coming-out ball, some months ago.

"Miss Merriville, will you do me the honour of dancing the waltz with me?" He bowed, with a twinkle in his eyes.

She curtsied to him in response, smiling as she did so.

"Thank you, Lord Alverstoke, I should be delighted!"

Alver took her in his arms, carefully distanced in the correct manner, and they circled the large room several times, twirling at the corners, until they were both out of breath. By the time they stopped, she was very much closer to him than the correct distance.

Alver, observing this, said with amusement, "You can see what I mean! Shall we do that again?"

So they did.

At the end, Frederica observed, "We dance very well together!"

"Yes, indeed we do. I really must go tomorrow morning to get a special licence from Doctors' Commons."

"What, and where, is that?" said Frederica.

"Doctors' Commons is the office that issues special licences from the Archbishop of Canterbury, so that people can marry quickly. Their location is close to St Paul's Cathedral, just off the main route to the City of London. I do not want to ask you to anticipate our vows, and I can already see that I shall be very tempted to do so! Rather than wait three weeks for the banns to be called in church, I should like us to be married, perhaps a fortnight on Saturday, and probably at Alver Park."

The Marquis took his betrothed back into the entrance hall, and to the foot of the staircase. There, he turned to Wicken, who was expecting them to leave the house.

But Lord Alverstoke told his butler, "Wicken, I am going upstairs to show Miss Merriville the rooms on the first floor. Will you please ask Mrs Jones to be available in 15 minutes' time, ready to show Frederica the staff accommodation?"

Wicken sent Walter, one of the footmen, to find the housekeeper, and Alver took Frederica with him up the main staircase from the entrance hall.

"You will see here, to the right, the rooms that are for the use of the Marquis and his wife. At Alver Park, there is a long picture gallery that is used for exercise in inclement weather, and there are many family portraits there. But in Berkeley Square, we just have these two portraits of my parents that are here on the landing. To the left, along that corridor, are the bedrooms for guests. The nurseries on the floor level above were used by my sisters and by me when we were young children."

But he walked to the right along the corridor and opened the first door for them to enter the room.

"My mother died whilst I was still at school, so this room has not been used for the best part of 20 years. As you can see, whilst the space has been kept clean, it needs updating as far as the decorations are concerned. Frederica, what sleeping arrangements did your parents have at Graynard?"

"There were two principal bedrooms, one for my father and one for my mother. But, as a small child, I can only remember them using my father's room. I daresay that there may have been some occasions when my mother slept elsewhere. When I was tall enough, and able to turn their door handle, I could enter my father's room by myself - but I was always welcome, and I used to get into bed between them."

Alver smiled at her and then said: "You were fortunate in having parents who loved each other, and who shared a bed."

He hesitated, and then after a pause, he said: "I have always slept by myself. I have never woken in the morning in bed with anyone, but I would love to share my room with you, Frederica?"

"That would be my preference also, Alver."

"Now let me show you the other rooms here. There are two dressing rooms, one for each bedroom. After my father's death, I also installed a bathroom, to be shared between the two bedrooms, together with a new water system and boiler to provide hot water. That saves the maids endless work, as they used to have to carry hot water in buckets up the back stairs from the kitchen in the basement."

Frederica was impressed by the bathroom arrangements and said so.

"The arrangements at Graynard are not so sophisticated. My father was not interested in altering the house after my mother's death, or perhaps he did not have enough money to do so?"

Alver walked across the lobby from the bathroom and opened the door to his bedroom. Frederica's immediate impression was of a large, dark and formal space, with heavy curtains at the windows. There was a wide and imposing bed in dark mahogany, with a canopy above, and a wardrobe and a chest of drawers in the same wood. In addition to the door from the lobby, there was a second door to the dressing room.

"Tell me what you are thinking, Frederica?"

"This bedroom seems rather old fashioned to me, Alver, perhaps a little depressing. Is that the way that you like it?"

"Depressing? - I had never thought of the room that way but, if you don't like the decor, we will make changes."

"Perhaps if the wall colours were lighter, the general impression might be more attractive. And would you mind if we purchase a more interesting bed cover?"

Alver looked down at his betrothed with a wicked smile in his eyes. Clearly, he could safely hand over the control of the furnishings of his home to his darling Frederica once they were married.

"There will no time to make any changes before we leave for Alver Park next week, of course, but I would be grateful if you will consider your preferences when we return to London; then we can agree together what should be done."

Frederica smiled at him before they left the room via the lobby and returned along the corridor towards the landing at the top of the staircase. At the end, they found a middle-aged woman waiting for them.

"Frederica, this is our housekeeper. Mrs Jones, I would like to introduce my betrothed, Miss Merriville? We are to be married, probably at Alver Park, before the end of the month. I should be grateful if you would show her the rooms on the upper floor, including the nursery and the staff bedrooms.

Meanwhile, I will go and find Charles, Frederica, and ask him to contact the agency about finding you an abigail. There may be time for you to interview some candidates on Monday afternoon."

Mrs Jones invited Frederica to walk with her along the corridor to the far end, where they found a narrower staircase leading up to the second floor.

At the higher level, there were several staff rooms on each side of the corridor. Beyond, there was an upper landing and then there were a series of rooms which had clearly been used as nurseries and associated space.

The first room had a table and several large cupboards, with a window overlooking Berkeley Square, but was otherwise empty. Beyond, another nursery had a bed, and pleasant views from large windows at each end.

As they walked together, Mrs Jones explained that she had been with the family for many years, and she had known the Marquis since he was about 10 years old. Frederica was very tempted to inquire what kind of child he had been, but she decided that this might not be wise on the first day of their acquaintance.

However, she did ask the housekeeper about Alver's youngest sister Lady Eliza, explaining that they had already met. The housekeeper told her some entertaining stories about the lively girl that she had been before she had married Mr Kentmere and left London to live on his extensive estate in the Midlands. After that discussion, they returned to the ground floor, where they found the Marquis in the hall talking to Wicken.

"Charles Trevor is going to visit the staff agency later this afternoon, Frederica, to ask for a selection of ladies with experience as an abigail who can be available on Monday afternoon. He will ask the agency to send them here to be interviewed by you. Now I had better take you back to your home, where no doubt there will be many things that you may wish to do."

Chapter 2

After he had taken Frederica in his carriage back to Upper Wimpole Street, the Marquis returned home.

"Wicken, can I have a word with you in your room?"

"Of course, milord."

When they had reached the butler's room, and he had shut the door behind them, the Marquis said, "How long have we known each other, Wicken?"

"We first met when you were in your second year at Oxford, sir. I believe that your father introduced us when you returned at the end of the Michaelmas Term."

"What would he have thought about Miss Merriville, Wicken?"

The butler, with his long acquaintance with the Marquis, was confident enough to reply frankly.

"If I may venture to say so, sir, your father would have been really delighted that you have been able to persuade such a attractive and competent young lady to agree to marry you. He would have wanted you to have what he had never enjoyed – a happy marriage - with a lady who will not let you dominate her but can make you smile every day!"

"I hope that, over time, Frederica will transform me into a more thoughtful and kinder person. But I must warn you that both Jessamy and Felix Merriville will be living with us."

"Master Jessamy is always a serious and courteous young man, milord – very like his elder sister in manner, although perhaps not as outgoing as a person. As to young Felix, perhaps together everyone here can manage to keep him under control most of the time, although your secretary has told me that he may be going away to school in the autumn?"

On the following morning, Charis Merriville returned to Upper Wimpole Street from her overnight stay with Mrs Dauntry. The sisters greeted each other cautiously in the drawing room, Frederica taking her sister's overnight bag from her hand, and inviting Charis to sit beside her on the sofa.

"How is Lucretia Dauntry today, Charis?"

"She pressed me to stay longer with her in Green Street, but I told her that I needed to return to you, Frederica. She has had no recurrence of the spasms that troubled her after ... after Endymion left the house with Mr Trevor."

"Charles Trevor came here yesterday and explained to me, to Cousin Alverstoke and to his sister Lady Eliza what had happened at the St Clement Danes' church."

At this, Charis hesitated, and then said in a very small voice, "Were you very angry with me, Frederica?"

"I was much more annoyed with our brother Harry than with you, Charis – he should not have suggested that you should marry in secret, without giving me or Lord Alverstoke the opportunity to discuss the matter with you and Endymion. However, that is all 'water under the bridge' now. Has Mrs Dauntry withdrawn her opposition to the match? I had heard that she wanted her son to marry an heiress with a substantial dowry."

"His mother was completely taken aback when Endymion shouted at her – as I was. He was so angry and agitated, I thought that he might strike her! I have never seen him so upset. He said that, if she dared to utter one more word against me, he would never speak to her again as long as he lived!"

"What is his mother saying this morning, Charis?"

"Lucretia Dauntry has decided that I am her 'dear, sweet child' and, if Endymion wants to marry me, she will not stand in our way. Tell me, Frederica, will you still oppose the match?"

Her sister paused, and then said very slowly, "It was not my preference that you should marry Endymion. He is a very handsome and friendly man, but he does not have the greatest intellect in the world. I had greater hopes for you, but I have agreed with the Marquis that I will not oppose you marrying his cousin any longer.

Talking of marriage reminds me, I have some very good news for you," and she smiled at Charis.

"What good news is that? Tell me straight away, Frederica!"

"This will come as a big surprise – Lord Alverstoke and I are to marry, quite soon, and Jessamy and Felix will live with us, except of course when they wish to visit Harry at Graynard after the lease ends to Mr Porth."

Charis stared at her, and it took her several seconds to reply to her sister.

"Marry Cousin Alverstoke – but I had no idea that you liked him in that way, Frederica, or indeed that he was the marrying kind? Everyone has told me that, at 37, he is a confirmed rake!"

"Alver tells me that he thought that himself, but he found that he could not live happily without me!"

Her sister said, slowly and carefully, "Frederica, you are not marrying him because of his title, or because he is so very wealthy, are you?"

"No, I promise you that I am not! I am well aware of all his faults, but I do love him, Charis. I find that I can be really cross, and not quite comfortable, or at all happy, when he is not by my side. You don't object, do you?"

"No, of course not! I do find him quite daunting, but you and I are very different. I know that he has been very kind to our younger brothers, and that he was a great help to you when Felix had his accident with the balloon flight. Are you planning to marry in a church in London?"

"No, we have decided that we prefer to wed in the country. The Marquis is intending to persuade Lucretia Dauntry to travel down to Wiltshire to be my chaperone at Alver Park, and to bring you and both of her daughters with her until the wedding day. Alver will use the Dower House, and Endymion can stay there when he wants to visit you.

Lady Eliza Kentmere has suggested that, once we are married and have returned to London, your engagement should be announced in the Gazette. Alver and I can give a betrothal party for you and Endymion in Berkeley Square, and you can be married from Alverstoke House. Would you be happy with those arrangements, Charis?"

"Oh, Frederica, that would be wonderful! Yes, of course I would be delighted with that!"

The sisters embraced, and then Frederica brought Charis up to date with the rest of the family news, including Sir William Knighton's visit to see Felix, and the eminent doctor's positive verdict about their brother's recovery from his rheumatic fever that had been caused by the flight in the balloon.

On Friday, the announcement of Frederica's engagement to the Marquis was published in the Gazette. During the morning, Frederica went to Madame Franchot's establishment in Bruton Street, where the proprietor (having already read the Gazette) was delighted to be informed that her new client was that Miss Merriville.

All Frederica's measurements were quickly taken by two assistants before she ordered several dresses, including her wedding gown and associated garments. Frederica explained to Madame Franchot that she would be leaving London on Wednesday for Alver Park, so the modiste hoped that, on Monday morning, some of the dresses might be completed, and be ready for delivery to Berkeley Square.

Frederica explained that, once she had travelled to Wiltshire, the wedding dress and any other outstanding items should be delivered to the same London address, so that Charles Trevor could then transport them to Alver Park.

Frederica then went on to visit Miss Starke's premises in Conduit Street, where Charis had purchased some hats a few weeks' ago. It was soon clear that Miss Starke had also read the Gazette, for Miss Merriville was greeted with congratulations on her engagement to the Marquis before choosing several hats to take with her.

At Frederica's request, Alver had invited her eldest brother Harry to visit his home in Berkeley Square for a discussion before they left London.

Harry found the Marquis waiting for him in the library. He had been given no reason for the invitation, so his guest was somewhat relieved when Lord Alverstoke began by saying, "The main subject that I would like to discuss with you, Harry, is your two young brothers. But perhaps we should start our conversation with talking about Charis and Endymion."

Since Harry had been complicit in the attempted elopement of his younger sister and Alver's heir, he was not expecting that his host would take a positive view of the event. But he was in for a surprise.

"You will already know that Frederica would have preferred Charis to make a different match – but she has realised that it is much too late for that now. Charis is determined to marry Dauntry, and Endymion's mother, Lucretia, has been persuaded to take a favourable view of the alliance.

Mrs Dauntry has agreed to travel to my country estate in Wiltshire next week with her daughters Chloe and Diana and with Charis, to act as our chaperone until Frederica and I are married there in two weeks' time. Endymion will be travelling to Alver Park a few days later, so that we can discuss with him the plans for the betrothal to your younger sister. He can stay with me in the Dower House.

However, to return to Frederica's marriage with me, we both hope that you will be available to give her away at our wedding, which will probably take place in the church in the village near Alver Park."

"Of course, sir, that would not be a duty but a pleasure!"

"The main house at Alver Park will be full of guests, as my sister Lady Eliza and her family will be staying with us. I will secure a room for you at the local inn, and you will be able to dine with Frederica and the family at Alver Park."

Harry was happy to agree to these arrangements. He then reminded the Marquis that he had mentioned a discussion about Harry's brothers Jessamy and Felix.

"I assume that you would prefer Frederica to continue to care for the boys, especially until the lease of your house in Herefordshire to Mr. Porth comes to an end? Your accommodation in London is presumably too small to accommodate either Jessamy or Felix?"

"Yes indeed, sir, I should be very grateful if my brothers can live with you and Frederica until the end of the lease for Graynard. After that, in term time I shall be continuing my studies at the university in Oxford, but I hope that my brothers will want to visit me in Herefordshire in the holidays."

"Frederica and I intend that Felix will be able to go to school at Eton next term, with my sister Lady Eliza's younger son Tom. Her elder boy, Jack Kentmere, is already studying at the establishment."

The Marquis had no intention of allowing his future brother-in-law to pay for Felix attending the school in Windsor, but this was not the time to have an argument with Harry about that. So, the discussion moved on to the financial provisions being made for Frederica after her marriage, and Harry was pleased to know that the Merriville's family lawyer, Mr. Salcombe, would be involved in the negotiations.

"Mr. Salcombe is a dry old bachelor, sir, but I don't doubt that he will have a proper regard for all the matters that should be decided in Frederica's interests."

"Your sister and I will be inviting Mr. Salcombe to be a guest at our wedding. Frederica has told me that he has been of great use in assisting your family since your mother died, during your father's unfortunate illness, and since his death. We shall be booking a room for him to stay at the village inn."

Lord Alverstoke then brought the discussion to an end, and Harry was ushered by Wicken to the front door, and out into the Square.

On Saturday evening, the Marquis arrived at the rented house in Upper Wimpole Street to collect Frederica in his carriage. He left Curry tending the horses while he was greeted by Buddle, the butler, in the entrance hall, and then went upstairs to find Frederica in the drawing room on the first floor.

He walked across the room before putting one hand on her shoulder, as he bent his head and kissed her gently.

She smiled up at him as she said, "You are looking very fine in your evening dress, Alver. I must admit that I am feeling a little nervous at the prospect of meeting Lord and Lady Ormond and their friends."

"There is no need for your concern, my love. We may perhaps be the centre of attention, after the notice of our engagement in the paper yesterday, but hopefully all the interest in us this evening will be benevolent."

When they arrived at the Ormond's home in Mayfair, Frederica left her pelisse with one of the footmen in the spacious entrance hall. Alver put her hand firmly on his arm before they paused, and then entered the ballroom, ready for their names to be announced by the butler.

There were about 50 people already gathered together in the large space, which was decorated with beautiful floral arrangements around the walls. There was a low sound of conversation as the couple ahead of them were announced.

When the butler then said loudly "The Marquis of Alverstoke and Miss Merriville", there was a sudden hush and then, after a short pause, the entire company turned towards them and greeted them with enthusiastic applause.

"Good heavens!" said Alver quietly to his betrothed, "I have never in my life had such a reception! That must be especially for you, my dear!"

"Perhaps," she replied, "the greeting might be for both of us!", and they turned to meet their hosts.

Lady Ormond was a small lady, with beautifully dressed white hair. She smiled at Frederica and said, "That was quite a welcome for both of you! I have often wondered if this moment might never come for the Marquis! You are most welcome to our house, Miss Merriville – I am Susan. May I call you Frederica?"

"Of course, you may, milady. Thank you for inviting me."

Frederica then turned to greet her host, Lord Ormond, who seized her hands in his, saying "Miss Merriville – Frederica – I am Edward, and I am so delighted to meet you. I must admit that I had despaired of my godson ever finding a lady who was not daunted by his difficult reputation and capable of matching his quick mind!".

At this, Alver laughed and said, "Please do not dwell on my past sins, sir. I have assured my darling Frederica that I am now a fully reformed rake!" And he smiled down at her, with a twinkle in his eyes, as she laughed back at him.

They moved on to greet the other guests, everyone being curious to meet her. Frederica's emerald and diamond engagement ring was much admired, and she explained the history of the ring to those interested. Alver and Frederica had anticipated being asked questions about where and when they were to marry, and they had agreed to indicate that the details were yet to be settled.

Many people seemed to assume that they would be married at the church popular with society in London's Hanover Square, and they said nothing to contradict that. Others were curious about the location of Frederica's family property. She whispered to Alver quietly at one point that perhaps she should have had the information printed on cards, ready to be handed out to anyone inquiring!

"Are you finding all this rather tedious?" he said to her after yet another question.

"No, love, they are just interested, or at least curious. You must remember that I am a novelty to most of them," she paused, with a wicked expression in her eyes, "and of course you have been such a very well-known rake!"

Alver squeezed her hand in his, before moving them on to greet the next couple anxious to make their acquaintance.

Lord and Lady Ormond's son James and his wife Marietta were very agreeable people, well able to tease Lord Alverstoke about his newly betrothed status, and quick to threaten him with stories of his past misdemeanours should Frederica need assistance in holding her own in social circles. Marietta explained that, now James was taking over the management of the family's estate from his father, they were spending most of their time in the country. But they came to London regularly so that the two grandchildren could visit Lord and Lady Ormond, and she hoped that she could meet Frederica for lunch from time to time.

Afterwards, on the way back in the carriage to Upper Wimpole Street after the ball, Alver turned to her and said, "We have been neglecting practising kissing, my love – but this seems to be a very good opportunity!", and promptly did just that!

By the time Frederica emerged from a passionate and lengthy embrace, the vehicle had turned around the corner of the street, and she was almost home. Curry opened the carriage door for her to alight and wished her a peaceful night as Buddle opened the front door.

Alver thought it prudent to say his goodbyes on the doorstep and advised Frederica to have a quiet Sunday before he returned on Monday morning with the carriage to take her to Ludgate Hill, and then to Mayfair.

"Where," he announced, "It will be my intention to purchase some jewellery for you in Rundell and Bridge, or perhaps at Garrards, to match your betrothal ring!"

On Monday morning, what was notable at both locations was the instant attention that the arrival of the Marquis commanded. He had clearly been a purchaser at both shops in the past, although perhaps it was not wise to wonder who his purchases might have been intended for! Frederica was happier with the more restrained and sophisticated designs of the jewellery at Garrards, and she emerged from their premises in Mayfair having chosen a lovely emerald necklace, a matching tiara and a pair of emerald earbobs, each item with its own box with the Garrards' crest on the lid.

"I suppose," she observed, as they left to travel to the house in Berkeley Square, "that I am not permitted to enquire how much all this will cost?"

"Quite right, my love. That is not something that my wife will ever have to worry about. I shall take pleasure in purchasing many more items for you in the future, once I know more about what your preferences may be. I suggest that, once we get to Alverstoke House, we should have something to eat before the young ladies arrive from the staff agency who you will be interviewing for the post of abigail."

Charles Trevor had arranged for three candidates to be considered. All three abigails had had previous experience in the role and were available to start work at short notice. The third candidate, Emily Leonard, had been employed by a titled lady in London whose husband was shortly to become the Ambassador in Vienna. Although her employer had hoped to take Emily with her to Austria, she had preferred to remain nearer to her family in England, and Frederica decided that she was the best choice of the three applicants. Frederica liked her quiet calm manner and amiable sense of humour, and Emily could be available to travel to Alver Park on Wednesday.

Lucretia Dauntry was planning to make the journey to Wiltshire on the Tuesday, with her daughters Chloe and Diana, and her companion Miss Plumley, as well as Frederica's sister. Charis had been packing her bags and, by the time her sister returned to Upper Wimpole Street, Charis had already left and was safely installed at the house in Green Street, ready for the journey on the following day.

Frederica was kept busy on Tuesday, making sure that her elderly butler Buddle and her housekeeper Mrs Hudson were ready to leave for their well-earned extended holiday. Jessamy assisted her with the packing for her younger brothers, and she did her own bags, not sorry to leave behind the rather shabby rented house in Upper Wimpole Street.

Chapter 3

The Marquis left Berkeley Square in one of his travelling carriages early on Wednesday morning and collected Frederica and her brothers from the house in Upper Wimpole Street to travel to Alver Park. The new abigail was to travel in the carriage with Alver and Frederica.

He had only met Miss Leonard briefly on the Tuesday afternoon, when she had arrived with her possessions in a travelling case. She had been taken straight away to the bedroom which she would be occupying on the top floor of the house in Berkeley Square. Once she had settled into her accommodation, he had taken the opportunity to get to know her better, and asked about her previous employment, and where she had lived as a child.

She explained that she had not wanted to travel abroad, as all her family lived in London, and so she had declined the offer to go with her previous employer to live in Vienna. Her voice was calm and soothing, and she seemed to have a good sense of humour. Frederica had already decided that Emily would be discreet and supportive in the years ahead.

Frederica's brothers Jessamy and Felix were travelling in the second carriage with their tutor Septimus Trevor, and Alverstoke's valet, Knapp. It was a very long day's journey to Wiltshire for everyone, but they arrived safely at Alver Park in the early evening to find everything in good order.

Frederica had been looking forward very much to seeing the main house, and it did not disappoint. After passing through the handsome entrance gates between two lodges and entering the drive, they soon passed the Dower House set back from the drive on the right-hand side, and then continued over a bridge spanning a wide stream. There, the main house came into view, with the front entrance framed by tall columns. The walls had a white stucco finish, with the many windows shining in the late evening sunshine.

Beyond colourful formal gardens, the stream widened into a lake, with an attractive garden house on the far side. The stables were set to one side of the main property, with a spacious yard between the two buildings and, after they had all alighted from the carriages, Jessamy wasted no time in going to see the horses housed there.

Lucretia Dauntry was to act as chaperone in the main house at Alver Park, instead of Alverstoke's original choice of a widowed cousin, Mrs Osmington. Mrs Dauntry had arrived from town on the previous day with her daughters Chloe and Diana, together with Charis Merriville. With her companion Miss Plumley, they were already well settled into their accommodation.

Frederica was greeted in the hall by the housekeeper, Mrs Edwards, who seemed to be rather flustered. When his betrothed commented on that to Alver, he remarked quietly in reply, "That is the effect that dear Lucretia has on most people, my dear. No doubt she has been overcome by yet another of her spasms, and hopefully has already retired to her bedroom for the evening, to be fussed over by the unfortunate Miss Plumley!"

Alver was to sleep at the Dower House for the sake of propriety. That property had several bedrooms, and he would be sharing the building until the wedding day with his close friend Darcy Moreton and Lucrecia's son, Endymion, when they arrived in a few days' time and, during his short visits from London, with Alver's secretary, Charles Trevor.

Over the previous weekend, Alver had received an affirmative answer from his sister Eliza and her husband, John Kentmere to his suggestion that their family with their two sons and two daughters should travel in advance to arrive at Alver Park seven days before the wedding. The children would be company for Frederica's brothers, Jessamy and Felix, since Jack Kentmere and his younger brother Tom were of similar ages.

Even better, in her response Lady Eliza had suggested that, after the wedding day, young Felix Merriville might return with the Kentmere family to the Midlands for a two-week visit, leaving Alver and Frederica to enjoy a peaceful honeymoon at Alver Park without him!

Her middle brother and his tutor, Septimus Trevor, would be remaining at Alver Park, but they would be fully occupied with Jessamy's studies in preparation for entry to Oxford University, with riding out in the park, and fishing in the stream or the lake during their leisure hours. But Alver and Frederica were planning to take Jessamy with them when they travelled to collect Felix from the Kentmere's estate in the Shires.

In mid-morning on the day after they had arrived, Alver walked down the drive with Frederica to meet the rector at the church in the nearby village, so that they could discuss the arrangements for their wedding. The building was small, but well situated not far from the inn, and the stained glass windows were unusual, having beautiful depictions of flowers instead of portraits of saints in each one.

Having established that a special licence had been obtained by the Marquis from the Archbishop's office at Doctors' Commons, the cleric readily agreed that the wedding could take place on the Saturday morning, 10 days after their arrival.

As they walked back from the church through the village towards Alver Park, Frederica had a question. "Did your mother ever get personally involved with the people here?"

"No, not as far as I can recall, probably because she rarely visited Alver Park, preferring to spend all her time in London in our house in Berkeley Square. Why do you ask?"

"Before my mother died, I began to accompany her, when I would have been about 10 years old, when she visited local people in the village near our home, to take food or other items to families in need. After her death, I continued that practice. Would you object, Alver, if I began to visit local people for that purpose here in the village, to discover whether I can be of any use to them?"

"I cannot think of any reason why I should object to that, Frederica. My father had a rather diffident personality, but he spent a good part of every year here, and he was friendly with the rector at the local church. I suspect that he used to make donations quietly, so that no one knew anything about it, to pay for food, or perhaps for firewood in the wintertime, to help local people in need. I should be very happy to accompany you, love, should you decide to visit the local people. It would be a good idea for you to start anyway, perhaps before our wedding next week?"

Frederica had decided to explore the main house every day after breakfast, so that she could become familiar with the layout on each floor level. There were about 20 main bedrooms in the building, together with accommodation for the female staff on the top floor, and with bedrooms above the stables for the grooms and the footmen.

The main entertaining rooms were on the ground floor of the house with access from several corridors leading from the entrance hall. These included a very spacious library and two dining rooms. One of the dining rooms was smaller for family use, and the other one much larger with an extending table for entertaining. That room adjoined the ballroom, which was illuminated by several beautiful crystal chandeliers.

The two principal bedrooms for the marquis and his wife were on the east wing of the first floor; each had a private dressing room and a bathroom. Except for the nurseries, which were on the topmost floor level, the other bedrooms were in the west wing. All the bedrooms were in good order, with pleasant decorative features enhanced by long curtains at each window.

On the first floor, the main east wing was occupied by a long picture gallery used for exercise in bad weather, with windows on one side facing the many family portraits on the other. Alver had already shown her the portrait of his grandparents George and Caroline, with their elder son, Alver's father, aged about 5 years standing beside them.

Having had lunch after visiting the church, Alver drove Frederica in a gig through the park for a tour around the locality, ending at the junction with the main road towards Bath. They passed Septimus Trevor during their return journey, riding with her brother Jessamy across the fields.

"When we get back to the stables," Septimus told them, "We plan to go fishing in the stream to end the day. By then, we shall have more than earned our supper!"

On the Thursday morning, Alver asked Frederica to accompany him in his curricle around the park. To begin with, Alver drove the vehicle from the house along the drive but, after crossing the bridge over the stream, he turned the curricle to the left, onto a winding track which then climbed up the hill on the contour of the slope. Then they passed through an extensive area of woodland until they reached open farmland, where he stopped.

Frederica was silent to begin with. Then she asked him what the size of the estate was at Alver Park. When he told her, she exclaimed, "3000 acres! That is a very large area of land!"

"Perhaps we need to have a conversation about my inheritance, my love. When my father died 10 years ago, I inherited not only the house in Berkeley Square and the property here at Alver Park, but also several large estates in other counties that had come into the family through marriage, and some houses in central London. Alver Park and the London houses are entailed – that is to say, if I were to die tomorrow, my cousin Endymion Dauntry would inherit them.

I am aware how fortunate I am to be such a wealthy man. I manage my business affairs through my secretary Charles Trevor, my lawyer Muirhead, and my land agent, Coleford. There is a steward living at and managing each country estate on my behalf, and I try to visit all of them twice a year. One estate, Fairworthy, is ideally situated on the Devon/Dorset border, quite close to the sea. You may like to go there with me, as it is a very good place to reside for a week or two in the summer months.

As you will have seen, I keep several horses here at Alver Park, as well as in London. When I was at Harrow, I often used to come to Alver Park with my friend Darcy Moreton to visit my father during the school holidays; and Darcy would return the favour – his parents' estate is to the north of London."

"Does Darcy have any brothers or sisters?"

"Only one sister, who is much older than he is. She has been married for several years, and has children of her own, and Darcy is a very fond uncle."

"Darcy himself needs to be married– perhaps to a delightful widow with small daughters!"

"Perhaps – are you planning to become a matchmaker, Miss Merriville!"

"Why not – there are worse occupations, I'm sure! But to return to your inheritance, I suppose that I find all your wealth rather daunting. I would not want to become an over-proud member of the Ton, as you say that your mother had been."

"You should not worry about that, my darling. You have a very different personality from hers, including having the ability to laugh at yourself, not to mention me! Now, would you like to take the reins, and I can teach you how to drive my curricle?"

"May I – I should really like to learn? Jessamy told me about your journey chasing the balloon and Felix, on the way to Monk's Farm. He assured me that you are a capital driver!"

"I should be pleased to teach you – and perhaps I could take him out as well in the next ten days. He might like to learn. Jessamy is so competent with horses, and your brother Harry told me that he is a very skilled rider to hounds in Herefordshire."

"Jessamy would love to use the curricle, I'm sure!"

"Did you ever have a curricle at Graynard, my love?"

"There was a very old one housed in the stables but, by the time that I was old enough to want to learn, the condition of the vehicle was so bad that it was no longer useable."

Frederica took the reins from Alver, and she was soon taught the best way to control the horses.

Then she started another topic of conversation.

"What I often used to do, although only within the estate at Graynard, was to ride my horse astride. My sister Charis is a very clever needlewoman, and she made me a pair of loose trousers, which appear to be a skirt when I am walking. I used them to ride astride whenever I wanted to! It is so much more enjoyable than riding side-saddle. Do you have any idea how difficult that can be?"

"Tell me, my love."

"The side saddle must be tailored both to the horse and to the rider. First you need a man to lift you on and off the horse, otherwise you risk twisting the saddle, or hurting the horse, or both. There is the possibility that you can fall, either when you are stationary or riding along. Your riding habit can rise above the ankle, so some women sew ribbons into the hem to keep the skirt tail in place by tying the ribbons to their boots. However, if the ribbon wraps itself around the spur, or your foot slips in the stirrup, you can fall and be injured."

"Good heavens, Frederica! I had no idea about all those hazards. Do you have your loose trousers with you here at Alver Park?"

"Yes, I do."

"Then why not wear them next time we go riding together? I never told my mother, who strongly disapproved of ladies riding astride but, when my father once brought us here to Alver Park, my sister Eliza persuaded her governess to adapt a skirt for riding astride. Like you, she much preferred that to riding side-saddle."

"Now, let's go on a little further in the curricle to the top of the hill. There is a small wooden summerhouse there, with a large window on one side. When my grandparents were alive, they often used it as a place to pause, and to admire the view south over the countryside."

"I remember that my father became a much happier person after my mother died, whilst I was still at school. That was about a year after Eliza was married to John Kentmere. Papa went to London more often, and I began to know him much better. After my father died when I was 27, I decided to have both the Dower House and the inn here in the village refurbished."

"At about that time, I walked up here to look at George and Caroline's favourite location. There were marks on the wooden floor of the summerhouse where there had been a long sofa, though my father had presumably had that removed because it had become old and worn. I had the leaking roof of the summerhouse replaced, and the rest of the building made weathertight. Then everything was redecorated, as you will see when we get there."

After another two or three hundred yards, the track went round a bend, and there was the summerhouse, backed by tall trees on the north side. Alver helped her to alight from the curricle, and then he took a key out of his pocket and unlocked the door. Frederica walked inside, and then across the space to look at the view from the window. She turned to see the location on the floor where the sofa might have been.

"Would it be possible to choose a new sofa for this space when we return to London, Alver? This would be such a glorious place to look at the view?"

"I agree, my dear. I hope that we can visit Alver Park much more frequently in the future, and we should be able to spend many happy hours here together. We may decide to make some new routes laid out within the park so that we can drive a carriage to see other views from the higher ground. Now, we had better drive back to the stables, in case those rather dark clouds in the distance decide to bring some rain with them."

On the Friday morning, Frederica decided to have breakfast early. The night had been hot and humid, and she was looking forward to enjoying a cool glass of fruit juice before having something more substantial to eat. She found Felix already in the dining room, finishing what he described as "only a few small morsels", although the appearance of his plate indicated otherwise.

"Are you quite sure that you have had quite enough to eat, Felix?!"

"Don't worry," her brother told her, "Mrs Edwards has said that I can come back later on when I get hungry, and have more food, as a second breakfast!"

And he left the dining room before she could reply.

Frederica had just chosen what she wanted, and had taken her plate to the table, when the door opened, and Alver entered the room. She was surprised to see that he was not wearing either his jacket or his cravat.

Before she could question him, he smiled at her ruefully, and said, "I did not wait for Knapp to dress me today. It had been such a humid night that I woke very early. and decided that I would wear only a shirt and breeches to begin the day, and to put my jacket and cravat on later. Will you forgive me?"

Frederica decided to tease him. So, she rose from her seat and crossed the room to walk around her betrothed. She viewed him from every angle. Alver began to smile, as he realised that she was intending to provoke him.

"Well, Miss Merriville, does my appearance meet with your approval?"

"It is somewhat unconventional, I would say, sir – but I do like your new look!"

"Minx!" he exclaimed, and before she could protest and could get out of his reach, he swept her onto his knee and into a deep kiss.

Once she had been allowed to resume her seat, Alver filled his plate, and sat down beside her. Then she informed him that she had some grave news to impart.

Alarmed, he blurted out, "What is that?"

"I have discovered that Felix has persuaded your housekeeper that he needs two breakfasts to sustain him. I found him here when I came downstairs, consuming the first one. He told me that Mrs Edwards, presumably succumbing to one of his melting-eye expressions, had agreed that he could have a second breakfast later this morning."

"You will be pleased to know, my love, that words fail me on hearing that news!"

Frederica and Alver had quickly settled into the habit of taking a walk together every morning in the park.

The next day after breakfast, Frederica met Alver (now fully dressed) on the terrace in front of the house. He took her hand, and together they walked down the steep path and past the lake in front of the property. Then they continued up to the top of the first hill, where there was an extensive view of the countryside around in several directions.

Alver had seemed to Frederica to be rather tense and anxious, but she waited for him to talk until they had reached a wooden bench looking back towards the lake, where he suggested that they should sit down.

"Tell me, my dear," she said after a few minutes admiring the scenery, "what is it that is bothering you?"

Alver stretched out his long legs in front of him, and then seemed to contemplate his toes, hiding in his highly polished boots. Then he turned to look at her, smiling slowly. But he did not immediately answer her question.

"I have been remembering the last occasion when I walked up this path with my grandmother, Caroline, when I was about 15 years old.

My father had arrived unexpectedly at our London house in Berkeley Square during the school holidays, just before I had been intending to make a visit to the country estate of my close friend, Darcy Moreton. Instead, I found myself travelling with my father to

Alver Park, to see my grandparents. My father did not tell me during the journey, but my grandfather George was by that time gravely ill with a heart complaint, and he had been asking to see me. On our arrival, we went upstairs straight away to his bedroom.

My grandmother was sitting by his bedside, but she immediately rose to her feet, and invited me to take her place, so that I could talk to her husband. I could see that my grandfather was weak and tired, but he was very pleased to see me, and we had a brief but genial conversation.

Then my father said that he would stay in the room with grandfather. He asked me to take my grandmama outside into the park to get some fresh air, since she had spent most of her time in the past few weeks in the house caring for her husband. She walked with me up this path, and we sat together on the bench, admiring the view.

I soon noticed that she was twisting her emerald ring, the ring that you are wearing now, Frederica, back and forwards round her finger, as though she was very anxious about something.

Then, she said, 'Vernon, there is something that I must say to you privately whilst I have the opportunity. You already know that, because of your family's wealth and your social position, you cannot often rely on most people to tell you the truth. They may have other, less desirable, motives."

"George and I have been very fortunate in loving each other all these years and having had such a happy life together. But unfortunately, that has not been the case with your father and your mother."

"To attract him, Esther had pretended to be in love with my son, when all she really wanted was to enjoy his wealth and his social position in the Ton. Yes, I know that she has done her duty, and produced four healthy children, including you. But it is significant that she does not like to visit Alver Park, or to see either of us. Your mother much prefers the social scene in town, and attending balls and other events in London, often without your father."

"What I want to say to you now, is that you should be very careful indeed about what choices you make for your life in the future. There could be nothing worse than being married to someone who does not love you, or who does not share your interests."

"I do very much hope that one day you will meet and fall in love with a nice girl who feels the same about you. But please promise me that you will never, *never* allow yourself to be deceived as your father was. Above all, I want you to be happy, even if it may take many years for you to find the right person."

"At the time, as I told you, I was only 15 years old, and perhaps did not really understand what she was asking of me. But, of course, I did make that promise, if only to please her."

"And did you keep that promise, Alver?"

"Yes, my dearest Frederica. But she was correct. As soon as I left university, and joined the social life in town, I was pursued by matchmaking mamas and their daughters, who were interested only in my title and income, and not in me as a person. But it has taken me *so* long to find you. I have had so very many years seeking selfish pleasures in London to distract me – empty occupations that, in retrospect, meant very little to me"

And he seized her hands in his own, and kissed her fingertips as he smiled up at her.

After a pause, Frederica replied.

"I assume," she said carefully, "that you were aware that your parents had had a difficult marriage?"

"Yes; I was. They never wanted to be in the same location, or even in the same room. They spent much of their time in different houses, my mother in Berkeley Square, and my father here at Alver Park, so it was not difficult to conclude that there must be a serious problem. You may tell me that I have copied my mother's rather disdainful attitude towards other people, and her critical views of others in the Ton. And you would be right. My very tiresome sister

Louisa's personality is too like that of our mother, so you will know exactly what I mean."

"But I am also my father's son. He had learnt the hard way to be wary of how people present themselves, and I am unlikely to commit to anything unless I am very certain. But then I do keep my promises."

Frederica looked at him for a long time, and then she raised her hands to his face, and kissed him thoroughly, until it seemed to be wise to stop.

"Oh, my darling," Alver said, "I would be happy if you could kiss me like that all day!"

Frederica looked at him steadily, aware that he was still avoiding her initial question to him.

"Alver, what did I ask you to begin with?"

He looked at her ruefully, for to give her a true answer would going to be awkward.

"My darling, we must start as we mean to go on. Please be honest with me, Alver, even if I do not like what you have to say. Tell me what has been bothering you."

The Marquis had not spent many years as a gentleman in society without being aware that there were certain subjects which it was not appropriate to mention to a young unmarried lady, including your betrothed. But this was a moment to break that rule.

"Frederica, we have discussed before now the fact that neither of us has previously been in love. But you are aware that I have had a long career as 'a rake'. That was my way, I suppose, of filling time in my rather unhappy life, and indulging in physical pleasures that I could easily afford to pay for. I did so either with young ladies who wanted a price for their services - those 'barques of frailty' that you once referred to - or with married women whose husbands were indifferent to their wives sharing their favours with other men."

"I am not at all proud of how I used to behave. But I have absolutely no intention of continuing either practice, now that I have been fortunate enough to meet and fall in love with you."

Frederica looked at him steadily, before she said, "Mrs Parracombe was at the dinner before the ball in Berkeley Square that you held for your cousins Jane Buxted and Chloe Dauntry, and my sister Charis. Jane Buxted told me that Mrs Parracombe had been one of your 'flirts'?"

"Good God! Where did she get that information from? Presumably from her mother, my sister Louisa!"

"Was that true?"

"Yes, my love. It was true - that woman has the heart of a courtesan, and the manners of an alley cat! I am very interested to learn that Louisa discusses such matters with her eldest daughter!"

But Alver was aware that it behoved him to change the subject, to what was really concerning him.

"Tell me, Frederica, how old were you when your mother died?"

"I was about 12 years old. Why do you ask?"

The Marquis cleared his throat nervously -- something that she had never seen him do previously.

"I can remember Eliza telling me that there was something called the 'night-before' talk, which our mother had delivered to her on the evening before her wedding. My sister did not give me the full story, but I understand that Mama explained some details about what would be going to happen when Eliza and her John Kentmere went to bed together for the first time. Married friends of mine at my club, Whites, used sometimes to make a joke about such explanations, that their wives had told them about after the event."

"Your mother is no longer alive, so had you considered whether you would want someone else, perhaps Eliza, to explain anything to you? I guess that my sister will do the same for Caroline in due course, when her elder daughter has met someone who she wants to marry."

Frederica suddenly felt embarrassed, and close to being overcome by the giggles, as Alver looked at her with considerable anxiety visible on his face. She tried to compose herself before replying.

"That would be very helpful, Alver, but I would prefer you to ask your sister on my behalf! I hope that Eliza would not mind assisting me. Is that really all that has been bothering you?"

"Yes," he said gratefully, "that is exactly it, and please forgive me for raising the subject. Some people would consider me ill-mannered to discuss such matters with you at all but, as you say, we have agreed that we should start as we mean to go on. I hope that my grandmother, Caroline, is looking down on us with a smile on her face, especially as you are now wearing her beautiful ring on your finger."

He thought for a moment, and then added "Would you to do something for me? I should love to see you with your hair down."

Frederica smiled at him, and then moved her hands to take out her hair pins.

"Please let me do it for you, Frederica."

"Shall I hold the pins for you?"

"No need for that, my darling. I will put them in the pocket of my jacket."

She turned her back towards him, and Alver began to take out her hair pins, one by one, putting them in his pocket until her hair fell down loosely to her shoulders.

Alver drew a sharp breath, and then said, "Why don't women always wear their hair down? You look so lovely like that, Frederica, with your hair hanging free."

"It is the current fashion to put one's hair up, I suppose, love?"

He gazed at her for several seconds before he spoke.

"Until I met you, I had no idea how lonely I have felt throughout my life, and what a bad effect that must have had on my character and behaviour. Your family may have had money problems, but you and your siblings have always had each other for support since your mother's death."

"That's true, but I have also been quite lonely, with my siblings being so young, and our father's illness to contend with more recently. I owe a great debt to Mr Salcombe who showed me how to run our estate in Herefordshire, both before and after my father's death. Since I met you, and especially after my brother's accident with the balloon, you have supported me, and I have felt that I could always turn to you to answer any problem."

Alver smiled at her, running his fingers through her hair as he did so. Then he held her face between his hands, and kissed her very slowly and gently, not with the passion that he had used during the past few days.

"That is the answer, love – we need each other, and that is why I believe that our marriage will be a great success, as my grandmother Caroline had hoped. Now, we had better walk back to the house, as it must be nearly time for lunch. May I try to put those pins back in your hair? You do not have a mirror here to aid you."

She turned her back towards him again, and the Marquis made a good job of re-creating her hairstyle.

Alver rose to his feet and extended his hand to her before they walked back along the path to the house.

On the previous day, Curry had driven the travelling coach back to London. There, he had told Charles Trevor that they should make a very early start on the Friday for the return journey. They had left Berkeley Square at dawn and had arrived at Alver Park in mid-afternoon. The coach had paused at the Dower House, so that Mr Trevor could deposit his overnight bag, and Curry then took the coach up to the forecourt at Alver Park.

Alverstoke's secretary had been accompanied by Wicken, the butler, and by Cook, ready to look after all the people who would be staying at Alver Park before the wedding. Charles had brought with him the correspondence that needed urgent attention from the Marquis, and the coach had also carried two boxes for Miss Merriville that had been left with Wicken by her modiste, Mlle Franchot.

Wicken descended rather stiffly from the carriage, and advanced into the hall, where he was greeted by the housekeeper, Mrs Edwards. He went with her to find two servants to carry the boxes from the vehicle which were intended for Miss Merriville. Frederica and Alver had heard the carriage arrive, and both came down the main staircase from the long gallery to see who was there.

"Charles, Wicken, good to see you both, and Cook as well!" said the Marquis. "I presume, Charles, that the box contains all the correspondence that it is essential for me to deal with?"

"Exactly, sir," replied Mr Trevor.

Frederica had spied the two packages sent by her modiste, and followed the house boys as they carried the boxes upstairs to her room. With her abigail to assist her, she unpacked their contents until her bed was covered with sheets of tissue paper, and Emily exclaimed at the beautiful materials and embroidery on each dress as they were revealed. Mlle Franchot had also included the petticoats and other fine underwear that Frederica had selected.

On Frederica returning to the hall, Mr Wicken asked her to take a small package which he had been carrying in his pocket.

"What do you have there, Wicken?"

"Mlle Franchot said to tell you, Miss Merriville, that these are gloves – but unfortunately not the ones that you preferred. That pair had been reserved for another customer, but in this package are a pair that she hopes might be acceptable instead."

Frederica carefully opened the tissue paper wrapping, and exclaimed, "How clever she is – the pale cream colour is just right, and the pale green embroidery will match my dress!"

"What is in that parcel, Frederica?" the Marquis asked his beloved, as he walked across the hall towards her.

"I am sorry, Alver, but that must be one of the many secrets to be kept until our wedding day!"

Earlier that morning, Alver and Frederica had been completing the list of the guests to be invited to the wedding.

As well as Alver's sisters and their families, and Frederica's three brothers and sister, the list included Lord and Lady Ormond, their son James and his wife Marietta; Alver's good friends Darcy Moreton, Lord Petersham and Lord and Lady Jersey; Lucretia Dauntry with her son and two daughters, the Merriville's lawyer Mr Salcombe, and the brothers Charles and Septimus Trevor. That should leave enough space in the small church for the staff from Alver Park, and some of the villagers, to attend the ceremony.

"Charles Petersham will come alone, for his lady love, Maria, is an actress who would be disdained by my sister Jevington and her husband, not to mention the Jerseys!"

With the recent death in London of Frederica's uncle by marriage, Mr Scrabster, her aunt Seraphina Winsham had already made it clear that she would be declining any invitation to attend the wedding, as her priority must be to support her recently widowed sister Amelia. So, the list of people to be invited was complete, and was handed to Alver's secretary, Charles, to despatch the invitations as soon as he returned to London.

"I very much doubt," observed the Marquis, "whether my sister Louisa Buxted or any of her family will come – I am sure that they will find some prior engagement to prevent their attendance."

"That will probably be just as well," Frederica replied, not adding that she would be very pleased if that happened, as the Buxted family would not be likely to contribute to her enjoyment of the occasion.

Endymion Dauntry had arrived from London in the middle of the day, unable to keep away from Charis Merriville any longer. Having left his bags at the Dower House, he walked swiftly up the drive to surprise her. His mother Lucretia, though nominally the chaperone for all the young ladies, seemed to be more concerned with her own health, and was spending most of each day in the large conservatory overlooking the formal gardens, tended by her faithful companion Miss Plumley.

Endymion and Charis took advantage of her indifference to meet each other elsewhere in the house. More quietly, Charles Trevor was taking the opportunity to renew his interest in Endymion's sister, Chloe Dauntry.

On the Saturday afternoon, John and Eliza Kentmere arrived from their estate in the Midlands with their four children and the governess, not to mention a considerable quantity of baggage in the third coach.

Frederica was pleased to meet John Kentmere, and she discovered that he was very good company and had an excellent sense of humour. Alver had told her that his brother-in-law was a very wealthy landowner with a large estate, but he showed no sense of entitlement and had a calm and sensible personality, ruling his lively brood of children with a benevolent but firm hand. It was also easy to see that there was a very happy relationship between Kentmere and his wife Lady Eliza.

Their elder daughter Caroline was already 16 years old and due to have her 'come-out' in London next season. She soon became friendly with her cousins Chloe and Diana Dauntry, as well as with Jessamy Merriville, and she was keen to question Chloe and Charis Merriville about what her London 'come-out' would involve.

Her older brother Jack was at school at Eton, and her younger brother Tom was due to start there in the autumn. Jack Kentmere and Jessamy Merriville were almost exactly the same age, and Septimus Trevor soon included Jack in their riding and fishing expeditions.

Tom Kentmere was rather wary, to begin with, about the experiments by Felix Merriville that kept him busy in the outbuilding beyond the stables that the Marquis had permitted Frederica's brother to use. However, once his father John Kentmere had visited Felix there, and established that his second son was unlikely to come to too much harm, Tom and Felix disappeared together for hours, only returning to the house for their meals.

Their governess was able to keep the younger daughter, Mary, fully occupied for most of the time, but Frederica had introduced Emily Leonard to the young woman, so that her abigail could keep her mistress informed about their various activities.

Frederica had received a letter from her eldest brother, Harry, to say that he had accepted a kind offer from Alver's friend Darcy Moreton to travel in his coach from London to Alver Park before the wedding day. They arrived late in the afternoon, three days before the wedding, and were greeted by Frederica at the front door.

Darcy shook her hand warmly, and her brother Harry gave his sister a warm embrace.

"Let me offer you both some refreshments in the drawing room. Alver is out in the park riding with Jessamy and his nephew Jack Kentmere, but they should be back here soon. Then Harry can settle into the inn in the village and, as it is about to rain, Curry can use the coach to take you there."

"How are you, Frederica? Is my friend looking after you properly?"

"Yes indeed, Darcy, he is trying hard to forget having ever been a rake, and he is learning to become part of a couple! I have noticed that Alver seems to be much happier and more relaxed here in the country. He has been showing me how to drive his curricle on the paths within the park. Did you and Harry have a good journey from town? And how are your parents?"

"Yes, the journey was uneventful. My father is very well, thank you, Frederica. It is my mother's health that is causing our family some concern these days, and I shall be calling in to see my parents for a few days on my way back to town."

After the refreshments had been brought into the drawing room on a tray, and consumed by the new arrivals, Alver with the two boys joined the company, having returned to the stables just in time to escape a heavy rain shower.

"Where is Felix, Frederica?" asked Harry.

"He is probably about to blow something up in another of his experiments, Harry!" replied Alver, smiling at Frederica as he spoke to her brother across the room.

"Alver has kindly allowed Felix to use one of the outbuildings here. He and Tom Kentmere, one of Alver's nephews, spend happy hours in a shed there every day, making loud noises and constructing we know not what!"

"That is most generous of you, sir, as my brother Felix has been known to create real havoc at Graynard with his experiments, given any opportunity!"

The days before the wedding passed by quickly, with the guests keeping themselves busy with various country pursuits. The last guest expected to arrive in advance was Mr Salcombe, who was due to arrive on Thursday, two days before the wedding.

Chapter 4

Lord Alverstoke had asked to be informed when Mr Salcombe had arrived from Herefordshire at the local inn, where arrangements had been made to accommodate him. When the message came, as it was raining quite heavily that afternoon, Alver went down to the village in his carriage, to invite the Merrivilles' lawyer to join the family for dinner at Alver Park.

Mr Salcombe's rather limited acquaintance with members of the aristocracy had led him to expect that the Marquis would probably be tall, and his manner rather distant. However, although his host certainly was well over 6 feet in height, he was courteous and welcoming to the newcomer.

During the journey back to the house, Lord Alverstoke had a question for his guest.

"Tell me, Salcombe, how long have you known the Merriville family?"

"I followed my father into the law, sir, and he had advised Edmund Merriville, then the owner of the estate, for many years. James was the elder son and therefore due to inherit the property, so Edmund made plans for Frederick to marry the heiress of another family living in Herefordshire, so that he would be financially secure."

"However, through mutual friends, Frederick met Harriet Winsham, a very beautiful girl – but she only had a small dowry. He fell headlong in love with the young lady, who was from a respectable local family. Frederick had a very persuasive manner, which his son Felix has inherited, and he persuaded Harriet to elope with him to Gretna Green, as they were both too young to marry in England without their parents' consent. Frederica was born nine months later, just after her father reached his majority."

"Edmund Merriville was absolutely furious about his careful plans being thwarted, and he refused to have anything more to do with his younger son, or his new family. But some years later, both Edmund and James died of typhus, about the time that Harry was born, and so Frederick Merriville became the owner of the Graynard estate."

After these disclosures, Mr Salcombe asked if he could mention something to his host.

"I don't know whether you already know, sir, that Frederica – Miss Merriville – has been the person managing the Graynard estate for more than 5 years, ever since her father was first taken ill? Even before that unfortunate event, her father spent most of his time in London after his wife died, so Frederica had begun to help me to keep the property running smoothly on a very limited budget."

"Her elder brother Harry has not taken any real interest in managing Graynard since he achieved his majority; he has preferred his life at Oxford University and, as his father did, in visiting London. Their personalities were very similar, although mercifully Harry does not seem to take any interest in gambling. His brother Jessamy is only 16, of course, but recently he has started to assist Frederica with the estate. He really enjoys living in the countryside."

"I particularly want to ask you, once you are married, to make good use of the knowledge that Frederica has gained over quite a long period. It would be a great pity if her experience were to be wasted. I appreciate that it is very unusual for a woman to help manage an estate, unless she is a sole heiress, and sometimes not even then. Please forgive me if I am being too forward in making the suggestion."

"Do not apologise, Salcombe. The idea had not occurred to me – but you are quite correct, and I shall be happy to ask Frederica to help me. I was telling her, a few days ago, that I own Fairworthy, a large estate on the border of Devon with Dorset and quite near the sea, where we may visit soon. Perhaps I could hand over the management of that property to her?"

"That sounds an excellent idea, Lord Alverstoke. Thank you for listening to me."

"You might be able to do me a favour, Salcombe. My heir, Endymion Dauntry, who you will meet this evening, is the owner of a small property in Buckinghamshire. There has been no formal announcement yet, but he plans to marry Frederica's sister, Charis Merriville, later this year."

"I intend to purchase more land in that county for him, so that Endymion has a sufficient income to support a wife, but Dauntry's steward Mr Taylor is close to retirement. He would not be capable of taking on any extra responsibilities. So I will be looking to find a much younger man, who is at present the steward of a smaller estate, or an assistant wanting to take on a bigger task. Should you hear of such an individual anywhere in Herefordshire, I should be very grateful if you could write to me in London?"

"Of course, sir, I will make some enquiries once I return home, and then I will let you know if I hear about a suitable person."

"Thank you. I understand that you have not been married, Salcombe?"

"No, sir. I was an only child and needed to care for my elderly widowed mother for some years. By the time she died, I was almost in my fifties, and rather too old to impose my fixed habits on a wife. But, if I had been fortunate enough to have a daughter, I would have hoped that she would have been as delightful, and as competent, as Frederica Merriville."

"I doubt whether most of her siblings realise how much she has done for them since their mother's death. You will know that Seraphina Winsham moved to live at Graynard after her sister's early demise, and she did provide some stability for the household, especially as Frederick Merriville often took himself off to London, gambling away his inheritance. He rarely returned to the estate at Graynard until his illness. By the time Frederica was 15, she was making a valuable contribution to running the estate."

"From my conversations with her brother Jessamy, I believe that he at least knows what she has done."

"Yes, he is a good-humoured, thoughtful boy. Personally, I would be sorry to see him enter the church as his profession. He has very considerable academic abilities, which would be much better used in a different occupation,"

"I am happy to agree with you about that, Salcombe, and I hope to widen Jessamy's horizons as we become better acquainted."

Mr Salcombe had been favourably impressed by his host's informal manner. He was perhaps expecting Alver Park to be only a little grander than the Merrivilles' home at Graynard. However, as the coach crossed the bridge on the drive over the stream, and the large extent of the building came into sight, he saw the tall columns framing the entrance doorway, and realised that Alver Park was a much more imposing structure with a long front facade three storeys high.

He had been looking forward to meeting the other family members, and they were all very welcoming towards him. What he had not expected was to be given the place of honour at the dinner table next to Frederica, with John Kentmere on her other side, who had been introduced as the husband of the former Lady Eliza Dauntry.

Lady Eliza was seated at the other end of the dining table, next to her brother the Marquis. On his other side was a well-preserved beauty, Lucretia Dauntry, who Frederica explained was the mother of Alverstoke's heir, Endymion. She also told him that the gentleman next to Mrs Dauntry was a very good friend of the Marquis, Mr Darcy Moreton. Sitting along each side of the long dining table were the younger members of the families, with Endymion Dauntry next to Charis Merriville, and her brothers Harry and Jessamy, Caroline and Jack Kentmere, and Endymion's younger sisters Chloe and Diana.

Mr Salcombe was relieved to see that Felix was not present, as the youngest Merriville had had his supper earlier in the evening with the other Kentmere children and their governess. Whilst Salcombe admired his enterprising character, his experience was that the presence of Felix did not make for a peaceful meal!

The lively conversations between the young people revealed that several of them had been busy creating wedding decorations for the ballroom and other spaces in the house. However, these tasks had not been completed, in part because some of the materials would be arriving on the following day from London with Charles Trevor, the secretary to the Marquis.

Towards the end of the meal, Alverstoke rose to his feet to offer a toast to his future bride, and to welcome the visitors who had joined the family for the meal. Darcy Moreton then spoke in reply, telling his audience several lively anecdotes from his schooldays at Harrow with Alverstoke many years ago, including playing cricket in the annual match against Eton at Lords, and later during their years together at the University of Oxford. These stories caused considerable merriment amongst the younger members of the family.

Darcy Moreton then resumed his seat, exchanging smiles as he did so with the Marquis.

As the conversations continued around the dining table, Alver stood up and walked quietly to the other end, to put his arm around Frederica. As she looked up at him with a question in her eyes, he tapped a wine glass with a spoon to attract attention.

"I should mention that I have a special surprise for you, and I have not told Frederica anything about what I have organised for tomorrow evening. As the dining table will have been moved by that time to the side of this room, ready for the wedding meal on Saturday, we shall all be enjoying a buffet supper followed by …," and there he paused for a few moments, tightening his grip on Frederica's arm as he did so, "… a family party with music provided by the same musicians who will be playing for us on Saturday.

I have every intention of dancing more than one waltz with Frederica tomorrow night. For those of you who are already familiar with the steps of the various dances, this will be an opportunity to improve. For the younger members of the family, and anyone who has not danced for a long time, you will be able to practice your steps."

Then he smiled down on her, and she smiled at him in return. "What a lovely surprise!" she said to him quietly.

Then she spoke more loudly to Mr Salcombe, "When did you last dance, sir?"

"So many years ago that I cannot remember when it was, Frederica – but I am very willing to try, if Lord Alverstoke intends to invite me to your party?"

"Of course, Salcombe, you will be most welcome!"

After dinner, Mr Salcombe thanked Frederica, and then walked across the dining room to speak to Jessamy Merriville, and be introduced to his new friend, Jack Kentmere.

"It is very good to see you again, Jessamy. How are you enjoying your visit to Alver Park?"

"Jack and I both prefer Wiltshire to London, sir. I am studying each day with my tutor, Septimus, getting ready to take the entrance examinations to enter Oxford University next year. But then there is time to go fishing with Jack in the stream and the lake. Have you ever done any fly-fishing, Mr Salcombe?"

"As it happens, I have, when my late father gave me a set of rods and took me to the River Wye in our home county of Herefordshire, to learn how to cast a fly. I became quite competent at the skill, but that was many years ago now!"

"Why don't you come with us tomorrow morning? Jack and I will be going fishing with Mr Trevor for a couple of hours, and I'm sure that we can find you a set of rods to use."

Mr Salcombe promised to return to the house at the appointed time, to discover whether he could still cast a fly and catch a fish (or two).

Charles Trevor arrived early on the Friday afternoon, carrying a large box containing all the items that Charis had asked him to purchase from the fascinating shop in the Pantheon Bazaar.

Her elder sister's request to view the contents of the box was firmly declined, and Alver was asked to take Frederica on an extended walk in the park to keep her out of the way. Meanwhile, the four young ladies were to complete the decorations for the evening's entertainments.

"Which way are we going today, Alver?"

"I am going to take you to the Sculpture Avenue."

"What is that?"

"Well, you may be interested in the story of how it came about".

"Philip Dauntry, my great grandfather, went on the Grand Tour, as did many other young aristocrats at that time. With his tutor, he travelled to France, Switzerland and Italy and, as well as becoming acquainted with the art and architecture, I have been told that he took the various opportunities available to meet and enjoy the favours of several young ladies in different countries. Like other young men, my grandfather bought paintings and statues in Venice and in Rome. In due course, Philip and his tutor returned to England, and he went to live in London, and developed quite a reputation as a 'rake'."

"Then he met his future wife, Jane, a very beautiful but rather prim and proper young lady; she was the heiress to the Fairworthy estate in the West Country. Perhaps there is something in the saying that 'opposites attract'? They married within a few months of meeting, and my grandfather George was born within a year. Some of the statues that Philip had purchased when he was abroad for Alver Park were wearing few, if any, clothes, and his new wife decided to have them moved out of sight of the house, to this Sculpture Avenue. You may have already noticed that the statues that are visible from the house have been chosen for their more decorous appearance!"

"Then tragedy struck. A second son was born, but he did not survive, and his mother Jane died within 2 weeks of puerperal fever.

At the time, it was said that the infection killed between 20 and 25 per cent of all mothers who gave birth. Strangely enough, Philip never remarried, so perhaps it had really been a genuine love match?"

"Are there any paintings of Philip and his wife?"

"No, none, the only portrait that we have is of Philip and his tutor. That was painted before they left for the Continent on the Grand Tour, perhaps in case he did not survive the journey!"

"How pessimistic! Why is that the only picture? I would have thought that Philip and Jane would have wanted one of them together?"

"Perhaps they were going to wait until their children were older, so that they could be included. But, with her dying so young, that never happened."

After they had been walking away from the house for about 200 yards, Alver had turned left, and Frederica saw the Avenue ahead of them – a wide grass path with statues on plinths evenly spaced on each side. The ladies and gentlemen – gods and goddesses – were indeed wearing few, if any, clothes.

"Are you shocked, Miss Merriville?" Alver asked her, with a twinkle in his eyes.

"No, I am not, for all the statues are beautifully carved."

"When I was very young, my grandmother Caroline used to bring me here, and I asked her once why there were so many statues here. Her answer was that, after dark, and when all the humans had gone to bed, the statues came alive and danced together!"

"Why are there no cherubs in the Sculpture Avenue? I always enjoy cherubs because they usually look so happy!"

"I don't know the answer to that question. But I could commission a sculptor to create some cherubs for you, or we could purchase some Italian cherubs in London, if that is what you would like to see here."

Alver paused, and looked at her thoughtfully for a moment, before saying, "Frederica, we have not yet had any conversation about children. My sisters have often criticised me because I haven't taken any interest in their sons or daughters, and they are quite correct. Perhaps that was because I was brought up as such a solitary child, with only my tutor for company until I went to school at Harrow. It wasn't until I met Jessamy and Felix that I realised that children could be very interesting and enjoyable people to be with."

"Some couples want to have children, but that doesn't happen, Alver. I have really enjoyed being part of a large family, and I would be very sorry if I am not able to have children of my own."

He took her hand in his own.

"That reminds me that you went out this morning riding in the park with my sister Eliza. Am I allowed to ask whether she has given you the 'night before' talk?"

Frederica laughed at him before replying, "Yes, she has - and it was very interesting. Whether it was accurate, I will tell you on Sunday morning, should you wish to ask me! Now, we had better continue our walk, as Charis told me not to return to the house within two hours."

Meanwhile, her sister was in the conservatory with Chloe, Diana and Caroline, busy unpacking the box from the Pantheon Bazaar. Charis had ordered a considerable length of stylish French grey and pale green striped ribbon, several rosettes in each colour, and a bolt of soft grey fabric for creating swags, to be pinned to the sides of the tablecloths in the dining room. The young ladies applied themselves with enthusiasm to their tasks and, after nearly two hours, had finished the decorations, and fixed them firmly to the tablecloths.

When Frederica returned to the house with Alver, she was told in no uncertain terms that she should not enter the formal dining room, but that she should join the young ladies for refreshments elsewhere. Meanwhile, Alver had walked down to visit the village inn to see Harry Merriville and Mr Salcombe, who had eaten a meal with Endymion and Darcy Moreton earlier in the day.

That evening, all the young ladies' hard work was on display when the family members and their visitors gathered in the formal dining room for the buffet supper, before moving on to the ballroom for the dancing to begin.

Frederica was delighted with the decorations that the young ladies had made. "How clever of you, Charis, to choose colours to match the wedding dress that I shall be wearing tomorrow!"

At the Dower House, the four men sleeping there before the wedding had agreed that they would have their breakfast in the dining room at eight o'clock wearing only their informal attire – shirts and breeches - leaving their waistcoats and jackets ready in their rooms to put on before Curry arrived with the carriage just before ten thirty.

It had been raining overnight, but the weather was beginning to improve as they began their meal.

"That was a very pleasant party last night, sir," said Charles Trevor as he sat down to eat, "and the children and the young people staying in the main house really enjoyed the dancing after supper."

"Well, that was certainly my intention," replied his employer, "and it was a good way for everyone there to become better acquainted."

"Mr Salcombe is a very sensible man," said Darcy Moreton. "I had a conversation with him during the evening, and he has a very high opinion of Frederica, for the way that she had managed the Graynard estate during her father's illness, and then after her eldest brother left to go to university."

Endymion Dauntry was not a loquacious person, but he then joined in the conversation. "You have not been to Graynard, sir, as Charis tells me that the house is still let to Mr Porth for a few months?"

"No, I haven't had the opportunity," said Lord Alverstoke "but, once the lease is up, Frederica will hope to take me to see the estate in Herefordshire". Once the meal was over, they all went upstairs to finish getting dressed for the wedding.

Darcy was ready first, and he made his way to his friend's bedroom door and knocked.

"Come in – Ah, Darcy, I am nearly ready. Thank you, Knapp, that will be all for now."

"Are you nervous, Ver?"

"Interesting that you should ask that, my friend. I am a little anxious, but I cannot tell you the reason why. Frederica is not someone who would call off the wedding at the last minute, we are only a few minutes' drive here from the church, and what else could go wrong?"

"It amuses me that, six months ago, you did not know that Frederica or any of her siblings even existed!"

"That's quite true, and I cannot tell you how very precious she has become to me over the past few months."

"I will promise you one thing, Ver. If you are ever unfaithful to Frederica, I shall kill you, and not suffer any remorse for doing so!"

"That will not happen, Darcy. My empty and thoughtless years are over. One day, I hope that Cupid's darts will find you as well."

Knapp knocked on the bedroom door, to say that Curry had arrived with the carriage, ready to drive them to the village before returning to the main house to collect Frederica and her brother Harry, and within a few minutes they were entering the church and walking up the aisle to their seats.

When Frederica awoke, it had taken her a few moments to remember where she was. Then she recollected that the room with the pale green wallpaper and the gold patterned curtains was that used by the Marchioness at Alver Park. After 10 days in the house, she had quite forgotten the shabby bedroom in the house in Upper Wimpole Street, and she had become accustomed to her new surroundings.

Then Frederica remembered this was her wedding day - and before noon she would be married. Soon, she pressed the bell on the wall beside her, and summoned her abigail, Emily, to bring her breakfast. She had decided last night that she would not go down to the dining room, but to have the meal in the privacy of her bedroom.

Looking at the betrothal ring on the third finger of her left hand reminded her that this had been the bedroom used by Alver's grandmother, Caroline, many years ago, who had worn the same ring for the whole of her married life. Frederica hoped to wear the emerald ring herself for a long time.

It took Emily about 15 minutes to appear in the doorway carrying the breakfast tray.

"Good morning, Miss Merriville," she said. "Unfortunately, it has been rather wet this morning, but I hope that the weather will be better in time for your wedding?"

"Yes, indeed, but there is nothing much that anyone can do to influence the weather today, or on any other day."

Having put the tray on the table by the fireplace, Emily went to the window and pulled back the curtains, so that her mistress could see the weather, and the view over the gardens.

"Will you have your breakfast in bed, Miss Merriville, or would you prefer to come and sit at the table?"

"At the table would be best, Emily, if you can bring me my dressing gown?"

Frederica wondered whether she was feeling hungry but, once she began to eat, she enjoyed her meal, and then asked Emily to run the water for her bath. The warm water was comforting on a rather dismal morning, and she did not hurry to get out and dry herself.

Frederica went to the window to see whether the rain was still falling, and it seemed to be easing. She wondered what the Marquis was doing this morning at the Dower House. She delighted in his lively sense of humour, his entertaining conversation, and - despite his protestations - his unfailing support when life had been very difficult for her during the illness of her brother Felix. Her betrothed was not good at allowing himself to be thanked for his better qualities, but that was something that she must try to change, once they were married.

She moved to the window again to look out; a little sunshine was beginning to appear in the sky, and it had stopped raining at last.

A knock at the door proved to be her brother Jessamy, come to enquire how she was, and to wish her well.

"You will not be surprised to hear that Felix has gone to do some experiments with Tom Kentmere in the outbuilding that the Marquis has said he could use. I suppose that he is better occupied there than making a nuisance of himself somewhere in the house!"

"I agree, Jessamy, I would always prefer to know what Felix is doing, rather than having to worry about it. Have you had your breakfast?"

"Yes, thank you. Septimus has said that we are not going to have time for any studying this morning. Is there anything that you need me for? If not, I will go and find him now."

His sister assured him that she had no special requests, and smiled at him as he left the room. What a contrast there was between the two younger brothers in both their personalities and their interests.

Emily had already walked down to the Dower House, to leave Frederica's bag with clothes for the following morning, but now the abigail was back, to help Frederica to get dressed in her gown, ready for the wedding. Then she sat in the chair in front of the mirror whilst Emily carefully pinned her hair in the style which they had agreed.

Wicken knocked on the bedroom door, to tell Frederica that her brother Harry was waiting for her below in the entrance hall, and that Curry had arrived with the carriage outside the house.

"You had better leave me now, Emily. The gardener will be waiting to take you to the church in the gig."

When she had closed the door, Frederica took a deep breath, and then crossed the bedroom and walked out to go down the staircase to join her brother.

"You look very lovely in that dress, Frederica, and I like your bouquet of lilies of the valley. I am just practising with this event today, for I will have the same duty to perform at the wedding between Charis and Endymion!"

"That will be a much grander affair than this, Harry, if Lucretia Dauntry has anything to do with it! I would have liked to be married in our village church near Graynard but, in any case, Alver and I prefer to have a quieter ceremony."

At the front of the church, the Marquis sat with Darcy Moreton beside him. The sun was now shining, showing the stained glass windows to their best advantage, and they could hear the sound of the carriage coming to a halt outside. Then the bride and her brother entered through the open doors, and the rector asked the congregation to rise as the organist began to play.

Lord Alverstoke turned his head to look down the aisle. Frederica was wearing a pale green silk dress with an embroidered border of white flowers and green leaves at the neck, and around the lower part of the skirt. She was wearing the emerald necklace and ear bobs from Garrards that he had given to her, and her white net veil, scattered with small pearls, was held in place with a simple embroidered hair band to match the gown.

Beside him, Darcy Moreton drew in a sharp breath and whispered, "Frederica looks absolutely wonderful!"

In her hands, the bride was carrying a bouquet of lilies of the valley with their white flowers and green leaves. When she reached the Marquis, she handed the flowers to her sister Charis in the opposite pew, and then turned to look up at him as he smiled at her and took her hand in his.

The music ceased, and the rector began the service with the familiar words, "Dearly beloved, …."

Before they both knew it, the service was over, the register had been signed and witnessed, and they were walking back down the aisle together, with their families and friends smiling as they left the church. The sun was shining as they got into the carriage and, as Curry told the horses to walk on, a cacophony of sound began. Someone (perhaps Felix with Tom Kentmere) must have been busy attaching metal cups and cutlery to the underside of the vehicle.

As the open carriage drew away from the church, Frederica began to laugh because of the noise, and Alver did the same. Once the vehicle was out of the sight of the congregation, he took her in his arms and kissed her soundly. "I cannot embrace you properly if they can see us, my love. Thank you, darling, for wearing your hair long at the back, just as I like it! You hinted at the colour that you had chosen for your gown, so I was able to choose an appropriate waistcoat."

"The embroidery is magnificent, Alver! Is that waistcoat new?"

"Yes, I must admit that I saw it in Weston's shop, and I hoped that you might approve of my choice. I believe that we should commission an artist to paint a portrait, so that we can both remember our wedding finery. Shall we do that, Frederica?"

"Why not? That is an excellent idea."

By some means or other, Wicken had contrived to return from the church before them, and he was waiting outside the front doors of the house. Most of the guests walked back to Alver Park in the sunshine for the reception, where the bride and groom were ready to greet them in the entrance hall.

Augusta Jevington and her husband came by coach, and were first in line, followed by their daughter and their son Gregory, and Anna's fiancé Mr Redmure.

"I see that you are not wearing a tiara, Frederica, and have a rather unconventional hairstyle!" proclaimed Lady Jevington.

Before Lord Alverstoke could intervene, Frederica replied to this rather provocative statement, deciding to ignore the comment about her hair style.

"To wear my new tiara would have looked very pretentious in a country church, Lady Augusta. I shall look forward to wearing the tiara in a more appropriate setting."

Lord Jevington, normally a quiet man, rebuked his wife.

"Augusta, that arrogant remark sounded just like your late mother! Frederica, you must call us Humphrey and Augusta from now on. You have met our children and Redmure previously, haven't you?"

She shook hands with each of the young people, and then suggested that they should all move on to the buffet in the dining room.

"Quite typical of my sister Augusta to try to dominate the conversation," said Alver.

Frederica did not recognise the gentleman approaching them in the distance, but the Marquis whispered in her ear.

"This is my friend Charles Petersham, who is the heir to the Earl of Harrington. You may remember I told you that Petersham has a close lady friend, Maria Foote, who is an actress at Covent Garden, but his father the Earl does not approve of the liaison, so there is no marriage – yet."

"Does Lord Petersham have any children?"

"Not as far as I know. Perhaps Maria uses Pennyroyal Tea. Do you know about that?"

"Yes, most women do. I would guess that my mother had used the tea to space out her family. Except for Harry and Charis, who were born within 18 months of each other, all my other siblings are well spaced. I am three years older than Harry; Charis is three years older than Jessamy; and Jessamy is four years older than Felix."

"You make a very interesting point, my dear. Assuming that we are lucky enough to have children, I would not want you to be constantly worn out by years of child-bearing."

Alver introduced her to his friend, who was a handsome man of about the same height as the Marquis, with thick dark wavy hair and a small, pointed beard, and very stylishly attired.

"Lady Alverstoke, may I call you Frederica? I am Charles Petersham. I cannot tell you how delighted I am that your husband has finally succumbed to Cupid's dart after all these years as a bachelor. I am sure that you will have already been told what a beautiful dress you are wearing today."

"Thank you, milord – Charles. Welcome to Alver Park."

"Alverstoke told me that you hope to send your lively young brother Felix to my old school at Windsor?"

"Yes, we are hoping that Eton will be able to curb his more dangerous enthusiasms!"

Waiting patiently further down the line was the Kentmere family, their children accompanied by Felix Merriville in deep conversation with young Tom.

Eliza embraced her new sister-in-law before saying, "What a very lovely gown you are wearing, Frederica – did you get that from Mlle Franchot? I must take Caroline there when we move to town for her come-out."

Last in the line was Mr Salcombe with Jessamy.

"Apologies, Frederica, Cousin Alverstoke, for being late – we have been walking rather slowly, as I have been busy catching up with all the news from Herefordshire."

"No problem, Jessamy, but I must admit that I am rather hungry now, and your sister is probably the same. We should all get to the buffet in the dining room before the food disappears!"

Inevitably they found Felix with Tom Kentmere in the dining room, filling his plate, probably for the second time.

Frederica and Alver made their choices, and they ate their meal before moving into the ballroom where chairs had been arranged around the walls. The musicians were already on the dais at the far end of the room, ready to play when the Marquis indicated that it was time for the dancing to begin.

"I suggest that we walk around the room first to talk to our guests before I ask for the music to start, Frederica."

After about 30 minutes, the Marquis spoke to the musicians. The younger guests took to the floor with alacrity, and soon the ballroom was full of couples dancing and busy with conversation. Alver and Frederica stood back for a while, enjoying the lively scene, before joining in the dance with their guests.

Earlier in the week, Darcy Moreton had agreed with his friend that he should propose the toast to the bride and groom, with the Marquis to reply. Wicken rang a bell to get their guests' attention before Darcy said a few words to acknowledge his pleasure about their marriage and wishing them well for the future.

After the guests had toasted the couple, their glasses were refilled, and Lord Alverstoke replied, thanking everyone for their support, and proposing a toast to his bride.

Then the dancing resumed, and the less active guests sat watching the younger people make use of the floor to enjoy themselves. By the late afternoon, those people who had a greater distance to travel began to say their farewells, and leave the house, and by 7 o'clock only the people who were staying the night, either in the main house or at the village inn, remained. The musicians had already packed up their instruments and departed.

"Time for more food, Felix?" asked Charis, smiling.

"Always!" he replied.

After supper had been served and consumed, Wicken came to say that Curry was waiting outside, ready to drive them down to the Dower House. Frederica and Alver said goodnight to their guests, and they went out to the carriage.

When they reached their destination, Curry halted the carriage and held the door open as Frederica and Alver alighted.

"Thank you, Curry. Don't bring the carriage tomorrow morning unless the weather is wet."

"Very well, sir. Goodnight, milord, milady."

When they entered the hall, there were two candelabras on the table with the candles already lit.

"We have this house to ourselves now, my darling. Darcy, Endymion and Charles are sleeping at the village inn tonight. Are you anxious – about anything?"

"No, Alver. I am just very happy to be with you."

"You have nothing to fear, Frederica. I promise you that you will awake tomorrow morning with a smile on your face!"

Chapter 5

Frederica opened her eyes and, for a moment, she did not recognise her surroundings. Then she realised that she was in a bedroom in the Dower House. Someone had carefully tucked in the blankets around her, so she was comfortably warm, despite the room itself being quite chill.

She turned over to face the window and realised that her new husband was not in the bed with her. Instead, she could see that the bedroom door was open, and she could hear sounds from the ground floor below.

Then her nose began to recognise a delightful smell. Could that be chocolate? But there were no staff in the house with them, so who could be making that? Then, as she heard steps on the stairs, the smell of chocolate grew stronger, and Alver entered the room with a tray containing 2 cups and saucers, small spoons and a sugar bowl.

"Oh, I had hoped to surprise you, Frederica, but I see that you are awake. May I offer you a cup of chocolate?"

He placed the tray on the chest of drawers by the window, and then came across the room to gently kiss her.

"Alver, who made the chocolate?"

"I did. When Cook came down from London in the middle of last week, I persuaded her to show me how to make the drink. I had remembered how much you said that you had enjoyed chocolate at Gunter's in Berkeley Square. Making the drink is not difficult, once you know how!"

"Darling Alver, how thoughtful of you to take the trouble to surprise me. What a lovely way to start our first morning together!"

Alver arranged her pillows so that she could sit up comfortably, and then put one of the cups and saucers with a spoon and the sugar bowl on her side table, ready for her to drink the chocolate. Then he put sugar in his own cup on his side of the bed, and they sat happily together, side-by-side.

"Are we going to make a habit of this, every morning?"

"Why not, although perhaps Cook will make it for us, rather than me, as she is more likely to be an expert. I meant to ask you - how did you get that long scar above your right ankle, my love?"

"Ah! That scar was from falling off my mount at Graynard, several years ago, when I was riding side-saddle. The horse tripped on a rabbit hole, and I slipped over the pommel sideways onto the ground. I gashed my leg on a tree root, and the doctor had to put several stiches in the wound. Fortunately, I did not hit my head as I fell, but there and then I decided to start riding astride whenever I could within our estate. As I told you previously, Charis made me a pair of trousers especially so that I could wear them for using a normal saddle."

"Perhaps men ought to try riding side-saddle, then they might realise how difficult it is?"

"I would not recommend that idea, for it is certainly much easier to fall from your horse. Have you ever damaged yourself, Alver, perhaps when boxing or in some other sport?"

"I did fall from my horse once, here at Alver Park, when I was out riding with my tutor when I was about 12 years old. But I was only winded and, quite rightly, he made me get back on my mount straightaway, and continue with our outing. That may sound harsh to you, but I soon forgot about the fall. At Harrow, I enjoyed the fencing lessons, and got some nicks during the contests from time to time – but nothing serious. As for boxing at Jacksons, I rarely have an injury that bothers me for long."

After they had finished the chocolate, Frederica was about to leave the bed when Alver ventured to ask her a question.

"Was Eliza's 'night before' talk helpful, Frederica?"

His expression was anxious as he waited for her reply.

"There are some aspects of life, Alver, for which it is very difficult to find the right words. You were so thoughtful and gentle with me last night. Thank you, my darling!"

They had agreed with the family that they would walk up the drive from the Dower House to the main property at Alver Park at about 10 am, ready to have breakfast with them. Her brother Felix had been given strict instructions not to enter the dining room before they arrived, however hungry he felt. This instruction had been reinforced by John Kentmere, Lady Eliza's husband, who was to be his host at their home in the Midlands for two weeks.

As they reached the garden gate and closed it behind them, Alver held out his hand to Frederica and she put hers in his. Neither of them was wearing gloves, and she found it delightful to have the warmth of his hands in hers.

After they had walked on a little way together, he said "How does that feel to you -- holding my hand in yours?"

Frederica thought for a moment, and then replied "Intimate, and very precious to me."

Alver stopped walking and turned to his wife. "It is the same for me, my darling."

Then he put his hands on each side of her face, and he gave her a long lingering kiss.

"Let me hold you in my arms for a few moments, whilst I calm myself, and then we can walk on towards the house, where the rest of the family will be waiting for us."

And he held her head against his shoulder and embraced her for several minutes. Then they both took a deep breath, smiled at each other, and resumed walking along the drive. Once the main house came into sight, they could see Felix at the big first-floor window at the end of the picture gallery, looking anxiously as he hoped that they would come into view.

"What is it," said Alver, "about that boy that he is perpetually hungry? Was your brother Jessamy like that when he was 12 years old?"

"No, Jessamy was never like that. He was always quite grown-up for his age, and much quieter than Felix, thank goodness!"

They walked on and, as they reached the foot of the steps, Wicken was opening the doors to welcome them into the house.

"Good morning, milady, milord. Everything is ready for you in the dining room, and young Felix in particular will be delighted that you are here!"

Alver whispered in Frederica's ear that they had better walk swiftly into the dining room, before her youngest brother expired for lack of nourishment!

As they entered the dining room, they could hear John Kentmere saying "Felix, will you please wait until the adults have walked down the stairs. Then you can follow us with my children."

In the dining room, a breakfast choice was laid out on the sideboards on each side of the room. The wide table had already been laid with cutlery, glasses and jugs of orange juice. Several coffee pots were on the sideboard on one side of the room, and the food was on the other. Frederica and Alver took a plate each, and filled it with their choice of cold meats, eggs and other dishes.

As they sat down at the head of the table, side by-side, the footman brought each of them a cup of coffee, together with the sugar bowl.

By this time, everyone else was coming into the room, choosing their food, and finding a seat along one side of the long dining table. Felix and the other children chose to sit on each side at the far end, whilst the other adults filled the spaces in between. John Kentmere sat next to Frederica, whilst Lady Eliza sat next to her brother the Marquis.

"Is your secretary Charles Trevor, with Darcy Moreton and Mr Salcombe, having breakfast at the inn in the village?"

"Yes, they are," said Alverstoke to his brother-in-law.

"Then Darcy will be bringing his coach up here to the house, for he has offered to take Endymion, Charles and Frederica's brother Harry to Basingstoke, where they can catch the stage to continue their journey to London. Darcy's mother is not very well, so he will be journeying on to Hertfordshire to see his parents there."

John Kentmere asked, "What about Mr Salcombe? What route will he be taking back to Herefordshire?"

"He will also be going to Basingstoke with Darcy, but then he will be taking a different coach to the West."

It took some time for all the guests to get ready to leave, including the Kentmere family, who were taking Frederica's brother Felix with them for a 2 week stay, so that Alver and his new wife could enjoy their honeymoon at Alver Park.

Jessamy Merriville was remaining at the house with his tutor, Septimus Trevor, to continue his studies for entry to Oxford University. But finally, by the late morning, all the visitors had departed, leaving Alver and Frederica with Jessamy to return to the entrance hall.

"How quiet it is!"

"That," said Jessamy, "is because Felix is not here!"

"Yes, two weeks without any experiments or loud noises. Happy days!" replied Alver. "Now, Wicken has asked Cook to provide us with a light luncheon – cold meats and some vegetables, to be followed by one of Cook's excellent cold desserts. So let us go to the dining room, to see if the meal is ready for us."

Jessamy and Septimus Trevor came to join them, and they spent a pleasant hour together in the dining room. Alver then left the room and returned carrying one of the cushions from the drawing room.

"Come with me now, Frederica. We are going to have a short walk together in the park. Jessamy and Septimus will be collecting their fishing rods, as they are off to the lake for a couple of hours. I am going to leave my waistcoat and my jacket here; I will be much too hot otherwise."

The warmth of the weather in the park was quite a contrast to the cool rooms inside the house, as the newly weds left the house and walked together towards the stream.

"What is the cushion for, Alver?"

"You will see in a few minutes. There is a wooden bench near the stream, which should be in the shade at this time of day."

When they reached the bench, Alver sat down with Frederica next to him.

"Now, love, I will put the cushion on my knees, and you can use it as a pillow if you use the bench as a bed. You had a very, very, busy day yesterday, and much less sleep last night than you usually do. So lie down now, and close your eyes. I will put my arm around your waist, so that there is no risk of your rolling from the bench onto the grass."

Frederica did as he suggested, and the gentle bubbling noise from the water in the stream soon lulled her to sleep.

With his arm around her, Alver relaxed on the bench in the shade provided by the trees behind them. He looked back towards the house, where Jessamy and his companion soon emerged from the front door, carrying their fishing gear, and walked in the opposite direction towards the lake.

After a few minutes, Alver himself began to doze, and he was not sure how long they had been there when his wife began to fidget, and he realised that she was getting restless because the sun had moved round and the bench was no longer in the shade.

"Time to wake up, my Sleeping Beauty. We must walk back to the house before we both get too hot. Wicken can find us some cooling drinks, and perhaps some of Cook's lemon biscuits. We will both feel much less warm once we reach the drawing room."

Frederica slowly opened her eyes, and smiled up at him, before she swung herself round so that she had both her feet on the grass. "That was just lovely, Alver. I had not realised how tired I was. We must do this again on another sunny afternoon."

"That, my darling, is a very good idea!"

By the time that Jessamy and his tutor had returned to the house, it was time for everyone to dress ready for dinner. After the meal, their companions went to play a game of billiards, leaving Alver and Frederica to have some private time together.

The following morning, after breakfast, Alver spoke to Frederica's brother.

"Jessamy, as your sister and I will probably be using this property more frequently than I have done for the past 10 years, I plan to create more hard-surfaced paths around the park, and to widen those that already exist. I want every path to be wide enough to take a carriage. Would you like to come with us, and help to decide where those paths should be?"

"Are you going to walk or ride, sir?"

"We shall get much more done if we all ride. Curry should come with us, and he can make notes about the routes that we decide on."

Frederica's brother promptly agreed to help them.

It took several hours to complete most of the task, and Jessamy agreed to go out again with Curry later in the week, to ride through the deer enclosure, and around the fields beyond that were used by the sheep, and to decide what paths might be needed there.

Alver and Frederica had been much too busy with Lady Eliza's family and with their other guests before their wedding to discuss what changes they might like to make to the furnishings at Alver Park. As there were rain showers the next day, that was a good opportunity for them to walk through the whole house, including the servants' quarters, to decide what needed to be done.

Frederica's abigail, Emily, went with them to make notes of what they planned to do. Once their task had been completed, she made 2 copies of her list, one for Frederica and one for Charles Trevor, as Alver's secretary would be responsible for placing the orders in London, once he had identified the best suppliers.

Meanwhile, Frederica and Alver went to have lunch in the smaller dining room. While they were waiting for the dessert course to be served, she had a question for him.

"After you left university Alver, did you go on a 'Grand Tour' on the Continent, to Italy and Greece as well as to France?"

"That might have been the plan, once Napoleon had been defeated. My father and I did go to Paris and on to the Loire Valley together, once the war with the French was over. But somehow a longer trip never happened. My mother was dead by then, of course, and my father preferred for me to be in England."

"Was it ever suggested that you should serve in the army, love?"

"When I was at Harrow, some of my fellow pupils were younger sons in their families, who were planning to join the military or the navy when they left school. The tradition seems to be that the heir should stay at home to help the father run the family estates, and that a commission should be purchased for a younger son to serve in the army or the navy. In my case, of course, I have no brothers. I remember my father and I discussing the subject when I was about 15 years of age, and we agreed that I should not join the military.

My mother died a couple of years after that conversation, and my youngest sister Eliza had been married for a few months. I missed Eliza's company when she moved to the Shires, to John Kentmere's estate. She had had quite a battle to persuade my mother to agree to the match, as Mama was determined that her daughter should marry a member of the aristocracy as both Augusta and Louisa had done. However, my father insisted that Eliza should be allowed to marry the man that she loved. Love was not a concept that my mother ever understood!

However, my father George had had a cousin, Henry Dauntry. My grandfather purchased a commission for him, and he served in the military for more than 10 years. Towards the end of that time, he met and married his wife Lucrecia in London.

As you know, they had three children together – Endymion, Chloe and Diana. About six months before he was intending to sell out from the army, and to move his family to live on the country estate that my grandfather had given to him, he was serving abroad when he caught yellow fever, and died very suddenly.

As you may imagine, that event was a most dreadful shock for Lucrecia and for their children. It was probably about then that Lucrecia began to have those spasms with which we are all now very familiar! But I should be fair, her husband's death in the same year as her mother's demise must have been very difficult for her. However, her mother left Lucretia the ownership of the house in Green Street, and also an annual income in addition to the money that she had inherited from Henry Dauntry. Lucrecia has always preferred to live in town, which is why her son and Charis will be able to live on the family's estate in Buckinghamshire without her."

"My sister seems to prefer country life to living in town, so that should suit her very well."

"Whilst I remember, my love, I have just had a letter from Muirhead. Endymion needs more income to support his wife, and the estate in Buckinghamshire does not have enough land to do that. I had instructed my lawyer to try to find some more land, not too far from Endymion's estate, which could be purchased for that purpose. I have just heard from Muirhead that there is a property available about 10 miles away. We will need to travel to Buckinghamshire soon after we get back to town to make a decision. I hope that you would like to come with me. I should like to give the new land to Endymion and Charis as their wedding present."

"Is there a house with that land, Alver?"

"No, it seems not, so that would be one less responsibility for the new steward. Your Mr Salcombe is looking for a younger man in

Herefordshire who already has some experience, and who would be ready to take on greater responsibilities. Dauntry's steward Mr Taylor is elderly, and very ready to retire from his duties when a replacement is available to take over."

On the sixth day of their honeymoon, Alver and Frederica were having breakfast in the small dining room with Jessamy and Septimus Trevor when the Marquis asked the tutor a question.

"Will you be going fishing on the lake later, Septimus? The weather has been rather showery, but I had wondered whether Frederica and I might join you."

"Yes, sir, after a couple of hours with his studies, Jessamy and I will take a break to have something to eat, and then we intend to go down to the lake to practise our skills. Of course, we would be delighted if you would like to join us."

"I suspect that my wife has never learnt to fish with a rod and line. Is that not so, Frederica?"

"I have never had the opportunity to try any kind of fishing. At home in Herefordshire, the River Wye is very popular for catching trout, and Mr Salcombe has told me that he learned to fish there with his father. Harry used to fish on the wide stream that flows through the far side of our estate at Graynard, and very occasionally he would catch a small grayling or a twaite shad – but not often."

"A grayling is the most beautiful fish with large fins, whereas I have heard that a twaite shad looks more like a herring," said Septimus.

"Thank you for the description, Septimus. How successful have you and Jessamy been here in Wiltshire?"

"We have caught some small grayling, sir, and a few brook lamprey – they resemble an eel. I believe that King Henry I died in France in 1135 after his last meal – a surfeit of lampreys!"

"How sad – hopefully, he enjoyed his last repast!" said Jessamy.

"I must warn you, Frederica, that you will have to be very quiet so as not to alert the fish."

"Can you explain to me how fly-fishing works, Septimus? I only know that you use a rod and line."

"The goal of fly-fishing, milady, is to present the fly to the fish in a way that mimics the behaviour of a natural insect or baitfish. You use a line that is weighted at one end, and the fly is then cast in front of the fish. Then you wait, and wait, and wait, hoping that eventually a fish will take the bait!"

"Well, Septimus, if you like to suggest the best time for us to join you at the lake, Frederica and I will be there."

Without telling Frederica, Alver had arranged for a bench to be placed inside the wooden summerhouse that his grandparents had loved so much, for use until he and his wife had the opportunity to purchase a new sofa in town for the same location.

"Let's ask Cook for a picnic meal, Frederica. We can take that with us, and several cushions, to find a comfortable spot to eat our lunch, before our fishing expedition with Jessamy and Septimus."

About an hour later, Frederica together with Alver holding the reins were travelling in the gig up the hill on the far side of the lake towards the summerhouse. When they got there, she exclaimed with delight at the sight of the bench.

"Curry found that bench in a dusty corner of the stables and he had it moved up here to the summerhouse."

"I have just realised that I am quite hungry," said Frederica, as she unpacked the picnic basket, to reveal ham, cheese, bread rolls and butter, as well as some fruit. There were plates and glasses, plus a bottle of Cook's lime cordial.

"No wine, I see, which is just as well if you are to concentrate on your fishing tuition later on, my love."

After the meal, they sat together on the bench with his arm around her, enjoying the view.

"How large a sofa will we need here, Alver?"

"I would say big enough for two, both in length and width, my darling," and there was quite a wicked twinkle in his eyes as he waited for her reaction.

Frederica turned towards him before replying, and then she said, with a wide smile on her face, "What a really excellent idea, Alver!"

After returning the gig to the stables, they walked down to the lake, where Jessamy and Septimus were setting up their rods and lines.

"I will sit on this stool over here, Frederica, well back from the water. My father taught me to fly fish more than twenty years ago, but I have too impatient a personality to be successful. I suspect that you will do much better!"

"If you come over here, milady, let me show you what you need to do. It's the weight of the line that carries the fly to the target. This is why you see fly anglers on the water holding so much line in the air. They are letting more line out to get their fly to the target. If you use too much force or strength in your cast, you will overpower the rod."

Septimus handed her a rod and line, and then demonstrated what she should do.

"Your thumb should be on the top with your fingers wrapped underneath. Fly fishing should be relaxing, so take the tension off your hand. Hold it firmly, but not in a death grip. Stand with your feet shoulder-width apart, slightly angled toward your target. Now, your cast starts with the rod tip low. To do the pickup, lift your rod until the rod tip reaches the 10 o'clock position. It's at this point that you'll start your back cast.

To make a back cast, you must accelerate the rod tip backward from the 10 o'clock position to the 2 o'clock position, making an abrupt stop with the rod tip at the 2 o'clock position. Just for a brief second that will seem like forever, allow the line to stretch out behind you before making your forward cast.

Then, once the line has stretched behind you, it's time to start the forward cast. That is made with the same motion as you made your back cast – that quick acceleration to an abrupt stop. You'll want to bring the rod tip back to an abrupt stop at the 10 o'clock position again, which will let the line shoot out in front of you. Imagine that you're painting an imaginary line in the sky for your rod tip to follow."

"That is quite a lot for me to recall!"

"Yes, but with practice you will find that you will remember what you should do. Do not take your eyes off where you want the fly to land, as that will just open your casting stroke and keep your rod tip from following that straight line. Remember to be patient as you learn. No one makes a perfect cast all the time."

The Marquis, sitting back on his stool and watching Frederica intently, kept very still for the next 30 minutes or so, as his wife repeatedly cast the line as she had been directed into the lake.

"Perhaps you should take a short break," said Jessamy. "You are doing very well, but I found it quite tiring to begin with, having to remember everything that I had been told."

Frederica put down her rod and line.

"Could you show me, Septimus, how to attach the fly?"

"Yes, of course. I have a box of flies here. The idea is that the fish are deceived into thinking that they are edible. First, pass the free end of the line through the eye of the fly hook. Then, wrap the free end over line to form four coils. Next, pass the free end through the loop that you have formed at the eye. Finally, tuck it back through the loop that you formed after making the coil. Now, you need to practice all that!"

Frederica had to make several attempts before she was doing all the actions on the correct order. She then continued with casting her line for another 30 minutes, until the action was beginning to seem more automatic.

Then a voice came from behind her.

"Now you know why I am not patient enough to be a fly fisherman, my darling!"

She turned to look at Alver, with a wicked smile on her face.

"Or perhaps you did not really want to learn, love?"

"Minx!" came his reply.

Whilst she was considering how to reply to this impertinence, a shout came from Jessamy, whose line had suddenly shot away from him. "A fish has taken my bait, Septimus, although not a very big specimen!"

The others watched as he eventually reeled in his catch and landed the fish on the bank.

"Very well done, Jessamy. I hope to be able to do that one day, although I must confess that I am now in serious need of a hot or cold drink. Perhaps we could stop for some tea and biscuits, to celebrate your success?"

Her brother and Frederica collected their rods and lines.

When they returned to the house, Wicken told Frederica that a letter for her had arrived from Lady Eliza. Hoping that there might be some news of how her brother Felix was doing at the Kentmere's home, she opened the message as they waited for the tea and biscuits to arrive.

"Eliza says that her husband has needed to reprimand Felix for various reasons from time to time, but that he and Tom have been allowed to do some experiments in an outbuilding. They have all been very surprised to discover that Felix is not interested in horse riding, but her daughter Caroline is insisting that he goes out with her around the estate to improve his skills."

"Excellent! Your brother is learning to do as he is told, Jessamy! Let's hope that the improvement is permanent once we return to London."

"I wish that I could share your optimism, Cousin Alverstoke, but I fear that he may revert quite rapidly once he leaves the Kentmeres' estate."

"Has Felix always been so enterprising?" said Septimus.

"Yes, is the short answer!" replied Frederica. "Since he was quite a small child, he could be relied upon to cause chaos at Graynard. His only redeeming feature is that most people seem to find him interesting – and they indulge his whims, which is not helpful when I am trying to restrain him."

"I must have a word with my brother-in-law when I see him next. John Kentmere, and his daughter, seem to be succeeding, whereas we are having much more difficulty. Will you reply to Eliza, or shall I?"

"I will write back to her, and perhaps you would like to send a letter to John."

The days seemed to pass swiftly as the end of their honeymoon approached. Alver and Frederica continued to go out each day in the curricle when the weather allowed, and Wicken and Cook were busy, ready to close up the house when the Marquis and his wife had left for their journey to the Shires. Charles Trevor wrote from town to say that a pile of correspondence awaited his employer's return, but that none of the letters were urgent enough to require him to travel to Alver Park.

"Time to leave, Frederica. I hope that you will remember our stay here with pleasure. I am so happy to have had two weeks here with you. Once we return to London, we must explore the options for making a visit to the Continent. Apart from my short stay in Paris and a few days in the Loire Valley with my father, I have never left this country."

"I shall be very sorry to leave this house, and I will never forget our honeymoon here, Alver. But a trip to the Continent sounds an enticing possibility. However, reality will return as soon as we reach the Kentmeres' estate. I am looking forward to seeing Eliza and

John, and of course their children – not to mention young Felix! Are Jessamy and Septimus ready to get into the carriage?"

"Yes, they are waiting for us in the entrance hall. Perhaps, next time we come here, there will be a new oil painting in the long gallery?"

When they arrived at the Kentmeres' estate, Frederica had expected to see a large mansion set in gracious gardens like Alver Park, with some farmland attached. There was a handsome modern house, which Alver told them had been built several years ago by John Kentmere for his growing family. But, as at Graynard, the Merriville's property, the primary purpose of the estate was the Home Farm and the many acres of productive land attached to it.

As the carriage proceeded up the drive, they passed the original farmhouse that the Marquis told them was now used by the Kentmere grandparents as their home in retirement. Jessamy was pleased to see that there was also a very extensive stable block set back to one side from the main house.

When the carriage arrived at the house, the front door opened and the children came running out to greet them, including Felix. The visitors were given a warm welcome by their hosts, John and Eliza, and their elder daughter Caroline showed Frederica and Alver to their bedroom, while her brother Jack welcomed Jessamy, and took him with Septimus to their rooms.

The adults settled in the drawing room for some refreshments. Lady Eliza was quick to compliment her guest on the pale-yellow dress that she was wearing.

"Is that another gown from Mlle Franchot, Frederica? The colour looks so well on you."

"Thank you. Yes, she made me several dresses before the wedding, and this is one of my favourites. May I ask whether you have had any problems with my brother Felix during his stay with you?"

"Well, your young brother is an engaging scamp, but he and our Tom have enjoyed each other's company for the past two weeks. I would guess that it has been good for Felix that one of our children is younger than him. Part of his problem may be that he has always been the youngest in your family, and therefore expects to be indulged. I took him aside one day and said that he should set a good example for Mary. I am not sure that he has any interest in young girls, and he has absolutely no concept of what that might involve, so I suggested some ideas to him. You would have been very amused at his efforts to act as a supportive elder brother!"

Leaving his wife to have an uninterrupted conversation with Lady Eliza, the Marquis went with John Kentmere to inspect some of the buildings at the Home Farm.

"You would perhaps not have been impressed, Vernon, at the determination of young Felix to persuade me that he needed to construct his own balloon - so that he could practice being an aeronaut and make an ascension (or two) from my field – the one that you can just see over there, beyond the stable block. When I refused my permission, he assumed the expression of an orphan without any means of support. He was mightily disappointed that I refused to change my mind!"

"That child is quite incorrigible! You would have thought that his accident near Watford would have deterred him from ever going up in a balloon again. He seems to be quite fearless, and with enough wind some balloons can travel at fifty miles an hour! Frederica will be horrified when she hears about his request to you."

"I told him that he was the most rambunctious scallywag that I have ever met up with! When he said that he did not know the meaning of those words, I gave him a notebook to collect words that he did not know, and to write down their meanings. I told Felix that there is a dictionary in our library that he could use, and that he should collect as many new words as he could before you leave for town."

"Good – that will give him a new task to think about."

"Felix does seem to have a great thirst for information about mechanical inventions, doesn't he? When I suggested that he should design a water pump for me, he asked if I was able to provide him with a book from my library with instructions on how to do so. I had to disappoint him. When you return to Berkeley Square, perhaps someone can take him to Hatchards Bookshop, to ask if they have a volume about designing water pumps?"

"I will ask my secretary, Charles Trevor, to take him to Piccadilly. Not a task that Charles will relish, I can assure you, for he is rather too well acquainted with Felix and his curiosity about anything mechanical! However, I console myself that Felix may one day become a famous inventor and bring great credit to our family!"

The Marquis and Frederica stayed for three nights with his sister and the Kentmere family before returning to town with Jessamy, Felix, and Septimus Trevor.

Before they left, Lady Eliza took Frederica aside to thank her.

"What for, Eliza – I do not recall doing anything in particular?"

"For making my brother very happy – I have never seen him so content with his life and his future."

Chapter 6

Before his marriage, the Marquis had ordered every aspect of his life in London to suit himself, but the situation was very different now, with Frederica and her siblings living with him in the house in Berkeley Square.

Returning to London from Alver Park after nearly a month away, Alver had looked at his town house afresh through his wife's eyes. The spacious home had been furnished more than 30 years earlier to his mother's taste, and the style now seemed rather pretentious, and expressly calculated to impress other members of the Ton.

Alver and Frederica were sitting together for a rare quiet moment in their private sitting room on the first floor, with his arm around her shoulders, and Alver decided to discuss the subject.

"Frederica, do you like the furnishings in this house? Please be honest with me."

"No, I don't. The style is too elaborate, too fussy, too 'show off'. If I could follow my own preferences, I would prefer a more understated style, that looks more like a family home."

His wife had identified the core of the problem, and Alver decided there and then to do something about it.

"From now on, why don't we use two mornings every week to visit the shops selling furniture and furnishings. To begin with, we will not buy anything – we should familiarise ourselves with the choices available. Then, we can decide together on what we like, place the orders and look forward to having a home that we can both enjoy."

Frederica embraced him and looked so happy that Alver wished that he had mentioned the subject earlier, and that she could smile at him like that every moment of every day.

"Can I ask you a question, Alver?"

"Yes, of course you can."

"There are some rooms on the ground floor where I find the colours particularly depressing – the library, for instance. There are grooved vertical wood panels at intervals between groups of books, but the panels are dark brown. And the lower part of the walls, about two feet deep below the books, are also painted brown. The curtains hang across the windows even when they are opened, and they too are brown. The only other colour in the room is the handsome leather armchair at the desk, which has a buttoned back and is a lovely deep blueish-green colour."

"Let's go downstairs, Frederica, and you can show me what you would like to do with the room."

A short time later, having seen the space through her eyes, the Marquis realised that his wife was quite correct. The room was gloomy and looked neglected.

"Frederica, please do whatever you wish to change the library– more light, more interesting curtains, and more colour. The only features that I wish to retain are the chair and of course the books!"

Three weeks later, the room had been transformed. The ceiling had been painted in a very pale shade of cream, reflecting more light around the spaces. The dark brown walls beneath the bookshelves were now a blueish-green to match the leather armchair, with gold detailing, and the vertical wood panels between the groups of books had been highlighted with gold paint, with blueish green borders. The wooden support across the top of each window had been replaced with a longer pole, so that the curtains when open could hang down clear of the window frames, and the new curtains had an attractive design of blueish-green leaves on a gold background.

When Darcy Moreton next visited the house, the Marquis took him into the library to see the transformation.

"Good heavens! Frederica has done so well! Such an amazing difference from the room as it used to be, and the whole effect is much lighter and more interesting. Please congratulate her on my behalf, Ver!"

"My wife is now turning her attention to the garden at the back of the house. We have agreed that the geometrical design with low box hedge borders should be replaced with a more informal layout, more like a country garden."

"I shall look forward to seeing the changes, perhaps when I next visit Berkeley Square?"

Earlier that day, the Marquis had lunched with Darcy and Robert Castlereagh at White's.

"I have an unusual outing to offer you, Frederica. We are invited to visit Robert and Emily Castlereagh to view the private zoo on their estate, which is a few miles south of London. He tells me that they have many species there, including an armadillo, a flying squirrel, kangaroos, emus, a pair of ostriches, a puma - and a tiger who I have heard is notably bad-tempered. You may be relieved to know that all the animals are kept in very robust metal cages! The Castlereaghs have no children, so perhaps that is the reason that they keep the animals at their home at Woollet Hall. Would you like to accept their invitation, my dear?"

"I would be quite bad-tempered if I was kept outside in a metal cage in the English climate! Yes, I would love to visit the Castlereaghs' home, Alver, and to see the animals. How sad that they have no children."

Frederica discovered that her hostess had quite an eccentric personality, but she and her husband seemed to have a very happy personal relationship. Emily explained that she frequently travelled abroad with her husband, since his duties as the Foreign Secretary often took him to the major cities on the Continent. Alver and Frederica enjoyed a splendid meal with their hosts, after which they went on a tour of all the animals, each species kept in an individual cage. There were so many varieties that it was difficult to recall all the names, but the visit was a very refreshing change from the normal events offered by the Ton.

Whilst she had been staying at Alver Park, Frederica had decided to move her sister Charis to Berkeley Square from Lucretia's house in Green Street as soon as she and Alver were back in town.

Charis was a very kind-hearted girl, and at Alver Park before the wedding she had patiently supported Miss Plumley, the companion to Endymion's mother Lucretia Dauntry, through Lucretia's various 'spasms'. These seemed to occur whenever Lucretia needed to be the centre of attention.

"Lucretia cares only for her own interests, Alver. The sooner Charis has a chance to settle into her new life with Endymion at their home in Buckinghamshire, the happier I shall be!"

"I entirely agree, my love, but several more weeks yet will be needed to organise their wedding. I am waiting to hear from Mr Salcombe in Herefordshire as to whether he has been able to find a suitable young man to take over from Endymion's elderly steward at the estate. And my London lawyer Muirhead is still progressing the purchase of more land to add to Endymion's property in Buckinghamshire. All these matters take time."

Septimus Trevor was still living in Berkeley Square as the temporary tutor for Frederica's younger brothers Jessamy and Felix Merriville, as he had a few more weeks before he must return to his graduate studies at the university. Jessamy was to take the entry exams for Oxford, known as 'Responsions', in early September, with the intention that he should go to the university in the autumn of the following year.

Eton College, near Windsor, had now agreed to accept Felix, so he would be starting at the school next term, by which time he would be 13 years old.

Septimus went to make a suggestion to the Marquis about an outing for Felix.

"Children are admitted to the weekly lectures at the Royal Institution by Mr Faraday, sir. The lectures are so popular that traffic in Albemarle Street is now only allowed in one direction.

Fortunately, we live so close that we can walk and would not need to take the carriage to get there, sir. May I have your agreement that I can take Felix to a lecture next week? I believe that the tiered circular lecture theatre can accommodate 400 people."

"What an excellent suggestion, Septimus. I am sure that Felix would be delighted to attend. Let me know the cost of the tickets."

After their visit to the Royal Institution, Felix went to find Lord Alverstoke, to explain everything that he had been told about Electrodynamics during the lecture by Mr Faraday.

That evening, Alver said to Frederica, "I can assure you, my darling, that I only understood one word in ten of what Felix said, but he obviously really enjoyed the experience. Perhaps Septimus understood more than I did!"

Frederica then asked Alver a question about a different subject.

"Tell me, love, what was the pattern of your life in London before we married?"

"Well, on a Friday I would go to White's, usually to have lunch with Darcy Moreton. Several of my other friends might be at the club that day, so that would give me an opportunity to catch up with all the news. I should like to continue to go to White's on a Friday, although not every week. Also, from time to time, I would visit my tailor to order some new clothes, although not as often as you might think that I do!"

"I have several horses in training at Newmarket, so I used to travel there every two or three months to monitor their progress. The trainer enters my horses for races at Ascot and Newbury, as well as at Newmarket. Have you ever been to a horse race, Frederica?"

"I have only been to small local meetings in Herefordshire, which I enjoyed very much. The last time I did so, I took Jessamy with me. As you know, he is very keen on anything to do with horses, and he really enjoyed the day at the racecourse. Why do you ask?"

"Well, why don't we go to the next race meeting at Newmarket, and then the meeting at Newbury at the end of the month? We can travel in our barouche, and stay overnight, and have an enjoyable day there in the grandstand. I have a very promising horse that I could ask my trainer to enter in one of the races. We could take Jessamy with us if you would like to go?"

"Oh yes, please, Alver, I would love to go with you, and my brother would be so thrilled to be invited."

The Marquis had another suggestion to make for an interesting outing, in this case accompanied by Felix.

"When I took your young brother to see the pneumatic lift at the foundry in Soho, he told me that he had read about Maillardet's Automaton. That mechanical device had been devised by a Swiss designer in London who built clocks and other machines".

"The automaton, which resembles a human child sitting at a table with a pen in hand, is apparently capable of making four different drawings and even writing out three poems — two in French and one in English. Charles Trevor has confirmed that the automaton is on display at 'Maillardet's Automatical Theatre' in Catherine Street. Would you be interested in going to see it, Frederica?"

She thought that was a very good idea, and Felix was ecstatic at the prospect. Curry drove them in the carriage to Covent Garden, and they were all very intrigued by the complex system of gears, levers and cams, which enabled precise control over the movements and functions of the device.

"The proprietor told me that the mechanical child can play 16 tunes on the miniature piano!" said Felix, as they made their way home through the busy traffic in The Strand.

"Mercifully," remarked Alver, whose distaste for amateur musical events was no secret, "the automaton is not for sale, so I will not have to endure 16 tunes being played in Alverstoke House!"

"Another of my occupations where you will not want to join me, Frederica, is going to Jacksons boxing premises in Bond Street! Not something for the ladies!"

"No, I believe that I might manage to do without that! Regrettably, I have never personally been interested in the more gentle pursuits for ladies, such as embroidery or dressmaking - unlike Charis, who is exceptionally skilled in doing both. Or perhaps I was always too busy looking after my family, and the estate, to learn. Did you know that Charis made the lovely dress that she wore for the come-out ball?"

Alver looked at her with amazement. "You are not serious, are you, Frederica? That was a most exquisite gown!"

"Indeed, I am perfectly serious. My sister is a very expert needlewoman, I can assure you."

"Is there any personal interest that you would like to pursue, my dear, now you will have the means to do so?"

"Is it normal for aristocratic ladies to support a charitable endeavour? I would like to do something useful, but I would need to investigate an interest very thoroughly before I became involved. I have never had sufficient funds to pursue such matters in the past."

"Why don't you ask my sister Eliza for advice, when you next write to her? She has more than sufficient funds if she wants to help any charities, since John Kentmere is a wealthy man."

"That is an excellent idea, Alver. I will do that."

"Tell me, my love, what has most surprised you about being married to me?"

Frederica was quiet for several moments, and then replied. "Whatever I had expected, I have been most surprised at how very tactile you are. You very often put your arms around me, or stroke my cheek, or hold my hand when we walk down the stairs, and you help me with putting on my pelisse - instead of allowing one of the servants to assist me."

It was now Alver's turn to pause for what seemed to be quite a long time before replying.

"My mother was not an affectionate person, and she never embraced me. I knew that my father loved me, but his very difficult marriage meant that he had not found it easy to demonstrate his feelings in a physical way. The servants who looked after me were competent, but it was not part of their role to what your brother Felix would call 'cuddle' me.

Your family are so different, and you all show how you feel about each other, both in the way you talk and in physical gestures. You are affectionate towards me in a physical way, Frederica, and I am very happy to develop the same habit. I do hope that you would like me to continue. You would not dislike that, I hope?"

"Of course not, my darling! I will encourage you to carry on!"

Alver and Frederica had developed a private language between them. Their butler Wicken had been trying to work out the significance of the words 'Tonic'. As Frederica was crossing the entrance hall one day, her husband came down the stairs, and accosted her.

"I had been wondering, Frederica, about 'Tonic', my love."

"Do you mean now, Alver?"

"I should like to. Would you like to come upstairs …"

"Of course I would," but, as she turned to go up the stairs, Frederica saw that Wicken wanted to ask Alver a question.

"Your secretary was looking for you just now, milord".

"Ah! – well, tell Charles that I should be available in about an hour's time. I will visit his office later this morning."

"Thank you, milord. I will inform Mr Trevor."

As Frederica and Alver entered his bedroom, she laughed, and said, "Wicken is beginning to wonder what 'Tonic' might mean, my darling."

"What we will be doing for the next hour will be much more enjoyable than Tonic, Frederica! That remedy will always remind us of my intention to ask you to marry me that day, even though the Tonic was to help the recovery of your brother."

When they walked along the corridor afterwards, Alver said to Frederica, "Do I bother you too often, love?"

"You do not bother me, Alver – you delight me, and never too often!"

It was very rare for the Marquis to be lost for words, but this was one occasion. His eyes twinkled at her, and his wife said, "Alver, please stop trying to make me laugh!"

A few days later, Wicken asked Frederica if she could explain to him the significance of the word 'Tonic'.

"When my brother was recovering from his unfortunate balloon accident, I remembered that Mrs Ansdell, our Vicar's wife in Herefordshire, had recommended Dr Radcliffe's Pork Jelly Tonic as a restorative treatment after illness, and my brother Harry brought me some from London for my brother to take."

Wicken thanked her for the information about the Tonic, although he was clearly puzzled as to why Alver and Frederica were still using the description. However, Emily Leonard came down the stairs at that moment to ask him a question.

"Wicken, do you know whether Mrs Jones might have a goffering iron in the housekeeper's room?"

"I am not familiar with that item, Miss Leonard. Can you explain to me what it is for?"

"A goffering iron is heated in the fire before being used to iron lace trimmings on a ladies' dress or a gentleman's shirt sleeve."

"Ah! I will ask Mrs Jones. If we do not have a goffering iron in the house, I'm sure that one could be purchased. That sounds to be a very useful item."

Later that week, Jessamy had gone on an outing with Septimus Trevor to visit the British Museum, followed by lunch together in Covent Garden. In their absence, the house seemed very quiet, and

Frederica had not seen Alver since breakfast time. She had been having a meeting with the man from one of the many furnishing shops, to choose the fabric for new curtains in her bedroom. Frederica had also retained some samples for Alver to consider, as the curtains in his room also needed to be replaced.

After lunch, they had not been expecting to see Jessamy and Septimus Trevor back in Berkeley Square until mid-afternoon. When the hands on the grandfather clock in the hall had reached past four, Frederica decided to ask Wicken to order some tea for them on a tray in the library. Alver came to join her, and he was sipping his tea by the fireplace when he realised that his wife was looking rather anxious.

"What is it, my dear, something is troubling you. Please tell me what it is?"

Frederica paused, before saying, "Tears in your eyes just now, Alver?"

"Ah, I thought perhaps that you have missed that, my love, but clearly I was wrong. I had never thought of myself as an emotional man before now. Cynical, yes, and critical of other people. But falling in love with you has changed me. When you saw those tears, I was realising that I had never in my life been so happy as I was at that moment. Now I only want to make you content, and when I can see that you are. How my friends at White's would wonder if they knew what changes my marriage to you have brought!"

"Some of them, of course, are not married like Darcy Moreton, so they are not troubled by domestic matters, or the comfort of their wives. Happily, there are some members of the club who are fortunate in their choice of partner, and only go to White's from time to time like me, to catch up with the latest news. I am sorry if you have had any reason for worrying, but I can assure you that those tears were for the best of reasons!"

Alver rose from the settee, and Frederica put her teacup and saucer back on the tray, and she went to join Alver by the fireplace. Then she hugged him fiercely and held him tight for several minutes.

They were interrupted by one of the footmen knocking on the door. When Alver called him into the room, James told them that Jessamy and Septimus Trevor had just returned to the house and were asking to see them.

"Please ask Master Jessamy and Mr Trevor to join us, James."

They both declined any refreshments, saying that they had had such a splendid lunch at Rules restaurant in Covent Garden that they couldn't possibly consume any more food. Jessamy was full of the delights of the British Museum, and the interesting objects and books that they had found there.

"It is just as well, Frederica, that Felix is now at Eton, and not here. If he had gone with us to Rules, he would still be there, eating his way through the menu! There were so many choices which he would have liked. I had the steak and kidney pie, and Mr Trevor chose the venison stew. Both dishes were excellent. If you haven't been to the restaurant, you must ask Cousin Alverstoke to take you!"

Alverstoke acknowledged that he had eaten there on several occasions, but that he would be very delighted to take his wife, and possibly Jessamy with them, for a meal.

One morning, Alver and Frederica met Charles Trevor in the drawing room to discuss a pile of outstanding correspondence awaiting a reply.

"In the past, my dear, before I met the delightful members of the Merriville family, I refused to attend many social occasions. I had long since tired of being pursued by ambitious mothers and conversing with young ladies half my age. I suspect that Charles noticed, about three months ago, when I began to return to the social scene after you and Charis had been introduced to the Ton at the come-out ball that I hosted here. Isn't that so, Charles?"

"It is always my duty, sir, as your employee, to follow your instructions relating to correspondence."

"Tactfully put, Charles, as ever. Anyway, from now on we must consult together, my dear, about every social invitation that we receive. I have no desire to follow my late mother's example and try to dictate what my father should do. Charles already knows those members of the Ton who I favour, and those which I much prefer to avoid.

You, my dear, will know those people who you have already met who you would like to see more frequently, and hopefully that number will increase as your acquaintance expands. I suggest that you should have a conversation with Charles about that quite soon. You might decide that we should hold some dinner parties here every month. I will leave it to you to suggest who you might like to invite. I suspect that there are few members of the Ton who would refuse such an invitation, if only out of curiosity to meet you!"

Frederica turned and smiled at Mr Trevor.

"There must be times when the role of being the secretary to such a demanding employer must be quite wearing, Charles?"

"Quite so, milady, but I was aware of that before I agreed to take on the task, for my father knew the Marquis and his family quite well before I had ever met him."

Lord Alverstoke threw back his head and laughed. "Touché, Charles! How well you know me!"

"There is an invitation here from your sister, Lady Buxted, that you would previously have refused, sir. The invitation is addressed to both of you. What reply do you wish me to send?"

Alver turned to his wife and raised his eyebrows at her.

"Well, Frederica?"

Louisa Buxted was not her favourite person, and none of the Buxted family had attended their wedding, but perhaps it might be wise to mend some fences now.

"What does the invitation relate to, Charles?"

"Her son Carlton, Lord Buxted, has invited an Italian pianist to perform at a musical evening at her home in Grosvenor Place next week, milady."

"So, there is not to be any singing, or performances by either of her daughters Jane or Maria?"

(Thank God for that, said Lord Alverstoke under his breath.)

"No, I believe not, milady."

"I suggest that we should accept, Alver. Carlton would only invite someone to perform who is a skilled exponent on the piano and, although Louisa and I are never likely to become close friends, it is probably sensible for us to be seen in her company from time to time."

"Very well, my love, I agree with you. What other invitations are there for us to discuss, Charles?"

"Two, sir, one from Lady Jersey and another from Princess Esterhazy – both ladies, as you know, sir, are patronesses of Almack's."

"And both invitations are for balls?"

"Yes, milady."

"Well, Sally Jersey is a close friend of your family, isn't she, Alver? We ought to accept that invitation, and we will not have far to travel, since the Jerseys live here in Berkeley Square! I have never met Princess Esterhazy. Do you know her, Alver?"

"No, I do not. She is the wife of the Austrian ambassador, I understand, and I have heard that she has a disdain of social climbers, which must be a recommendation? Perhaps she is curious to meet the new Marchioness of Alverstoke?"

"Well, Emily Leonard was previously the abigail for the wife of the new ambassador in Vienna, so perhaps that might be a source for conversation. What do you think, Alver?"

"I agree – I have heard that the Princess has quite a very lively personality, so why not? Let's accept that invitation as well, my dear."

"There is also your summons to attend the opening of the next session of the House of Lords, milord, following the recent election for members of the House of Commons."

"How many peers are there currently in the House of Lords, Alver?"

"I believe that there are about 230 of us, perhaps as many as 240, although some are too old or too infirm to go to the House, and many like me do not choose to attend."

"May I ask which party you would support, Alver?"

"I suppose that you could describe me as a lapsed Tory ..."

At this remark, Charles Trevor cleared his throat, and the Marquis fixed his secretary with a mocking gaze.

"Well, Charles, what is it that you want to say?"

"I believe, sir, that to be described as 'lapsed', one must first participate!"

Lord Alverstoke laughed. "That is quite true, Charles. I will attend the summons for the opening of the Lords next week, as I should, but I will not see it as my duty to do more than that, since I am not persuaded by the proposals currently being made by the Tory party, or by the Whigs. Our politicians do not inspire my confidence."

At this point, Mr Trevor decided to leave the room, allowing the Marquis and his wife to continue their discussion without him, with Alver caressing his wife's hand as they sat together on the sofa.

"When I was at Harrow, our history master once discussed what careers we might pursue after we had left school – as a landowner, joining the army or the navy, entering the church, or taking up a position in government. He told us a story about the diplomat Sir Henry Wotton, who remarked in 1604 that 'An ambassador is an honest man sent abroad to lie for the good of his country'."

"You could employ a similar phrase about any politician seeking to protect his party's interests, whether he sees himself as a Tory or a

Whig! To be a successful politician, it seems to me that you need to be capable of deceiving yourself as well as others. I have very many faults, my darling, as you well know, but my father impressed upon me that I must never deceive myself about a situation or a person, even though I might sometimes intend to mislead other people, as my mother did."

"I promise you that I have never lied to you since we first met, nor will I ever try to mislead you in the future. Your confidence and affection are far too precious to me to do that, Frederica."

Earlier that day, she had told Jessamy about a brief letter that had arrived from Felix, dated on Monday, saying that he was keeping his promise to Cousin Alverstoke to write every week, so that he could continue to receive the modest allowance that he was given by his family!

"I have also had a letter, from my sister Eliza," Alverstoke told Jessamy. "Her son Tom, who as you know went to Eton at the same time as Felix, is a much better correspondent than your younger brother! He says that Felix is being kept well under control by his housemaster at the school, and he is not being allowed to do any scientific experiments that might endanger his fellow pupils. I sincerely hope that he is correct!"

Frederica laughed but did not comment. She had had many years experience of trying to keep her youngest brother in order. If the teachers at Eton were succeeding where she had often failed, she would be delighted!

Alver had recently heard from his lawyer Muirhead that land in Buckinghamshire had come up for sale, not very far from Endymion Dauntry's residence.

"Frederica, I should travel soon to inspect that estate. I hope that you would like to accompany me?"

"Of course I would, Alver. Will we also visit Endymion's property whilst we are in the county?"

"I see no reason why not. I have not told my cousin about my plans for his wedding present yet, so please do not mention the idea to Charis, or to Lucretia Dauntry. I very much doubt whether Lucretia would be capable of keeping that secret."

The day was rather cloudy and overcast when Curry brought the carriage to the front door of their house in Berkeley Square. However, the journey went well, and they made good progress towards their destination, stopping at an inn on the way for an early lunch.

"We shall be meeting the representative of the current landowner in the nearest town; he will show us round the estate. I shall be interested in hearing your opinion afterwards, my dear. There is no house on the land, which matters little, since Endymion's estate already has a property where he and Charis intend to live. What I want to see is whether the land for sale is in good condition, well-arranged, and capable of producing an extra income for the newlyweds."

Accompanied by the landowner's steward, they drove on the roads and tracks around the land. Some of the boundaries to the fields were fences; others were hedges, and parts of the land were well wooded, including some handsome oak trees. Wheat and other arable crops could be seen, as well as sheep and cattle in some of the fields.

"Would it be possible to purchase the animals from the owner?" asked Alver.

"I don't know, milord, but I could ask that question if you would like me to do so."

"All the sheep and cattle look to be in good condition," remarked Frederica, who had already surprised the steward with her knowledge of agricultural matters, to Alver's amusement.

"My wife has been managing her brother Harry's estate in Herefordshire. I have yet to visit that county, but I look forward to doing so later this year."

"Could we pause the carriage just here, please? I should like to get out and look at that lovely view."

Alver called to Curry to stop the carriage for a few minutes to meet Frederica's request, and they got out of the carriage to look to the south. They were at the top of a hill, and the view in that direction was indeed very wide and interesting, with a stream beyond the field and with a small village visible in the distance.

The steward told them that the route that they had been following was named Meadowsweet Lane.

"Are there any farm buildings on the estate?"

"Yes, milady, they are about a mile or so ahead of us as we descend the road on the other side of this hill. They have been quite well maintained, as you will be able to see."

After they had completed their inspection of the estate for sale, and had parted from the steward, there was enough time left to make a short visit to Endymion's property. Alver had met the housekeeper on a previous occasion, and she greeted the Marquis with a friendly smile. Having been introduced to Frederica, the young woman explained that she was Annie Taylor, the daughter of the steward who would soon be retiring from his post. She showed them around the house, which was in need of redecoration throughout, as well as new furnishings in every room.

Then it was time for Alver and Frederica to begin the return journey back to town, and they took the opportunity to discuss what they had seen during the day.

"There were a few repairs needed to the farm buildings on the estate for sale, my darling?"

"Yes, I agree, but the land is being offered at a fair price. The house on Endymion's estate really needs to be entirely updated, and the stream there is rather too close to the building if they have young children. I do wonder, Alver, whether it might be worth Endymion and Charis building a new home on the land which you will be giving them? There was one location along Meadowsweet Lane, where we stopped the barouche, that had an absolutely splendid view towards the south over the nearby village."

"Goodness, Frederica, you really are planning for their future, aren't you, my love? Am I to pay for that new house as well, my dear?"

"That should not be necessary, Alver. Endymion's existing home could be sold to someone who only wants a house and a garden, and not any land for farming. The property should be valuable enough to pay for a new home for Endymion and Charis, I would guess?"

"But the location in Meadowsweet Lane was close to the top of a hill, Frederica – how would they supply a new house there with water?"

"I agree that might be a serious problem. Do you plan to purchase the extra land, Alver?"

"Yes, Frederica, I do. Endymion will need to sign the contract for the land, not me. My role is only to provide the money! We can wait to discuss any future ideas with them once they return from their honeymoon trip to the Continent. I suggest that we wait to tell them about our gift until a couple of weeks before their wedding. Hopefully, that will be a happy surprise."

As the Marquis had promised Frederica, he had arranged to commission an artist to create a portrait of them both wearing their wedding clothes. The artist that he chose was Sir Thomas Lawrence, who was a great favourite of the Prince Regent. He had recently completed a much-admired portrait of the society beauty Frances Vane, who was about to marry the half-brother of Lord Castlereagh, the Foreign Secretary. At the suggestion of the Prince, Sir Thomas was about to embark on a tour of the Continent, and Lord Alverstoke's commission would be the last to be completed before he left England to go abroad in September.

"He comes very well recommended," Alver told Frederica, "But we must make ourselves available at No.65, Russell Square whenever

Sir Thomas asks us to do so, or the painting will not be finished before he leaves for Aachen and Vienna."

Sir Thomas was a brilliant draughtsman and known for his gift of capturing a likeness, so Alver and Frederica had high hopes for their portrait. They were not disappointed, with the artist capturing her lively personality, and the delightful details on her pale green wedding dress, and her husband was portrayed with a small smile, but looking very distinguished standing beside her.

Over the next few weeks, the Marquis and his wife settled into their new life, becoming acknowledged leaders of the social scene in town, although a keen observer might note that they were always very selective about those invitations that they had agreed to accept.

Occasionally they would encounter Lord and Lady Jevington at a ball in Mayfair, and Frederica began to realise that Augusta's husband Humphrey had a rather enjoyably dry sense of humour.

"I hope you realise, Frederica," he said, with a twinkle in his eye, "that you are getting quite a reputation – for very stylish dresses, and for wearing jewellery that is really beautiful without being ostentatious?"

As Lady Jevington invariably wore her rather magnificent but very ugly tiara to every ball that she attended, Frederica thought carefully before replying to him.

"Alver is very generous. Now that he knows what style of jewellery I prefer, he often calls into Garrards' premises in Albemarle Street, and comes home with the most delightful presents for me!"

"But you are not going to try to persuade me that he selects your gowns as well?"

"No, those are my choices, and I thank you for your very kind remarks, Humphrey!"

"I wish that you could encourage Louisa Buxted to dress her daughter Jane in something more flattering. They aren't here this evening but, at the last ball we all attended, the girl was wearing pink yet again, which really does not suit her red hair and rather freckled complexion. I ventured to suggest another colour that would suit Jane better, but neither she nor Louisa would consider a reasonable alternative!"

Frederica was inclined to agree with him but decided that it was best not to comment.

The Marquis had been standing back from this conversation. However, when their relatives had moved on to speak to other guests, he said quietly, "You seem to get on very well with Humphrey, Frederica? I had not realised previously that he has such a good sense of humour."

"I have been coming to the view that I prefer to talk to them separately. Augusta relaxes more, and does not sound so overbearing, and Humphrey can be quite talkative at times, instead of being almost silent."

"Little do they know what an acute observer my wife can be, darling! May I say that you look very fine this evening in your new diamond tiara, but I still prefer you with your hair down!"

"There is a time and place in my life for everything, love!"

Having lived in rural Herefordshire all her life, Frederica had never had the opportunity to go to the theatre. Now Alver often took a box at the Theatre Royal in Drury Lane, which had had gas lighting installed in 1817. They invited close friends to join them at the performances, and Jessamy developed an enthusiasm for watching plays. With all the lights in use throughout every performance, other people in the audience could be seen very easily from the boxes above.

"Shall we visit other theatres, Alver?"

"Well, there are quite a few to choose from, as you may know. The Theatre Royal has used many famous actresses, several of whom have married members of the peerage. I am quite fond of the Haymarket Theatre with the circular vestibule lined with mirrors. Sadler's Wells is a little out of town, but I have heard that their naval dramas are quite dramatic. The Lyceum was the first theatre to install some gas lighting, but they feature opera performances and, as you know, I am not keen on music as a leisure pursuit!"

Frederica enjoyed all the opportunities to visit these theatres. Indeed, she and Lord Alverstoke agreed that, in general, they preferred a visit to a theatre to going to a ball!

Since neither Charis nor her elder sister could play the piano, Alver did not have to suffer music being heard in his own house. However, Frederica persuaded her husband to visit the Hanover Square Rooms for the annual benefit performance of Handel's Messiah for the Royal Society of Musicians. The Marquis told her firmly that he should not be expected to listen to any other music or for a less worthy cause.

Meanwhile, with Felix now away at school in Windsor, and Harry at the university in Oxford, only two of the Merriville siblings were living in the house in Berkeley Square. Jessamy had been fully occupied with his studies with Septimus Trevor and exercising Alver's horses, and Charis was looking forward to the preparations for her marriage to Endymion Dauntry, who was a frequent visitor to the property.

Lady Eliza had come to town for a few days to stay with her brother and Frederica while she completed her preparations for her daughter Caroline's come-out next Season. She had a list of tasks to complete during her short stay, so her hosts only saw her at mealtimes. However, Eliza and Frederica did manage to include an enjoyable visit to Gunter's, to consume some excellent cakes as well as more than one cup of coffee.

"Presumably John is happy about all the expense of launching your daughter next Season, Eliza?"

"I suspect that he always takes a rather jaundiced view of the Ton, Frederica, as he is a countryman at heart, but he has never shown any concern about what the rented house or the Season will cost him. He and Caroline are good friends and share many interests. He will want her to have the best of everything for her come-out."

On her last day in Berkeley Square, the Marquis had a conversation with his youngest sister.

"It is very interesting to see London through Frederica's eyes, Eliza. Apart from a short visit to her Aunt Scrabster in Harley Street some years ago, she had never been to town until earlier this year, so nearly everything is new to her. By contrast, I have lived in London my whole life, except for being at school in Harrow and then going to Oxford. I am now learning about places and activities that I knew nothing about previously and, with her by my side, I am really enjoying myself."

"You seem very happy to me, Vernon, and with no regrets about leaving all your rakish years behind you. Although you might probably not want to admit the fact, you even find the occasional antics by young Felix quite intriguing?"

"That might be pushing me too far, Eliza, since I am enjoying how quiet the house is in his absence. However, I shall miss Jessamy when he goes to university next year. He is good company when we occasionally share an outing with the horses. I suppose that he, amongst his siblings, is the most like Frederica in personality, though he is sometimes much too serious for a boy who is only 16."

A few days after Lady Eliza had returned home, Wicken told the Marquis that the tutor, Septimus Trevor, was hoping to have a few words with him.

"Do you know where he is, Wicken?"

"When I saw him last, Mr Septimus was talking with his brother Charles in the corridor, sir."

Lord Alverstoke walked through the house to his secretary's office, to find the tutor.

"Come with me to the library, Septimus. Wicken tells me that there is some topic that you would like to discuss?"

When they had sat down together, the tutor said that he was concerned about Jessamy working too hard.

"We have covered everything that he needs to know for the entry examinations very thoroughly, milord. I would like to propose a rather unconventional outing later this month as a distraction – Bartholomew Fair. I was in Fleet Street a few days' ago, and picked up a handbill that I can show you."

Septimus unrolled the poster for Lord Alverstoke to read.

"That all sounds very entertaining, Septimus, I must confess – particularly Madame Giradelli, the Fireproof Lady! Is it possible that she can withstand boiling oil and melted lead? What about Toby, the learned pig that can count, and answer questions? I must admit that all that sounds so intriguing that I might like to go to the Fair myself – but perhaps not. Sadly, I am now too old for such diversions!"

"There are also more conventional attractions at the Fair, milord, puppets, musicians, wire walkers and roundabouts and, of course, no shortage of stalls selling food and drinks."

"I have heard that many people visiting the Fair can get quite rowdy, Septimus? However, I am sure that you would take good care of Jessamy?"

"I suggest that we should wear our oldest clothes, sir – no cravats or well-ironed shirts – so that we don't stand out in the crowds. We should take a hackney to Smithfield, if you give us permission to go."

"Very well, Septimus. Ask my secretary to give you as much money as you are likely to need, and in small coinage."

Jessamy was thrilled to hear about the treat in store for him, and they set out early for what proved to be a long but exciting day at the Fair.

Two weary but happy young men returned to Berkeley Square late that evening, keen to describe everything that they had seen to the Marquis and Frederica, including the prize fights, the Living Skeleton, the famous Dutch Dwarf and other extraordinary persons, and several wild animals.

"The Lord Mayor of London opened the fair last night, on St Bartholomew's Eve. However, when we reached Smithfield, we were just in time to see the Merchant Taylors Guild in their traditional procession to the street named Cloth Fair, to test the measures for cloth using their standard silver yard."

"That sounds very interesting to watch. But do me a favour, Jessamy. Please do not describe to your brother in too much detail what Madame Giradelli endured, or we will have Felix trying to copy her display by dipping himself in acid or touching red-hot irons!"

After the success of the visit to Smithfield, Lord Alverstoke decided to take Frederica, Jessamy and Septimus Trevor to the Egyptian Hall in Piccadilly. Completed some six years earlier, the façade was like a temple with windows of stained glass with lead panes, having a statue on each side of the central window, above which was the Royal coat of arms.

Inside, Mr William Bullock was exhibiting stuffed wild animals 'grazing' in an imitation of an African landscape. However, Frederica was more interested in several Napoleonic artefacts, including the dictator's carriage that was said to be bullet-proof and that had been captured at the battle of Waterloo. There seemed to be thousands of curiosities, including arms and armour, and many objects brought back to England by the explorer Captain James Cook from the southern hemisphere.

"Perhaps this exhibition is not as exciting as Bartholomew Fair, Jessamy, but the location is probably rather more peaceful?"

"Yes, Cousin Alverstoke, I would certainly agree with that remark."

"Now, let us walk further along Piccadilly, as there is something else that I would like to show you."

When they reached a substantial house set well back from the street, he stopped.

"This property is now owned by my friend George Burlington, who purchased the property from his nephew, the Duke of Devonshire, some three years ago. He has a large family with his wife Elizabeth. George has made changes to the interior of the house, but that is not why we have come to view the site.

To one side, you will see a building under construction where there used to be a lane. George and Elizabeth have had many problems with passers-by throwing oyster shells and other rubbish over their boundary wall.

This time next year, when the builders have finished, you will see a narrow covered arcade with top lighting, and a total of 72 small shops on each side of the pedestrian walkway, on two floor levels, and with fully glazed front facades."

"What an excellent idea," said Jessamy. "When the weather is wet, people wanting to shop will not be disturbed by the rain."

"What kind of shops will they be, sir?" asked Septimus.

"George Burlington told me that he will only accept shopkeepers who sell goods of the highest quality. He hopes to have a milliner, some linen shops, a shoemaker, at least one hairdresser, a jeweller or watchmaker, tobacconists and florists, as well as a goldsmith, an optician, a wine merchant, a bookseller, and a stationer."

"He was an army officer in the 10th Royal Hussars, and he will be employing several beadles hired from former soldiers who served in that regiment; they will wear frock coats and top hats. Their instructions will be to prevent any singing, humming, hurrying or any other boisterous behaviour."

"In that case, we will have to make quite sure that we do not bring Felix here!" said Frederica.

They concluded their visit to Piccadilly by calling in to make several purchases at Fortnum and Mason, the grocers whose premises were at the corner of Piccadilly with Duke Street.

The updating of the decorations and furnishings in the house in Berkeley Square was now well advanced, and Alver suggested to Frederica that they might take Jessamy to a race meeting at Newmarket and that they should include Septimus Trevor in the excursion.

A few days later, they all had a most enjoyable visit to Newmarket, though Alver's horse did not win his race. However, the Marquis was more successful at Newbury a week later, with his filly many yards ahead of the other horses at the winning post.

Chapter 7

Sometimes, Alver decided, the mornings when he woke up first could be the best part of the day. Frederica was not restless during the night, and she usually slept soundly beside him. However, and it was quite uncanny, if he woke early, within five minutes or so she would stir and, with her eyes still shut, she would turn and put her arm around him. Then Alver would tickle her ear until she opened her eyes and smiled at him. Nothing would be said, and they might go back to sleep, but on other mornings they didn't, and they would revisit their delight in each other.

Jessamy's studies during the summer at Alver Park with his tutor, Septimus Trevor, had been successful, so much so that when he had gone to Oxford to take Responsions (the entrance tests for the university) in early September, Jessamy had passed the examinations with flying colours in all three subjects - Latin, Ancient Greek, and Mathematics. Indeed, the university had said that Jessamy could go to Oxford this autumn if he wished to do so, a year earlier than was usual.

This suggestion had been discussed in private between Frederica and Alver, and they had given Jessamy a few days to consider the idea and make his decision. They were not happy about Jessamy's intention to enter the church as his profession; both Frederica and Alver considered that Jessamy's academic competence as well as his personality might be better suited to joining the diplomatic service.

"There are reasons why I would like to go to Oxford straightaway", her brother told them, "But would you mind very much if I say No? It would be great to have a few months without having any studies to think about, and to just enjoy myself. If you will permit me to continue to exercise your horses, Cousin Alverstoke, both here in London and at Alver Park, that is what I would like to do. And perhaps I could also be of use in assisting Charles Trevor with some of his duties?"

That idea had not occurred to the Marquess but; as he told Frederica later, the more he thought about it, the better he liked it. Frederica and Alver agreed that both of Jessamy's suggestions should be accepted, and that he should go to university in the autumn of the following year.

"All I ask, Jessamy, is that you do not seek to emulate some young men who, when they arrive in town, parade the streets and wrench off door knockers, or kick over the small huts in which the night watchmen sit, trapping them inside, not to mention pinching shop signs, barbers' poles and even other people's hats!"

Jessamy was about to assure the Marquis that he had no intention of behaving like that when Frederica intervened.

"I cannot think of anyone less likely to behave in such a stupid way, Jessamy. My husband is bamming you!"

Alver had the grace to apologise, and to say that there was no one of his acquaintance who was more sensible than Jessamy, and less likely to behave in such a fashion.

"When I was at Harrow, I was taught fencing, and I enjoyed the sport enough at school to continue since then. You probably haven't had the opportunity to learn, Jessamy? Perhaps you would like to go to Angelo's School of Arms in Bond Street for regular lessons? Darcy Moreton and I go for a bout now and then, usually at least once a month. My secretary might also be interested, as he hopes to join the diplomatic service; fencing is a very popular sport on the Continent."

Jessamy enthusiastically agreed with this suggestion, and he went with Charles Trevor to enrol as a subscriber. The premises seemed to be like a club, with the walls hung with foils, padded practice sleeves, crossed single sticks, and framed illustrations showing various techniques. Mr Angelo showed Jessamy the padded plastron worn under a fencing jacket to protect the chest, and he told them that he organised frequent amateur matches and competitions for his clients.

Charles Trevor reported back to his employer that he thought that Jessamy might be well suited to the sport, as he was calm and patient, and yet quick on his feet and very good at observing his opponent's tactics.

When her brother Harry had called into Berkeley Square to see Felix before he started school at Eton, Frederica had noticed that Jessamy must have grown in height, as he was now almost as tall as his elder brother. With the wedding day only a few weeks away, she realised that Jessamy was going to need some new clothes for the occasion. In Herefordshire, her brothers had used a tailor in the nearby town of Ross on Wye. But their home at Graynard had been let to Mr Porth for several more months, so the local tailor was not an option, and Frederica discussed with her husband what should be done for Jessamy.

"That is quite simple, my love. I will take your brother to my tailor, Weston, at 27 Old Bond Street to be fitted for a new jacket and a stylish waistcoat. He probably needs new boots as well, so we can go to Hoby's shop at the corner of St James' Street and Piccadilly. Has Jessamy a hat for wearing to the church?"

Frederica laughed. "No, he has not. Who can supply that, Alver?"

"Well, James Lock's premises are also in St James' Street – they are the best source. Your brother and I had better go on a shopping expedition tomorrow morning! Should Harry tell you that he wants to pay for Jessamy's new finery, you can tell him that such expenses will fall to me while his brother is living here with us."

On their return to Berkeley Square after a busy morning on the following day, Jessamy told his sister that it was just as well Cousin Alverstoke would be paying for the new jacket and other items, since the Marquis obviously patronised some of the most expensive shops in Mayfair!

About 10 days' later, Jessamy returned home after collecting his new jacket and waistcoat from Weston's, and he put them on to show his sister. His snowy white cravat had been tied by Alver's valet, Knapp, the pale grey waistcoat was embroidered with blue flowers, and he had new breeches, as well as black boots from Hoby's.

She was silent as she looked him up and down.

"Is there some problem, Frederica? It is not like you to be so quiet."

"There is no problem, Jessamy. It is just that you look much older, and - Oh - so stylish, Jessamy! You have changed from a boy into a handsome young man. I have always thought that you resembled our mother's family, and indeed now you look quite like our uncle Richard Winsham."

"I am still the same person underneath as I ever was, Frederica – but the jacket and waistcoat do go well together, don't they?"

"Indeed, they do, Jessamy!" said Alver from the doorway as he came into the room. "You will be quite the swell at the wedding!"

Meanwhile, there were many other matters demanding the attention of Frederica and Alver. Since their marriage, Charis Merriville had been living with them in their home in Berkeley Square.

The betrothal between Charis and Endymion Dauntry had already been announced in the London Gazette. Frederica had suggested to Alver that they should host a ball for Charis and Endymion to celebrate their engagement. Those arrangements had taken time, but the occasion had proved to be very popular with the younger members of the Ton. Now the time had come to plan for the wedding itself.

Frederica and Alver soon realised that their decision to have a quiet country ceremony at Alver Park had been very sensible. Endymion's mother Lucretia was absolutely determined that her son should be married, with all the members of the Ton in the congregation, at the church where she and her late husband Henry Dauntry had been united many years before.

Frederica and Alver thought that Charis and Endymion should be the people to make the decision about where their wedding should be held, not to mention all the other matters that needed to be agreed, especially as Lucretia Dauntry seemed quite unable to plan any task without creating a crisis. Both Alver and Frederica found this very tiresome. They decided that Lucretia should be excluded as far as possible from making any decisions relating to the wedding, in favour of the bride and groom.

However, there was some sense in the ceremony being held in London, since Charis and Endymion had a wide acquaintance amongst members of the Ton, who they wished to invite together with the members of both families. The church, St George's in Hanover Square, was large enough to easily accommodate all the people who they wanted to invite.

Harry had agreed to escort his sister up the aisle to give her away, and the chosen date was in the middle of the term at Oxford, when he would be permitted to travel from his university for a few days in London. Endymion's sisters Chloe and Diana were to be the bridesmaids, together with their cousin Caroline Kentmere. Caroline's younger sister Mary would have an important role as the flower girl to hold the bride's bouquet once Charis had reached the altar.

Being only too familiar with Lucretia Dauntry's ability to overspend whenever she was given the opportunity, Alver had already told her how much he was willing to contribute for the wedding arrangements, including the reception which was to be held at the house in Berkeley Square. Alver had informed Lucretia of his financial offer in the presence of both Endymion and Charis, who considered the amount to be very generous, so she had been unable to complain as was her normal habit.

Lucretia Dauntry was a well-preserved beauty who always looked very stylish in the clinging gowns that she habitually wore. No doubt she was planning to attend her son's wedding in a suitably elaborate dress for the occasion. But Frederica had no intention of allowing Lucretia to choose what Charis, or any of the bride's attendants, would wear.

Frederica had told her sister firmly that she would not be allowed to sew her own wedding dress, as Charis had initially suggested. Instead, Frederica took Charis, together with Chloe, Diana, Caroline and Mary Kentmere, to visit her modiste Mlle Franchot, so that Charis could choose the dress design that she favoured for her attendants. They were measured for their gowns, and Charis also chose what she wanted to wear herself on the day, and placed orders for the other items that would be needed. Visits were also needed to shoemakers in Piccadilly and Old Bond Street.

Alver knew how much all this was likely to cost, and he arranged to transfer a generous amount of money to Frederica's personal bank account.

A visit was also needed to Miss Starke, the milliner in Conduit Street where, guided by her elder sister, Charis purchased several delightful hats to wear for starting her married life, although she insisted that she would not need so many, as she and Endymion planned to spend most of their time on his country estate, rather than in London.

"Perhaps, if we were to have several daughters, you need to start saving up now for their weddings, Alver?"

He replied that to do so, until those happy events had occurred, he was content to cope with the current nuptials, giving himself some years to recover!

"What are you going to wear for the wedding, Frederica? With so many members of the Ton likely to be present, I assume that you will also require a new hat as well as a lovely dress."

"I shall decide nearer the date what I prefer, when all the other details have been settled. But for now, shall I choose the menu for the reception? Charis does not seem to have any preferences at all about the food to be served, and I very much doubt whether Endymion will have any opinions."

"Very wise, my love. Why don't you have a discussion with our chef and pass on his suggestions to Charis and Endymion. The happy couple will probably agree without asking for any changes. Then we can present my cousin Lucretia with a 'fait accompli'!"

Frederica escorted Charis and her wedding attendants on a return visit to Mlle Franchot's salon to try on their dresses, and she reported back to Alver that the bride and the other young ladies would be looking very fine on the happy day.

She had spoken to Charis about the decorations to be used in the house for the wedding reception, and they visited the Pantheon Bazaar together to make some purchases. Alver's secretary Charles Trevor had placed a large order for the flowers to decorate the ballroom. Charis wanted there to be an opportunity for dancing, so the musicians who had been at her coming-out ball had been asked to play during the reception.

Endymion Dauntry visited Berkeley Square for a discussion about the outstanding matters relating to the wedding with Charis, Frederica and Alver. He was planning to wear his military uniform at the wedding for the last time before he left the army. There was a discussion about the speeches at the reception, as it was customary for the bridegroom to say a few words, followed by the bride's father.

"I have no abilities whatsoever in public speaking, Cousin Vernon. Fred Merriville died twelve months ago, and his son Harry is very reluctant to speak in his father's place. What do you suggest that we should do?"

The Marquis and Frederica exchanged looks, and then he said, "Endymion, Charis, if your preference is that I should say a few words to welcome the guests to Alverstoke House, then I could propose a toast to both of you, the bride and groom. Would that be appropriate?"

"We would both be very happy with that suggestion, Cousin Vernon. Thank you."

Alver then revealed that his wedding present to the happy couple would be the land in Buckinghamshire that had recently been found to add to the Dauntry estate. He also told them that Mr Salcombe's search in Herefordshire for a younger man had been successful, to take over the management of the estate from Endymion's elderly steward.

The information that Alver did not pass on was that Salcombe had told him in a letter that the young man seemed to be very competent, so that they need have no worries about the Dauntry estate income being insufficient to support the newly-weds.

"That is an exceptionally generous wedding gift, Cousin Vernon. Thank you both very much."

Charis, in her soft gentle voice, agreed with her betrothed. Frederica was an amused onlooker, as she knew how much trouble the Marquis had taken to achieve a satisfactory solution for the Dauntrys' future income from their estate.

"Are you determined, Endymion, to 'sell out' and leave the Army?"

"Yes, Frederica. I have enjoyed my time with my brother officers, and made good friends, but Charis and I both prefer to live in the countryside. We are really looking forward to returning to Buckinghamshire after our honeymoon. I have already agreed with my mama that we will visit London regularly, as she much prefers living in Town."

"For a change from all this talk of weddings, why don't I take you and Charis, as well as Frederica and Jessamy, to Astley's? Have you been there before, Endymion?"

"No, Cousin Vernon, I have not. What an excellent suggestion!"

Astley's popular show was held in a large building on the south-west side of Westminster Bridge, and Alver had told Frederica that it was the biggest amphitheatre in London.

As she entered the venue, Frederica exclaimed, "What an absolutely enormous space, Alver!"

"Yes, indeed. There have been two fires on this site, and each time Astley has rebuilt the amphitheatre bigger and better!"

Before them, they could see a large stage, separated by the orchestra pit from the circus ring, with ramps between the two ready for dramatic gallops by the horses. Below the ceiling, there were three tiers of seats for the audience, in addition to those people who were seated close to the circus ring. As they looked up above the first tier where they were sitting, the centre of the ceiling had been painted with a detailed design in gold below a large chandelier. Charis was entranced as she watched the show, which included acrobats, strong men, dancing dogs, jugglers and clowns, as well as the horses which were used for the Human Pyramid act.

After this very enjoyable diversion, the preparations for the wedding continued smoothly without any intervention by Lucretia Dauntry – too much so, the Marquis thought, as his experiences in the past had taught him that she would find some excuse to draw attention to herself, and soon he was proved to be right.

Alver and Frederica had just returned home to Berkeley Square after spending a few days attending the races at Newmarket when Jessamy came into the drawing room, breathless from searching for them.

"Thank goodness you are both back home! There has been such a fuss here, with Charis at her wits end about knowing what to do."

"What is the problem, young man? Something to do with Lucretia?"

"Yes, sir. Miss Plumley has not been in Green Street for several days, as she has had to visit a family member who lives up north and is unwell. While her companion was away, Mrs Dauntry was taken ill with one of her spasms, and she insisted on a new doctor being called to attend her. When he told his patient that he couldn't find anything wrong with her, Mrs Dauntry lost her temper and insisted that her previous medical adviser should be summoned."

"But it turned out that the other doctor was not in town, as he was in Richmond attending to another client. Lucretia then wanted her son to come to her, but Endymion is on guard duty at St James Palace today, and he sent a message that he would not be able to get to Green Street until later this evening."

"Then Charis was summoned to Green Street, and I went with her, but she had no idea what to do next. When we got to the house, Mrs Dauntry wanted me to go to St James Palace to persuade Endymion to change his mind, but I said that I was not willing to intervene. She called me all sorts of rude names, and eventually I told Charis to come back with me to Berkeley Square! So that is the current situation, sir. Charis is upstairs in her room, feeling tearful and guilty about not knowing what to do. Have you any good ideas, Frederica?"

"Yes, I do. I suggest that you and we do nothing at all. Endymion will be back in Green Street this evening. Meanwhile, unless you believe that Mrs Dauntry is really unwell, she will not come to any harm. Do you know whether Chloe and Diana are with her?"

"No, they are not. Charis told me that they are away for a few days on a visit to one of Chloe's friends who lives in Brighton."

Alver had been listening to all this excitement with a cynical smile on his face, but now he intervened in the conversation.

"I have often thought that a little 'benign neglect' is much the best way of dealing with Lucretia. The more attention she manages to attract, the more tiresome she becomes. Go and find Charis, Jessamy, and bring her downstairs. We can console her, and make sure that she eats some supper. Eventually, Endymion will arrive here in Berkeley Square, and tell us what has happened in Green Street since you were there earlier today."

Between them, they were able to assure Charis that she had done her best, and to persuade her that Endymion would arrive sooner or later, to tell her the outcome. When he finally arrived, Endymion's normally placid demeanour had been seriously ruffled in trying to cope with his mother's complaints about her treatment, including Jessamy's insistence that Charis should return to Berkeley Square.

"I must admit, sir," he said, addressing the Marquis, "that whatever amount my mother pays Miss Plumley to be her companion could not be too much to compensate her for carrying out her duties! I am quite exhausted, and I really cannot see that there is anything at all wrong with my mama. She told me that she had called Jessamy several names that I will not repeat, and she complained about Charis returning here."

Charis, with his arm around her shoulders, was already reassured. "When will Miss Plumley be returning to town?"

"My mother said probably on Friday or Saturday. It cannot be too soon, as far as I am concerned!"

Later that evening, Alver and Frederica reviewed the events of the day before they went to sleep.

"I had thought that Endymion did not realise how good his mother was at play-acting. What is your opinion, Frederica?"

"Well, he has had 25 years to find out, I suppose. He must be looking forward to living at least two hours' travelling distance from Green Street!"

"With the wedding date approaching, I suppose that we can expect Lucretia to produce more regular 'spasms' to get everyone's attention? Why don't we go down to Alver Park for a few days, Frederica, taking Charis with us? Jessamy can come as well, and Endymion can probably arrange for a few days' leave from his military duties. If we leave tomorrow morning, Lucretia will not be able to ask for an invitation to travel to Wiltshire."

Frederica was surprised how quickly this idea could be set in motion, and by Thursday night they were all at Alver Park, and enjoying a pleasant supper prepared by their housekeeper, Mrs Edwards. Endymion was able to join them on the following day.

The new wide paths around the estate were almost completed, and Frederica continued her driving lessons with Alver in the curricle. Endymion offered to teach Charis how to drive, but she lacked the courage to learn, so they spent their time together walking in the park and looking at the views of the countryside around.

The large sofa that Alver and Frederica had ordered for the summerhouse had been delivered some weeks ago, and it had been taken up the hill on a cart to the intended location. On a showery afternoon, they sat together admiring the wide views to the south, remembering Alver's grandparents George and Caroline who had used the summerhouse for the same purpose.

On a rather wet morning a few days later, Jessamy rode on one of Alver's horses for the short journey to visit Septimus at his father's rectory near Bath. The Trevor family congratulated him on his excellent results in the Responsion examinations for his university entry due, as Jessamy was quick to tell them, to the helpful tuition that he had received from Septimus.

Alver's secretary Charles wrote to Frederica from London to say that a very short note had come from Felix at school, but that the news therein was as limited as usual. A letter had arrived in town from Lady Eliza Kentmere for the Marquis, but Charles had not opened that communication, having set it aside for Alver's attention when he returned to London.

When Lucretia Dauntry discovered that her son was out of town and staying with Charis at Alver Park, a complaining message arrived for him, and a second for Charis. Both letters having been passed to Alver and Frederica to read, they advised the recipients not to reply, but to continue to enjoy the visit to their country estate!

They had a welcome diversion during their return journey from Wiltshire towards London, as Alver had a horse running in a race at Newbury. They all stayed overnight at an inn a short distance away, so that they could travel to the racecourse on the following morning.

It was the first occasion when Charis had watched a horse race, and she really enjoyed the experience. Endymion told her that, as in Herefordshire, there were local races near his country estate that they would be able to attend, once they were married.

Once back in town, Endymion went to visit his mother without Charis. Miss Plumley had returned from her family visit, and order had been restored in Green Street. He took the opportunity to have a long private conversation with his mother's companion, including asking her how much she was paid by Lucretia for her rather onerous duties.

Frederica had asked Charles Trevor to make enquiries at the staff agency as to what an appropriate amount would be, and how much demand there was for well qualified ladies' companions. Armed with this information, Endymion frightened his mother by telling her that, if she did not want to lose Miss Plumley's services, she needed to increase her salary by a substantial amount. Lucretia, always more generous towards herself than to others, jibbed at this suggestion, but she was even more concerned about the possibility of her companion leaving for a better paid position in another household. Miss Plumley soon had a pleasant surprise – and Frederica with Charles Trevor were congratulated by the Marquis on a job well done!

The letter from his sister Lady Eliza had included a request for the Kentmere family to stay in Berkeley Square so that they could attend the wedding. She very much doubted whether they would enjoy a visit to her sister Louisa Buxted's household, and her eldest sister Augusta Jevington would be hosting other guests for the wedding celebrations, so she was unable to offer enough bedrooms for the four Kentmere children as well as their parents.

Frederica and Alver were happy to be of use, provided that the young people could share their bedrooms. Jessamy would be pleased to see Jack again, and Felix to share his bedroom with Tom, although the Marquis had made it very clear that no experiments of any kind were to happen inside the house!

A few days later, Frederica was walking along the corridor towards the entrance hall. As she passed one of the footmen, she stopped.

"Walter, good morning. Have you seen Lord Alverstoke?"

"Yes, milady. He is in the library with Lord Buxted."

After thanking him for the information, she went to join them.

Unusually, Carlton did not seem to be pleased to see her, but Alver smiled at Frederica as she entered the room.

"We have a surprise visitor, my dear. My nephew has come to ask our advice on a family problem."

At this, Lord Buxted demurred.

"Alverstoke, I really don't think that the subject is suitable for a lady's ears!"

"Carlton, I can assure you that Frederica knows exactly what a 'barque of frailty' does, don't you, my love?"

"Yes, I remember that you once said that you had been an expert on the ladies who provided services of that kind. But why are you having to trouble yourself on that subject, Carlton. Surely you ..."

Lord Buxted looked outraged.

"I do not need the advice on my own behalf, Frederica! But I have received a letter from the headmaster at Harrow. Apparently, my brother, with two friends, has been ... visiting a particular location in the town on a regular basis, and the headmaster thought that I should know about his activities."

"I don't believe that I have met your brother George. How old is he?"

"He is 17, and in his last year at the school."

At this point, Alver intervened.

"Carlton wants me to visit Harrow to remonstrate with his brother. I have told him that I do not believe that would be a sensible course of action. The problem is that it is several weeks before the school term ends, and my cousin does not want to wait until George returns home to Grosvenor Place."

"May I make a suggestion, Alver?"

"Yes, of course you may, love."

"Carlton, you and your family - your mother, brother and your three sisters - have already accepted invitations to my sister's wedding in two weeks' time?"

"Yes, we have, Frederica."

"Well, the reception afterwards for Charis and Endymion is to be held here in Berkeley Square. The reception could give Alver several opportunities, before or after lunch, to take George aside to have a few words on the subject. Would you be willing to help in that way, my dear?"

Alver sighed, smiled at her and then said to his cousin that, yes, he would undertake to speak to George during the reception.

Carlton Buxted, who from the expression on his face had been ready to disagree with any suggestion that Frederica might make, could find no reason to object to her very sensible proposal.

Alver, secretly amused at his cousin's reaction, ended the conversation by mentioning the various preparations being made for the wedding, and then took Lord Buxted to the front door.

When he returned to the library, he laughed and then remarked, "Poor Carlton, he tries so hard to look after his family, as indeed he should, but he has no idea what to do when his much more enterprising brother gets into a scrape! Perhaps Felix will not turn out the same way when he is older, as your father did."

Frederica did not reply to this suggestion, but inwardly hoped that Alver's words would be correct when her youngest brother reached the same age.

Frederica visited her modiste Mlle Franchot to choose the material for the dress that she would wear to the wedding, to be made in a simple design that she knew would suit her. Both the new gown and the matching hat from the milliner Miss Starke would be in a pale green shade, so that she could wear the emerald necklace and ear bobs that the Marquis had given her.

Felix came back from school two days before the wedding and, unlike Jessamy, the new clothes that had been purchased for him before he had started at Eton were still a good fit.

Frederica was surprised how calm Charis was on the morning of the wedding, and the bride was dressed in good time before her brother Harry arrived at Berkeley Square to take her to the church. She had borrowed the diamond necklace that Frederica had inherited from their mother, to wear with the new diamond ear bobs that her sister had given to her as a wedding gift. The bridesmaids would be waiting in the entrance to the church in Hanover Square, with Mary Kentmere ready to hold the bride's flowers once she had reached the altar.

The Marquis and Frederica went to see Charis in the drawing room before their carriage was brought to the front door.

"That is a most beautiful dress, Charis, and your floral bouquet is delightful. May I wish you well for the ceremony, and the reception here afterwards?"

"Thank you, Cousin Alverstoke, and for letting me live here for the past few months. Endymion and I will look forward to hosting both you and Frederica in our home in Buckinghamshire, once we return from our honeymoon."

"Now where have Jessamy and Felix got to? They are supposed to be travelling to the church with us."

"Your brothers are already waiting in the hall, my love. Let us all go now and be on our way."

When the Marquis's carriage arrived at Hanover Square, the church was almost full, with most of the friends and relations of the bride and groom already sitting in the pews. The bridesmaids were waiting just inside the building, and they smiled nervously at Frederica as she passed by. There was a floral archway as she entered the church with Alver beside her, and they walked up the aisle to take their seats at the front. Many people in the congregation turned their heads to see who the smartly dressed young man was, as Jessamy walked with Felix behind Frederica and the Marquis.

A few minutes later, the organist began to play as Charis and her brother Harry entered the church, and they began their walk up the aisle towards the altar, followed by Mary Kentmere and the three bridesmaids. Mary took the flowers from the bride, and the service began. Frederica wished that her mother could have been there to see how beautiful Charis looked in her lovely gown. The time passed by very quickly, and soon the clergyman was pronouncing that Endymion and Charis were now man and wife.

Harry Merriville and Lucretia Dauntry witnessed the signatures as the register was signed in the vestry. Then the happy couple walked back down the aisle to the sounds of the wedding march, followed by their guests ready to throw confetti over them as they settled themselves into their open carriage, ready for the journey to the reception in Alverstoke House.

"Tell me, Frederica" said Lady Ormond, as she waited beside the Marquis and his wife outside the church, "who is that handsome young man who walked behind you into the church?"

"That is my middle brother, Jessamy. He would be very flattered indeed to know that you consider him to be handsome, Susan. So may I thank you on his behalf?"

"Indeed. I thought that there was a family resemblance. Charis and her brother Harry perhaps take more after your father?"

"Yes, you are correct. My youngest brother Felix, who was walking beside Jessamy, is a mixture of both sides of my family. But one of Felix is quite enough!"

Frederica and Alver found Curry waiting with the barouche to drive them home with Jessamy and Felix, and soon their house was full of guests arriving for the wedding reception. The family dining room had been set aside for the younger guests, supervised by Mrs

Jones the housekeeper, with a generous buffet on the sideboard full of tempting dishes for Felix Merriville and the other guests of a similar age.

Charis and Endymion greeted their families and friends just inside the doors to the ballroom, and Frederica and the Marquis circulated around the room, greeting everyone present. Eventually they met, and Frederica asked her husband, "Have you had a chance yet for a private conversation with George Buxted?"

"I can see him over there on the other side of the room, talking to Jessamy and Diana Dauntry. Why don't we join them, and then I can perhaps take him aside for a few private words."

George seemed to be a very pleasant young man, with a rather livelier personality than his elder brother. Frederica started an interesting discussion with Jessamy and Diana about how the service in the church had gone and, when she next turned round, she could not see either Alver or George.

Then Chloe Dauntry came across the room to talk to her sister, with Charles Trevor beside her, and by the time Jessamy suggested that they might like to take a glass of wine from the tray being offered to them by one of the footmen, George Buxted was back, standing next to Frederica.

"Are your sisters Maria and Kitty in our family dining room with the other younger people, George?"

"Yes, they are, milady, and they both said that they are enjoying the occasion. Your brother Felix was there with Tom Kentmere, busy eating the food on the buffet table!"

This news did not surprise either Frederica or Jessamy, who was standing beside her.

"Can you see my husband anywhere? – there is something that I want to speak to him about."

Jessamy pointed to his right.

"He is over there, standing by the glazed doors to the garden, talking to Lord Ormond with his son James and his daughter in law Marietta. But Wicken has just come into the room, which may mean that Cousin Alverstoke is about to say a few words to the guests about Charis and Endymion?"

His comments proved to be correct, as the butler called for everyone to be quiet as Alver came across the room to put Frederica's hand on his arm, and they walked together to stand on the raised dais at the end of the ballroom. Endymion and Charis joined them to listen to the speech by the Marquis. Before he began speaking, he lifted his wife's hand to his lips, and kissed it.

"First, may I welcome you all to Alverstoke House on this very happy occasion? It is a particular pleasure for me to do so with my wife Frederica by my side. I can advise the newlyweds that I can thoroughly recommend the married state, and I hope that Frederica is able to say the same!"

She laughed at him - but remained silent as he continued.

"Sadly, Frederick Merriville died a year ago, so Charis does not have her father here to speak on her behalf."

"The groom has told me that speechmaking is not his 'forte', so I hope that you will find me an acceptable substitute for both. Charis met Endymion in this house a few months' ago at her coming-out ball and, from that moment on, it seems that their affections for each other have grown ever stronger."

"When Frederica and I married, we agreed that we should do so in the church near my estate at Alver Park. Charis has lived with us here since we returned to London, whilst the arrangements have been made for her wedding to Endymion in the church where his parents were married many years ago."

"They are delighted that so many of their friends are here today to support them and to celebrate the occasion. Charis and Endymion would like me to thank her attendants – Chloe and Diana Dauntry, and Caroline and Mary Kentmere - who I hope you will agree look delightful in their beautiful dresses, and they have all performed their duties in an exemplary manner."

At this point, the Marquis paused to allow for the guests to applaud the young ladies.

"Now it is my very welcome task to ask you to raise your wine glasses, to wish Endymion and Charis a very happy future life together. Here's to their health and happiness! Endymion and Charis!"

And he raised his glass to his lips and, after pausing briefly, he called for three cheers for the newlywed couple.

"So well done, my dearest Alver!" said Frederica to him quietly after the cheers had died down. "Thank you, love!"

Chapter 8

"I have a proposition for you, Frederica."

"I should like to take you for a short visit to my estate at Fairworthy, which adjoins the boundary between Devon and Dorset. Most of the 250 acres of land lie within Dorset, in the direction of the attractive town of Beaminster. I had an interesting conversation with your lawyer Mr Salcombe in the days before our wedding. He told me how well you had managed your family's estate at Graynard, and he suggested that it would be regrettable if your skills were not to be used in the future. The Fairworthy estate came into my family through my great grandmother Jane – the lady who had the idea of creating the Sculpture Avenue. I hope that you will be willing to take over the management of the estate from me; the steward in charge there, Mr Bugler, is a very competent man."

His wife was speechless for a few moments after Alver had made this proposal, but she soon regained her voice.

"I should absolutely love to do that, Alver, after we have visited the property together."

"Well, that was the reason for my suggestion. Why don't we travel to Fairworthy quite soon, and we could take Jessamy with us. Felix may have other ideas!"

The Marquis was correct about Felix, who asked his elder sister to write to Lady Eliza, as he would like to travel to the Shires to see his friend Tom Kentmere. Having established that Septimus Trevor would be willing to accompany Felix on the journey by stagecoach, Frederica wrote to her sister-in-law, and received a rapid and favourable response.

Having despatched Felix and his companion on their journey to the Midlands, Alver and Frederica left town for the Fairworthy estate, with Jessamy with them in their travelling carriage, and Emily Leonard and Knapp in the second vehicle. After two stays overnight in hostelries on the route, they passed through Beaminster, a pleasant stone-built small town with an attractive square in the centre. Alver then pointed out a steep escarpment on their right, which he said was named Pilsdon Pen and was thought to be a prehistoric earthwork. A further 15-minute journey took them to their destination.

The house had been built on a gentle rise in the ground, with a wide panoramic view and the sea in the distance. The steward, Mr Bugler, and his wife greeted them on arrival, and they entered a spacious entrance hall with a highly polished oak floor. Two hours later, after an enjoyable meal in the dining room, the three of them sat together in the salon to decide what they wished to do during their stay.

"Perhaps we could start with a discussion with Mr Bugler tomorrow morning, followed by a tour of the farm buildings and then parts of the estate, Alver?"

"I agree. I do not keep any horses here, Jessamy, although there is a gig in the stables if you would like to harness one of the carriage horses for an outing."

"Yes, I could do that, Cousin Alverstoke, whilst you are both busy with the steward. Are we planning to climb Pilsdon Pen during our visit?"

"If the weather stays favourable, why not! Curry can drive us to the foot of the steep slope, and we can walk up to the summit from there."

Frederica asked what other places in the locality were worth a visit.

"Both Beaminster and Bridport, which is closer to the sea, are towns with good shops, and inns for a meal. They make ropes for the Navy in Bridport, so you might like to visit the Rope Walks where long hemp strands are twisted together into rope before they are sent to Chatham Dockyard in Kent. Lyme Regis, to the west, has an interesting harbour, but the place can get rather too busy with visitors."

During the return journey towards London after their visit to the estate, Jessamy said that he had enjoyed the climb up Pilsdon Pen the most, although it was just as well that the weather had not been any warmer. Frederica had preferred their day in Bridport, and the meal of fresh fish that they had enjoyed in the town.

"Everyone who we met there seemed to be called either Bugler or Loder, Jessamy! I assume that those are local names."

Alver did not state a preference but said how happy he was that Frederica was willing to take on the management of the Fairworthy estate.

The morning after their return to town, Alver and Frederica were in their private upstairs sitting room.

"I seem to remember you mentioning Diana a few months ago, when we were talking about her elder sister Chloe Dauntry and Charles Trevor. You were quite correct, Frederica."

"You mean that Diana is promising to become a most lovely girl?"

"Yes. But having talked to her briefly at the wedding reception for Charis and Endymion, you were quite right - she will be a beautiful wet-goose like your sister whereas, despite her youth, Chloe has the makings of becoming an excellent wife for a diplomat!"

"Are you matchmaking now, Alver, and planning a new career for your secretary?"

"Perhaps. I will hate to see Charles leave, as he is by far the most competent and pleasant young man who I have ever employed to assist me. But he is clearly very smitten with Chloe, and she with him. If they are to marry, he will be needing a larger income, and to have some clear plans for his future. Maybe I should speak to Edward Ormond, as he has high level connections in the Foreign Office. Often, being employed by an ambassador in a foreign country can be a beginning for a very successful career in our government."

"My abigail, Emily, said when I interviewed her for the position, that she had previously worked for the wife of the diplomat who is now the English ambassador in Vienna. Would Edward be acquainted with him, I wonder?"

"I had forgotten that, love. I will ask Edward to answer your question."

"Have you ever spoken to Charles about his future career, Alver? Or perhaps I should ask him about Chloe?"

"Would you, my darling? That discussion would be better coming from you than from me, if you could find a suitable opportunity."

It was during a discussion about the management of Fairworthy, the large estate on the borders of Devon and Dorset, that Frederica asked Mr Trevor about Chloe Dauntry.

"Would you consider me impertinent, Charles, if I enquire about your intentions towards Endymion's sister? When I lived in the house in Upper Wimpole Street, I remember you being a very welcome visitor, but you were really coming to meet Chloe, weren't you?"

Charles flushed, and then admitted that she was quite right.

"I saw Chloe very frequently before Endymion Dauntry married your sister, but it is much more difficult now that he and Charis are abroad on their honeymoon. You are quite correct – I do love her, and she tells me that she loves me in return. But her mother is hoping for a much better match for Chloe than I can offer at present, someone with money and good prospects in the future."

"The Marquis has told me that his godfather has high level connections in the Foreign Office. Would you like Lord Alverstoke to arrange for you to meet Lord Ormond at his home in Mayfair, to see whether he could be of any help?"

"That would be wonderful, milady! I have thought that my work here would be a good preparation for a junior role in government, but I have had no idea about how I could achieve that."

Having heard about this conversation with his secretary, the Marquis went to see his godfather. He told Edward Ormond about Charles Trevor, and the previous connection of Frederica's abigail with the wife of the ambassador to Austria. Two weeks passed, and then Charles Trevor received an invitation to visit Lord Ormond at his home.

"Vernon Dauntry speaks very highly of you, Mr Trevor," said Lord Ormond. "May I ask how old you are?"

"I shall have my 24th birthday next month, milord."

"Alverstoke told me that, although he would be very reluctant for you to leave him, he would like me to make some enquiries on your behalf. It seems that the man currently in post in Vienna assisting the new ambassador may be promoted during the next six months, most likely after next April, to a more senior post elsewhere. If you would be willing to work abroad, it might be possible for you to replace him. You would need to be interviewed at the Foreign Office, of course, and Vernon tells me that there is a young lady involved in your future. She would have to be happy to accompany you abroad, if you plan to marry?"

Charles could hardly believe what he was hearing, but it all sounded very positive.

"I would need to discuss what you have mentioned with Chloe – Miss Dauntry - sir. But the suggestion that you have made is most welcome. May I speak to her and then send you a note about the outcome?"

"Indeed, you should. But don't delay, for these matters can take time to arrange, and I should hate you to miss the opportunity, if the idea appeals to you."

After his return to Berkeley Square, Mr Trevor told his employer what had been suggested. Frederica immediately invited Chloe to join her and Charles Trevor for tea at Gunter's, so that the two young people could discuss what Lord Ormond had proposed. Chloe had no qualms at all about moving to live abroad, and the main hurdle would seem to be whether Lucretia Dauntry would agree to the marriage taking place.

Frederica spoke to her husband afterwards.

"Emily has told me that her previous employer, the ambassador's wife, is a very pleasant person, as is her husband, so Charles need have no worries on that score. As for Chloe's mother, I will deal with her. Diana Dauntry is due to make her come-out, and I could suggest to Lucretia that her younger daughter's entry to the Ton would be much easier to organise if Chloe is already betrothed to Charles, and if he has positive plans for their future."

Alver was highly amused at all this plotting, and he was happy to stand back and watch whilst Frederica's intentions were achieved!

In due course, Lord Ormond was able to arrange for Charles to be interviewed at the Foreign Office, and Mr Trevor was delighted to be added to the Government list for the candidates for the posts to be filled next year.

Meanwhile, the next letter sent to them by Felix was rather longer than usual. John Kentmere, the father of his schoolfriend Tom, was apparently employing a dowser to find water on part of the family's large estate in the Shires. Felix was very intrigued by the idea, and he wanted to know whether Lord Alverstoke had ever tried to locate water on his estate at Alver Park.

When told about this request, the Marquis remarked, "At least Felix looking for water cannot cause an explosion, for which we should all be very grateful!"

"Have you ever searched for water on your estate, Alver?"

"No, Frederica, I haven't, although the subject of dowsing has been discussed several times between my friends at the club."

"And what equipment would dowsing require?"

"I will write to John Kentmere today for some more information. Then Felix can enjoy looking for water when we next travel with him to Alver Park. Indeed, perhaps he might like to try to find water under the ground in our garden here in Berkeley Square."

Frederica and Alver had continued their practice of drinking chocolate on Saturday and Sunday mornings, but it was more convenient to do so in their private sitting room, rather than in Lord Alverstoke's bedroom.

It was in the sitting room that Emily Leonard found them on the following Saturday morning, to deliver several letters that had just arrived. The first was from John Kentmere, in reply to the correspondence from the Marquis earlier in the week. The second was from Lady Eliza for Frederica, reminding her that the rental for the house that the Kentmere family had hired for their daughter Caroline's coming-out ball would commence in a week's time.

"Your sister with Caroline would like to stay with us for two nights next week, whilst Eliza completes the arrangements for the staff who need to be hired for the Season, and then they will move into the property in Mayfair. I don't see any problems with that, do you, Alver?"

"No, my dear, that will be fine. I shall be delighted to see them both. John Kentmere writes to say that Eliza will bring with her in the carriage several Y-shaped twigs from a hazel tree. Apparently, they would be needed for any dowsing that we might attempt. The elderly man who they had employed to search for water in the fields on his estate was successful both in finding new water sources, and in locating existing pipes. John also remarks that we have a pond here at the rear of our property, which must be supplied by either a water pipe or a spring. You and I could see what we can locate here?"

Once during each term, the parents of scholars at Eton were sent a letter from their pupil's housemaster, to report on their boy's progress at the school, and a letter had arrived from Windsor for the Marquis.

"The housemaster writes that Felix is a most unusual pupil, both in his interests and in his persistence in pursuing his current enthusiasms. However, they seem to be coping quite well with keeping his exuberance under control."

"Perhaps we should ask them exactly how they manage to do that, my love! As you know, my young brother can be very persuasive at times, with his melting-eyes expressions!"

From their first acquaintance, Frederica had taken to Alver's youngest sister Eliza, and she had enjoyed her company at Alver Park when her family had stayed in the house during the week before the wedding. Lady Eliza shared her brother Alverstoke's very lively sense of humour, but her personality was less abrupt and more open than his. Caroline, the eldest of the Kentmere children, had inherited her mother's direct character but looked more like her father.

When the two visitors arrived in Berkeley Square, Jessamy Merriville was on hand as well as Frederica and her husband to welcome them. Their luggage, including the parcel of hazel twigs, had been unloaded, and it soon became clear that the two young people were very keen to explore the rear garden and to test their dowsing skills.

"Will you come with us, Uncle Vernon? asked Caroline Kentmere. "Jessamy and I have one of the hazel twigs here, and I know how to use it, as I went with my Papa and the dowser when they were searching for water all over our estate."

"Very well, Caroline. I am sure that your mother and Frederica will have plenty of news to exchange before dinner, so let the three of us go into the garden now and see what we can find."

The rather formal design of the space behind the house had been changed recently at Frederica's request, but the pond remained in the same location. Jessamy and Lord Alverstoke watched as Caroline held the hazel twig, with one of the two short branches in each hand, and the longer arm pointing away from her. Starting with the façade of the house to her right, she walked slowly back and forth, getting closer to the pond each time. Suddenly the long arm of the twig dipped and twisted away from her, and Caroline stopped walking.

"Goodness!" the Marquis exclaimed. "That wasn't you, Caroline, moving your hands, was it?"

"No, that is what happens when there is water, or a water pipe, below my hands."

"May I try, please?" said Jessamy.

So, he repeated what Caroline had done, and the twig twisted in his hands in exactly the same location.

"It's not possible to stop the twig turning in my hands when it wants to do so, sir. Would you like to have a go yourself?"

Alverstoke took the twig, holding it in his hands as Caroline had shown them, and he felt the strong sensation as the tip of the Y-shape dipped away from him.

They extended their exploration to other parts of the garden and discovered two other locations where there seemed to be a reaction. Caroline told them that there were probably underground water pipes in all three places leading to the pond, and that they could create a map, if that would be useful.

"Your brother Felix is going to be fighting with you when you try dowsing at Alver Park, Jessamy, and for once you will know more about something practical than he does!"

"Well," said Caroline, "we have brought several hazel twigs with us, uncle, so there should be no need for a fight!"

At dinner, Lady Eliza told her brother that the staff agency recommended by his secretary, Charles Trevor, had identified several candidates for the temporary posts of butler, footmen, maids and kitchen staff that she would need, and that she would be interviewing them at the agency on the following morning.

Both her sons were now away at school in Windsor, and she had left her younger daughter at home with her father and her governess. Mary would be accompanying John Kentmere when he travelled to join Lady Eliza and Caroline at the house in Mayfair in a week or so.

"Frederica has wondered whether I would consider including Diana Dauntry in the come-out ball for Caroline, Vernon. I understand that her sister Chloe may wish to marry soon, so that Lucretia will have the expense of that event in any case, without having to pay for Diana's come-out."

"Eliza, that would be most civil of you," said her brother. "I am sure that Lucretia and Diana would be delighted with that suggestion. Caroline, would you be happy to agree to that idea?"

"I don't see why not, Uncle Vernon. I began to know Diana better when we met at Alver Park before your wedding, and since then, when Charis married her brother Endymion. Perhaps Diana and I could support each other during the Season?"

At this point, Lady Eliza joined in the conversation.

"Although Caroline has already had several dancing lessons at home in the Shires, I shall be employing a dancing master in London for a few weeks to perfect her skills. Would you like to join her, Jessamy, for those lessons?"

"Am I to be invited to the come-out ball, Lady Eliza?"

"But of course you are. You are part of the family, although I am told that your brother Harry is not keen to attend any social events."

"Then I will be very happy to accept your offer – although I should warn you that I have never had a dancing lesson in my life!"

"Jessamy, do you have a chess set in this house? I often play with my father at home and would enjoy a game."

"Yes, we do, Caroline. It is in the library. Shall we go, and have a game now before it is time for bed?"

"If there is no chess set in the house that Eliza has hired, I should be pleased to buy one for Caroline and Jessamy to use."

Later that evening when they were alone, Alver spoke to Frederica about her suggestion concerning the come-out ball.

"Are you sure that your idea is a good one? Diana is likely to be the star debutante of the season. Caroline is not in the same league, is she?"

"Not in beauty, I agree, but Caroline is a pleasant and confident girl, who has a livelier intelligence. Diana has not needed to learn to ride, as she has only ever lived in London. Caroline knows how to manage a country estate, and she regularly rides to hounds. She has been better educated than her cousin, and she is able to speak Italian as well as French. I do not believe that she will be at any disadvantage in the social scene."

"I noticed, when we were at Alver Park in the week before our wedding, that Caroline went riding several times with Jessamy and her younger brother Jack."

"Yes, both Jessamy and Caroline seem to enjoy country pursuits."

Having successfully hired the staff that she needed for the rental property, Lady Eliza and Caroline moved to live in the house, which was in the next street to the home of Lord and Lady Ormond. However, Alver's sister had chosen very well, as her property was in a cul-de-sac with less than a dozen houses, and with no passing traffic. Jessamy had to walk for less than 10 minutes to attend the dancing lessons with Caroline, and he made good progress in the first week. However, an unexpected event disrupted this pleasant situation.

"No letter from Felix today," remarked Lord Alverstoke, when the post arrived. "However, there is one from his housemaster. Let's see what he has to say."

As he read the communication, which extended to two pages, his expression grew more and more serious.

"What's the matter, love? What does the letter say?"

"A quite extraordinary message – the housemaster writes that Felix has disappeared, and they have no idea where he is. The school has been searched, but he is nowhere to be found."

Frederica sat down heavily on the sofa and put her head in her hands.

"The housemaster must be wrong. How can Felix have just disappeared? He has no money until his small allowance arrives at the end of the month. Perhaps Eliza may have had a letter from her son Tom – those two boys are very close friends, and he might know something about what has happened."

"Eliza told me earlier this week that Tom does not yet have her London address, so his letters will still be sent to their country estate. However, I will go and see her now, in case she has had any news from John Kentmere. Why don't you come with me, Frederica? If necessary, I will have to travel today to Windsor to have an urgent discussion with the housemaster."

They walked together to the hired house in Mayfair, but his sister Eliza knew nothing about Felix and the disappearance. They went to interrupt the dancing lesson, and Jessamy and Caroline were horrified to hear that his brother was missing. Lord Alverstoke decided to take charge of the situation.

"Frederica, you had best stay here in town, with Charles Trevor to support you. We can send you a letter before we return, should there be any news of Felix. Eliza, may I have your permission to speak to Tom and, if necessary, to bring him back to town with me?"

"Of course, Vernon. You must do whatever the situation requires."

"Jessamy, would you like to come with me on the journey to Windsor? We should leave Berkeley Square as soon as Curry can harness the horses to the carriage. My valet Knapp will travel with us, and you ought to pack a small bag, in case we need to remain in the town overnight. I stayed once at a comfortable old inn in Eton - The Crown & Cushion - so hopefully there might be space available there if we need to find some bedrooms nearby."

When the carriage was ready to leave Berkeley Square, Frederica waited nervously outside the front door.

Alver took her hands in his, and said gently, "Don't look so worried, my darling. Remember what happened when Felix went on the steam-packet by himself down the River Thames to Margate, so that he could see how the paddle wheels worked? He has a happy knack of making friends with everyone, and the master of the ship let him return to London as a stowaway. This will probably prove to be yet another of your brother's hair-raising adventures. As your aunt Seraphina once told me, that boy will always land on his feet like a cat."

Frederica looked at him doubtfully, but Alver took her into his arms, and hugged her tight in front of Wicken standing by the front door, and with Curry waiting by the horses. She did not sleep well that night, busy worrying about what mishap may have arisen.

However, the search party returned from Windsor to Berkeley Square on the following afternoon, without Felix, but they had brought Tom Kentmere with them. After being reunited with Frederica, they all walked the short distance to Mayfair together to see Lady Eliza and Caroline. Tom, although normally quite a serious boy, was in a high state of excitement at the prospect of having a few days away from his studies at school, and the possibility of seeing more of the London sights.

His elder sister soon took Tom off to explore their rented house, leaving his mother, the Marquis, Frederica and Jessamy in the drawing room.

"I have a letter here for you, Eliza, from Jack. He did not tell me what the contents refer to."

Whilst Eliza was busy reading the long letter from her elder son, the Marquis said to Jessamy, "If one of your friends asked you to keep something secret that he had told you, would you do that?"

"If the person was the same age as me, yes, I would, sir."

"And if he was younger, like Felix or Tom?"

Jessamy hesitated for a long time before he replied.

"If it was Felix making the request, then I would eventually say something. My brother is enterprising, but he can be very volatile. He is not someone who ever considers the consequences of his actions affecting other people."

Eliza had finished reading her letter from Jack, and she seemed to be rather puzzled.

"I must confess that I find some parts of his message rather complicated. Jack says that a lecturer came from the university at Oxford to talk to them about what an orrery can do. The lecture was intended only for the most senior boys at the school, but he smuggled Tom as well as Felix into a side alcove in the room, as Felix particularly wanted to hear what was said. The lecturer explained that the orrery had been made in brass, and that it had been given in 1763 to his college by a group of benefactors. Because it was much too precious to be taken to Eton, the lecturer drew pictures on the blackboard to explain how the various parts worked.

Jack says that an orrery is a mechanical model of the solar system, capable of predicting the relative positions of the planets and the moons in the sky. He said that the device is named after Charles Boyle, the 4th Earl of Orrery, who was educated at Christ Church in Oxford."

"That sounds just the type of mechanical device that would interest Felix," said Frederica.

"Yes, but the letter from Jack does not explain why Felix has disappeared?"

"No, it doesn't, Frederica."

"Jessamy, do you believe that Tom knows anything useful about why Felix cannot be found, or where he has gone?"

"Tom seems to be a thoughtful boy, sir, and someone who would be very loyal to his friends. Felix is quite different. He is, as we all know well, very single-minded. Perhaps Lady Eliza could speak to her son, to see if she can persuade him to explain anything that Felix might have told him?"

"Let me order a tray of tea for you all, and then I will take Tom aside when he returns with Caroline from viewing the house."

After tea, Caroline, Jessamy and Tom went off to the billiard room, to pot some balls in an informal contest.

"Did Tom tell you anything helpful, Eliza?"

"He mentioned two, apparently unrelated, matters. Felix had been very excited after hearing about what an orrery can do, and he mentioned that he knew someone called Richard who owned one. Felix and Tom share a study bedroom at Eton, and Tom has noticed that the very handsome telescope that Vernon gave him for his birthday has disappeared from the shelf where it was kept. He wondered if Felix might have taken the telescope to the pawnbrokers in Windsor, who are in Peascod Street? Apparently, many of the boys use that shop towards the end of the month, when they are running short on cash."

Frederica looked at her husband with dismay, and he went quickly across the room and put his arm around her.

"Tell me what you are thinking?" said Eliza.

"Perhaps I should explain. My mother was the youngest in her family of four children by several years. Amelia Scrabster, recently widowed in London, is the eldest. Then came the twins, Aunt Seraphina and my Uncle Richard, and finally our mother, Harriet, who died twelve years ago.

My Uncle Richard is open and friendly; as a child he was clever and studious. Although they did not have very much money to spare, the parents managed to pay for him to go to Edinburgh University to study to become a doctor."

"And where is he living now?"

"After he qualified, he returned to Ross on Wye, which is the nearest town to our estate at Graynard, and he still lives there with his family. My uncle often argued with my father about Papa's gambling, and Papa refused to see him after that. We had to use another doctor who was based in the county town, Hereford, which is only a little further away from Graynard.

My mother was not happy about that decision, but she did not see any benefit in provoking an argument every time we needed attention for some medical reason. After Papa died, Aunt Seraphina took us to see my uncle and his wife in Ross on Wye, although we continued to use the doctor in Hereford. Last year, we were invited to spend Boxing Day with Richard and his wife, who was born in Wales. They have three children; both the two daughters were married last year, and the son is studying at the university in Edinburgh. He plans to become a doctor like his father.

After the festive meal, Uncle Richard showed us all an unexpected gift that he had recently been given by a grateful patient. It was a very handsome brass orrery – something that my uncle could not have afforded to purchase for himself. Felix did not seem to be particularly interested, and I don't think that he was in the room when my uncle explained to the rest of us what the orrery was for and how it worked.

My uncle is the only person named Richard who I know. I wonder whether Felix has pawned his handsome telescope so that he has enough money for the journey to Herefordshire, so that he can ask our uncle if he can borrow the orrery to show to his friends at school."

"That would be a journey of at least 110 miles by the shortest route, my dear, and most people would want to stop for at least one night in an inn on the way. Surely, your brother would not have had the money to pay for an overnight stay, as well as for the coach fare?"

"What direction could Felix have taken?" asked Eliza.

"Probably the popular route via Newbury and Bristol, and then he would have to take another coach to Hereford before finally using the local service to reach Ross-on-Wye."

"All that travelling would be a major undertaking for a schoolboy of his age, Vernon?"

"True, but Felix is not your average schoolboy, Eliza. There are regular coaches to Bristol that only stop to change the horses and the coachmen at intervals on the route, with the passengers snatching a meal wherever they can. Felix can be very persuasive with his melting-eye expressions, and no doubt he would manage to find some benevolent fellow passenger to pay for his food."

Frederica had been silent during this conversation, considering what their best plan of action might be. Perhaps she could 'kill two birds with one stone'.

"Well, if that is what he has been up to, Felix should have reached his destination by now. If so, we can expect a letter to arrive from Uncle Richard very soon; he has our address in Berkeley Square.

I have just been wondering what the best method would be to retrieve him, and it may be that I can make good use of the situation. I am sure that Uncle Richard will not lend Felix the orrery, and he would not have the time to accompany his nephew on the return journey to Windsor. Mr Salcombe, whose office is in the same town, would not relish the task either. He finds Felix very tiresome at the best of times.

However, if I were to travel with your secretary, Alver, and if I invited Chloe Dauntry to accompany me on an interesting expedition to Herefordshire - an area that she has probably never visited - that would leave space remaining for Felix in our travelling coach. There would be absolutely no need to mention to Lucretia that Charles Trevor would be involved."

"No space left in the coach for me then, Frederica? Don't forget that you should also take Emily with you. I must admit that the thought of two or more days travelling with Felix on the journey back to Berkshire does not tempt me!"

"Exactly, my darling! Charles Trevor has a very firm way of dealing with Felix if we need him to keep my little brother in order. What do you think of my plan, Eliza?"

"I seem to remember at Alver Park that I suspected Chloe and Charles shared a romantic interest? It sounds as though I was right about that, Frederica?"

At this point, her brother explained to Eliza the plans that were being made for Charles Trevor's future diplomatic career, following the efforts by Edward Ormond on his behalf.

It was two days later that the letter arrived for Frederica from Richard Winsham.

He wrote, 'You will not be surprised to learn, my dear niece, that young Felix shows no remorse whatsoever about his mad escapade. I shall expect either you or the Marquis to collect him from Ross-on-Wye at some time during the next week. Meanwhile, I shall do my best to ensure that the miscreant does not commit any more follies. You will, of course, be very welcome to stay here with us. I shall not allow him to borrow my orrery, although I will try to find the time to demonstrate to Felix how it works.'

Frederica sent a rapid reply, to advise her uncle that she would be travelling with Charles, Chloe and Emily as her companions on the journey. The Marquis, meanwhile, wrote to the housemaster at Eton to advise him that Felix had been located, and that he would soon be returning to the school.

The main beneficiary of all this excitement was young Tom Kentmere, who was able to persuade his mother that he ought to make the best possible use of his unexpected presence in London, and that the date for his return to Eton should coincide with that of his best friend!

Chapter 9

It was on a Friday, several weeks later, that Lord Alverstoke returned to his home in Berkeley Square accompanied by Darcy Moreton, having had lunch with him at White's in St James' Street.

They had been joined for their meal by William Arden, Lord Alvanley. He was a witty man, very good company and well liked, but he was an incorrigible gambler. He was anxious to write a new bet in White's famous book, and so Alvanley had left their table soon after the meal was over. It was said that he had once bet £3,000 on which of two raindrops would reach the bottom of a pane first on the bow window overlooking the street outside!

"I suspect, Ver, that Alvanley's finances are now in very dire straits. He is hoping against hope that his uncle dies soon, so that his inheritance can rescue him from penury. It is just as well that he has neither a wife nor any children."

"Yes, I agree with you. It would be best if you do not mention Alvanley's name to Frederica. She is understandably very wary of anyone connected with gambling after her experience with her father. Fortunately, that has never been a pastime that has attracted me."

Having stayed to speak to several other acquaintances at the club, it was mid-afternoon before they reached Berkeley Square. They were admitted by one of the footmen to the entrance hall and, when they saw Wicken, they noticed that he seemed to be rather upset, so the Marquis asked the butler what was concerning him.

"There is a young man waiting with your secretary, milord. I should go and tell Mr Trevor that you have returned, and he will explain."

"Very well. You will find me with Mr Moreton in the library."

In a few minutes' time, Charles Trevor entered the room, and the Marquis invited him to sit down with them.

"I understand that there is a problem, Charles. Please explain."

"About an hour ago, sir, a young man knocked at the front door. His name is William Brown, and he had come here in great haste from Hounslow Heath, where he had been riding with a group of other young men. They had been travelling in a westerly direction and saw, in the far distance, two curricles coming towards them which appeared to be racing, with one overtaking the other.

Suddenly they saw that a wheel of the second curricle was clipping the rear corner of the other vehicle, and then tipping over. When they reached the accident, they saw the driver lying under his curricle, pinned to the ground, and very obviously dead. His companion had been thrown clear, but he had been seriously hurt."

"And the first vehicle, Charles?"

"Mr Brown said that the curricle had stayed upright, and that the two occupants were unharmed although, not surprisingly, they were very shocked. He dismounted and ran to the injured man. He was drifting in and out of consciousness, but then he muttered 'Hurry', and told Brown to look in the driver's pockets for a card, and to 'tell Lord Alverstoke'."

Charles held out his right hand to his employer, which held one of the Marquis's business cards.

When he turned the card over in his hand, Lord Alverstoke's face was suddenly white with shock, for written on the other side was the message about Jackson's boxing saloon that he had scrawled on the card for Harry Merriville on the day that they had first met.

There was silence for a few moments, before he said slowly and in a very shaky voice, "I believe that the injured passenger in the curricle was probably Barny Peplow, and that what he had said was not 'Hurry', but 'Harry' – meaning Harry Merriville."

"Good god!" exclaimed Darcy Moreton, "Frederica's brother!"

"Yes, I fear so, Darcy. We had better go with Charles and speak to Mr Brown."

They found the messenger in the secretary's office, his clothes and boots covered with dust from his journey. He was just finishing the tray of refreshments that had been offered to him.

"This is Lord Alverstoke, Mr Brown," said Charles. "Please repeat to him what you have already told me about the accident on the Heath."

Mr Brown's account, although more detailed, was essentially the same as the explanation that Charles Trevor had already given to them. Lord Alverstoke asked his secretary to recompense the young man for his trouble and, after that had been done and Mr Brown had left the house, he turned to Charles.

"We need to recover Harry's body as soon as possible, Charles, and to bring him back here. Will you do that for me? The body may have been taken elsewhere by now, perhaps into Hounslow? It may be some time before you are able to discover where he is.

Wicken can ask Curry to prepare a coach ready for you, and to harness the horses. I suggest that one of the footmen goes with you, as you may need some assistance – perhaps Walter would be best, as he is the more experienced man. Make sure that you have plenty of money on you, as various payments may need to be made. If you can obtain more news about Mr Peplow's injuries, that would be very helpful."

As Darcy went back with his friend to the library, he asked, "Where is your wife, Ver?"

"Frederica was going to visit the new art exhibition in the Strand this morning, at Somerset House. Then our town coach was to take her to have lunch with Lucretia Dauntry at her house in Green Street."

"So, she may be back here quite soon? It will not be easy to break the dreadful news to her?"

"No, indeed. Perhaps, when she does arrive, you can give us some time alone in the drawing room? Could you ask Wicken to arrange for a tray of tea about half an hour later?"

"Would you prefer that I leave the house?"

"No, you will be a welcome distraction once I have broken the sad news. Frederica is always pleased to see you."

"How long do you think it will take Charles Trevor to locate the body, and to return here?"

"I do not expect him to be back until quite late this evening, Darcy. Curry and Walter are both very competent and they will do whatever they can to assist him."

Frederica returned to Berkeley Square about 30 minutes after this conversation and, while the Marquis took her with him to the drawing room, Darcy went to find Wicken to carry out his friend's instructions.

When Darcy joined them, Frederica was sharing the sofa with Alverstoke, and he was holding her hands tightly in his. Her face was tear stained, but she greeted Darcy in a quiet voice, and then began to serve the tea for the three of them.

Darcy took a quick look at the Marquis; he looked very strained and anxious.

Then he said, "Frederica, I seem to remember you telling me when we first met that your father had died without making any will?"

"Yes, that is correct. Why do you ask?"

"Your brother Harry had his 21st birthday last year. That would have been the first opportunity when he could have made a legal will. Do you know whether Mr Salcombe had suggested that?"

"Yes, as a matter of fact he did ask Harry, when he came home to celebrate his birthday, and Mr Salcombe was very insistent that the will should be drafted and signed, and that the signature should be witnessed, before Harry returned to Oxford."

"Frederica, do you know who had been appointed as the two executors for the will?"

"Yes. He was to be one executor, and the other was my uncle, Richard Winsham."

"Well, you had better write to Salcombe to tell him the sad news, and to Richard Winsham."

"Alver, who will be inheriting the estate?"

"Your brother Jessamy, of course. He is the next to his brother in age."

"Oh! I cannot imagine how Jessamy will react to that news."

Darcy Moreton echoed those sentiments in his first contribution to the discussion, and then said, "Frederica, Vernon - I should leave you now, before Jessamy returns home, if you will excuse me?"

"Yes, of course, Darcy - let me see you to the front door," said Alverstoke.

When Alver came back into the drawing room, he sat down swiftly on the sofa next to Frederica and held her in a firm but loving embrace.

"Where is your secretary? I have not seen him since I returned home."

"I have sent Charles Trevor with Curry, and Walter the footman, to discover where Harry has been taken, and to bring him back to us. I hope that they will return here before nightfall."

"Quite apart from Jessamy, what are we going to do about telling Charis? She and Endymion are not due back from their honeymoon in France and Italy for at least another two weeks."

"I see no advantage in trying to contact them in Paris, Frederica. We might as well wait until they return to England. We can arrange for Harry's body to be embalmed, and for the funeral to take place in Herefordshire in about a month's' time. Would you be happy with that?"

"Yes, I suppose so. And what are we going to do about Felix?"

"Telling him the sad news can wait for a few days. He is happy and busy with his studies at Eton, and I can see little benefit in travelling to tell him now, when we have so many other things to arrange."

As he spoke, they could hear Wicken talking to someone in the entrance hall.

"That is probably Jessamy now, back from his outing with Septimus Trevor," and Frederica rose from the sofa and went to open the door.

She could see the tutor talking to the butler as Jessamy came across the hall to her with a smile on his face. But that smile rapidly disappeared as he saw her expression.

"What is it, Frederica? You look very upset?"

"Yes, please come into the drawing room, and shut the door. We have some very unhappy news to tell you."

After her brother sat down in a chair, Frederica explained what had happened on Hounslow Heath earlier that day.

Jessamy exclaimed, "Are you telling me that I am now the owner of Graynard? I have only just had my birthday, so what will happen until I reach my majority in four years time?"

This time, it was the Marquis who answered him. "As Harry had made and signed his will last year, the two executors Mr Salcombe and Richard Winsham will act as your trustees until you reach 21. However, I'm sure that they will consult you about managing the Graynard estate. Frederica and I will be happy to assist you, should you want that."

"What about telling Charis and Felix? She and Endymion will not be back in England for some weeks."

His sister explained that it seemed best to await their return before informing them, and that there was no urgency about giving the news to Felix.

"Frederica, could you ring the bell, and ask for some tea for me? I can see that both of you have had some refreshments."

"I will go and ask Wicken to arrange for that to be done, Jessamy."

By the time that he had finished his tea, Jessamy was beginning to recover his equilibrium, and said, "At least Harry died driving his curricle – he enjoyed doing that so much. I suppose that Charles may be able to bring some news about Barny Peplow? Harry never mentioned to me where Barny's family lives."

"Did you and Septimus Trevor enjoy your river outing to Greenwich, Jessamy?"

"Yes, the river was quite busy with boats both on the way there, and on the way back. But there were many things to see at our destination, so -yes - I really did enjoy the outing."

As Alverstoke had foreseen, it was almost dark when Charles Trevor returned from his mission. Curry drove the coach directly to the stables, where a safe space had been found for Harry's body to be unloaded from the vehicle and placed on a table.

Jessamy was accompanied by Cousin Alverstoke, and by Frederica, when he went to see his brother lying there.

"How very peaceful he looks," remarked his brother, "and I can see no sign of any injuries, beyond that nasty bruise on his forehead."

"No - hopefully he was killed instantly when the curricle fell on top of him. We should be grateful for small mercies, Jessamy," said the Marquis, trying to console him. "Charles says that Harry's body had been taken to Hounslow, where a doctor had confirmed his death."

"Did he have any news about Barny Peplow?"

"Only that the same doctor had examined his injuries, which are severe, and he told my secretary that Mr Peplow's life was hanging in the balance.

Charles had said to the doctor that Oxford University should be contacted as a matter of urgency, as they would know where the Peplow family lived. He had written a note to the Master of the college and he had asked the doctor to send the letter tomorrow morning. Charles had asked the college for the Peplow family's home address, and for the Master to send that information urgently to the doctor, and to the Marquis at Berkeley Square. He had also assured the doctor that Lord Alverstoke would pay for Mr Peplow's care and for any treatment that might help save his life."

They returned to the house, and the Marquis went to find his secretary. "Charles, you have done very well," said Alverstoke, "so allow me to thank you on behalf of both of us."

Meanwhile, Frederica told Jessamy that, in the morning, an embalmer would be asked to come to the stables, so that he could begin the process of preserving Harry's body, as it was likely to be at least a month before the funeral could take place in Herefordshire.

It had been a long day for everyone, so Frederica suggested that it was time for Jessamy to go to bed. After he had left them, Alver and Frederica talked through the day's events before they too decided that they needed some rest. At the top of the staircase, Frederica said to him, "I had better go and make sure that Jessamy is ready for bed. He has had a very difficult evening."

"Very well, my love. I will be waiting for you in our sitting room when you have settled your brother," said Alver, and he kissed her hand before he turned right along the corridor.

Frederica went in the opposite direction, to Jessamy's bedroom, which had a window facing the garden at the back of the house. She knocked on the door, and then turned the doorknob and went in to see him.

She crossed the room and sat down on the edge of the bed. He was lying on his back with his eyes wide open. When he saw his sister, he smiled at her.

"Are you finding it very difficult to go to sleep?" asked Frederica.

"Yes, I am. There's been so much to think about, and especially the news about Harry. But don't worry about me - you probably remember that I am usually quite good at drifting off."

"It would not be too surprising, Jessamy, if tonight might be different?"

"I suppose that I could try counting some sheep. That is the traditional way of getting to sleep, isn't it?"

"I'm not sure that we have any sheep in Berkeley Square. But I can ask Alver if he could arrange that if you like!"

Her brother smiled at the joke.

"I'm trying very hard to be sensible, Frederica, but it is not easy. It is not that I am particularly worried at becoming the owner of Graynard. I love being at the estate, and Mr Salcombe and Uncle Richard will help me, I'm sure. It's just that, until yesterday, I thought my future was clear – that I would be a student at Oxford, and that then I would study to join the Church. Now everything will be different, and I am the new owner of a property in Herefordshire. But all that is only at the expense of Harry losing his life."

"Yes. One can never know what the future holds, can we? Now, you should try to go to sleep, so I will leave you in peace. But do not hesitate to come along the corridor to see us if you're worried about anything during the night."

Frederica kissed his cheek, and then left the room, closing the door quietly behind her.

"How is he, Frederica?" said Alver when she had joined him in their sitting room.

"Trying to be very sensible, as usual. I will check him in the morning before breakfast. By then, I expect that reality will have begun to kick in and will remind him of yesterday's events. I see that you have already changed into your banyan, Alver?"

"Yes, someone I know who is very good at choosing presents gave me this very handsome quilted dressing gown."

"I wonder who that could have been?" I already have some good ideas for your next present."

"I hope that those ideas do not include giving me a nightshirt! I have not worn one since I left school in Harrow twenty years ago, and I have no intention of starting now!"

After breakfast on the following day, Frederica composed a long message to Mr Salcombe in Herefordshire, and she asked Wicken to arrange to have the letter taken to the Post Office in Lombard Street immediately. Frederica and Alver tried to keep Jessamy fully occupied all morning.

Charles Trevor had left the house earlier in the day, to find someone with a knowledge of embalming. Just before lunch, he returned with Mr Ebenezer Crow, a thin serious man of middle years, who arrived carrying a large wooden box. Wicken took him to the stables to begin his work, and sometime later the secretary found Frederica and Alver with Jessamy in the drawing room.

"If you please, sir, Mr Crow is ready to explain what he has to do to preserve the body."

"Do you want to come with us, Jessamy?" said Alver.

The boy hesitated for a few moments, and then said slowly, "Yes, I suppose so, sir." And all three of them went out to the stables.

The embalmer explained that it had been the Scottish anatomist William Hunter who, some 40 or 50 years ago, had been the first to report fully on arterial and cavity embalming as a way to preserve bodies for burial. The technique was to replace the blood with an embalming fluid. No organs needed to be removed during the process.

Alver was very relieved to hear this, as he had feared that some damage to the body might be necessary, which would have distressed both Frederica and Jessamy.

He said, "It is just as well that Felix is not here. I fear that he would be much more interested in the details of the embalming process than in the death of his elder brother!"

Jessamy smiled weakly. Yes, I'm quite sure that you are right, sir!"

They all three agreed that it would be best if Frederica wrote a letter to her youngest brother, saying that she and Alver would be visiting Felix at Eton in about 10 days' time, but making no reference to the reason for their journey.

Mr Salcombe replied promptly to Frederica's letter, and he had some good news to tell her.

The tenant at Graynard, Mr Porth, was about to complete the purchase of an estate about 15 minutes' drive from Ross-on-Wye, and he would therefore be happy to end his occupation several weeks earlier than had been expected, without expecting any refund on the monthly rental that had been agreed for the property. So, Graynard would be available for the family to use before the funeral.

Their lawyer would wait to hear from Frederica that Charis and Endymion had returned to England before making the arrangements.

When they arrived at Eton to see him, Felix was in very good spirits and happy to show them around the school premises. After a pleasant lunch in a nearby inn, Alver and Frederica broke the news about Harry's death.

For once, Felix was speechless -- at least to begin with.

Then he said slowly, "You are sure that Harry was killed instantly?"

"Yes, and apart from a bruise on his head, there was no other sign of injury," said Frederica.

Felix was uncharacteristically subdued for the rest of their discussion, and it was not difficult to guess that he was processing the sad news. Unlike Jessamy, Felix seemed to realise immediately who would be the new owner of Graynard.

Alver and Frederica explained that the funeral would probably not be for several weeks, until Charis was back from her honeymoon with Endymion.

"Unless you have any views to the contrary, Felix, it might be best if you stay at school, and don't travel to Herefordshire for the funeral?" said Alver.

For once, Felix was hesitant before replying.

"I would prefer to remember Harry as I last saw him, very happy as he drove his curricle with Barny Peplow away from the house in Upper Wimpole Street. Yes, I would rather stay at Eton when you go to the funeral with Jessamy, Charis and Endymion, if that would not be seen as being disrespectful to Harry's memory?"

About a week after Frederica and Alver had returned from Windsor, a letter arrived from Charis in France, to say that she and Endymion would return to London in about 10 days' time. The letter was full of excited comments about the sights in Paris, where they were currently staying. On their return to London, they proposed to call in at Berkeley Square for lunch, before going on to Green Street to stay with Endymion's mother Lucrecia Dauntry.

A few days before the newlyweds were expected to return, Alver was in his secretary's office, discussing with Charles Trevor various papers that needed his attention, when Wicken entered the room.

"There is a Mr Peplow in the hall asking for you, milord. He told me that he has travelled from Lincolnshire, near Stamford, to see you."

"Mr Peplow, you say. What age of person would he be, Wicken?"

Wicken paused and considered before replying.

"I would say that he might be a few years older than your brother-in-law, Mr Kentmere, milord. And not unlike him in appearance, sir – probably a country landowner?"

"Ah. Perhaps he may be the father of Harry's friend, young Barny Peplow? Charles, would you please take Mr Peplow to the library, and tell him that I will join him there very soon."

"Wicken, my wife is probably in the stables with Jessamy, inspecting that new horse that I purchased last week. Please send a footman to ask her to join me in the library as soon as possible. And Wicken, as Mr Peplow may have had a long journey to get here, please organise some refreshments for our visitor."

When Alver met Mr Peplow, he decided that Wicken's description of the visitor had been accurate. The man had the ruddy complexion of a person who spent much of his time in the open air. He also had a pleasingly open manner of speaking.

"Mr Peplow, good morning. I am Lord Alverstoke, and my wife Frederica will be joining us shortly."

"Milord, I am pleased to meet you. I am Edward Peplow, Barny's father. He was injured in the accident on Hounslow Heath a couple of weeks ago. I have been told that his close friend, Harry Merriville, was killed in the accident? Please accept my sincere condolences for your family's loss."

"Thank you, Mr Peplow. Harry was my brother-in-law, the eldest of Frederica's three brothers. May I ask how your son Barny is now?"

"Once we received the news of the accident, I immediately travelled with my elder son, William, from our estate in Lincolnshire to the doctor's home in Hounslow where he had been taken."

He wiped tears from his eyes with a handkerchief before continuing.

"He was in a very bad way to begin with, sir, and the doctor feared for his life. One of his legs had been damaged in several places, and he had broken ribs. He had a head wound, and internal injuries were also matters for concern. My son was unconscious for a couple of days after our arrival. But Barny is made of good sturdy Lincolnshire stock and, once he awoke and saw us, he began to rally.

The doctor had put splints on his leg, although he has told me since that my son may always walk with a limp, as it was a very bad break. After a few days, we were told that Barny was well enough to travel home, and so we took him back to Lincolnshire. My estate is not far from Stamford, near Burghley House, the home of the Marquis of Exeter.

I have come here to see you today, Lord Alverstoke, as I understand that you paid all the expenses for my son's care. I wish to reimburse you, and to sincerely thank you for your support."

Alver was torn between refusing any payment, which would probably offend his visitor, or making some alternative suggestion.

However, at that moment Frederica came into the room, with Jessamy, followed by a footman bearing a tray of refreshments.

"Mr Peplow, this is my wife – Harry's elder sister Frederica - and this is Harry's younger brother, Jessamy Merriville.   Frederica, Jessamy - Mr Edward Peplow is the father of Harry's good friend Barny, and he has come from his home in Lincolnshire to visit us."

"I am honoured to meet you both, Lady Alverstoke and Mr Merriville. I met your brother Harry twice, but I must admit that I do not see a strong likeness to him in either of you?"

Jessamy decided to reply to this remark.

"Most people say that our sister Charis, as well as Harry, resemble our late father, whereas Frederica and I look more like our mother. How is your son's health, sir?"

The visitor repeated what he had told Alver, while Frederica poured the tea for them all, and offered Mr Peplow a choice of the pastries on the tray.

"It is very kind of you to offer to pay for the expenses of your son's care, Mr Peplow. However, we all valued your son's friendship with Harry, so I would prefer not to accept any contribution towards the cost of Barny's medical expenses. Perhaps you could tell us when Barny hopes to return to Oxford to resume his studies?"

"The university has been very helpful, but I explained to them that he will probably not be well enough to return until the autumn of next year. Meanwhile, as well as my elder son William, Barny has three younger siblings – all sisters - who are keeping busy entertaining him, and often making a nuisance of themselves. Until his leg has healed, he is quite unable to pursue them around the house, so the girls are taking all kinds of liberties with their brother."

"Jessamy will be starting at Oxford next autumn," said Frederica, "so perhaps he will meet Barny there at some time."

During the visit from Mr Peplow, the Marquis had an interesting discussion with his visitor about the meeting known as the Norfolk Shearings that was held every year by Thomas Coke at Holkham House. His guest told Lord Alverstoke that he had been one of the 300 people attending the Shearings for several days in the Spring, including the American ambassador and the French consul.

Mr Peplow said that he was keen to pursue any new ideas that might increase the income from his Lincolnshire estate. He no longer left his land fallow for a year, having introduced Thomas Coke's idea of the four-crop rotation method using turnips in the first year, followed by wheat, barley and clover. He was not so keen on Coke's suggestion of using oxen instead of horses for tilling his fields.

"Thank you, Peplow, for this very useful conversation. I must consider sending my land agent, Coleford, to the Shearings next year."

Charis and Endymion arrived in London during the following week, and they were keen to explain all about their travels through France and Italy. Frederica and Alver waited until after lunch was over before breaking the news about Harry.

As Alver had expected, his sister-in-law immediately burst into tears, and it took her husband several minutes to calm her. However, Frederica was impressed at Endymion's skill in dealing with Charis. He had certainly succeeded in quieting her much more quickly than she would have been able to achieve.

"Now that you are both back with us in England, we will make the arrangements to travel to Herefordshire," said Frederica.

She explained that their tenant, Mr Porth, had just purchased an estate in the area, and so he would be vacating the house at Graynard rather earlier than planned.

"I wrote soon after Harry's death to Mr Salcombe and to Uncle Richard, to tell them the sad news. Once we have agreed on the date for the funeral, Alver has suggested that we all go down to Graynard several days in advance, so that we can meet him and Uncle Richard. There will be a great deal for Jessamy to discuss there, as well as for us."

After the newlyweds had left Berkeley Square to stay with his mother in Green Street, Alver remarked that Endymion seemed to have matured during his honeymoon, and that Charis would hopefully do the same in due course.

"If you mean that my sister won't burst into tears at any unexpected news, Alver, I fear that you may be sorely disappointed. That has always been her personality, and I very much doubt that she will change."

The Marquis smiled at his wife's pessimism, but he conceded that she was probably correct.

"Can I suggest that your brother's funeral should be held in two weeks time, now that Endymion and Charis are back in England? You can write now to Mr Salcombe and to your uncle. Then we can plan to travel with Jessamy to Graynard, arriving there about a week before Harry is to be buried in the village churchyard."

Frederica walked to Green Street with Emily to suggest these arrangements to the newlyweds and, as soon as they heard back from Herefordshire, preparations began at the house in Berkeley Square.

Chapter 10

When the day came to leave London for Herefordshire, Jessamy travelled with Alver and Frederica. Knapp and Emily were in the second coach, together with a quantity of baggage for everyone.

The long journey towards the west took several days, although Alver's comfortable carriage meant that the time passed pleasantly enough, and the inns where they stopped each evening were clean and well appointed. Curry was kept busy, with his assistant, changing the horses for both carriages at regular intervals during each day.

To Frederica, so much had happened to her in the past few months that it seemed to be quite a different world that she had left behind at Graynard.

"Am I going to like the house, and the estate?" asked Alver of his companions when they had only a few miles left to travel.

Frederica and Jessamy smiled at him, and Jessamy replied, "We are biased, sir. You need to ask that question of a more disinterested observer, as we have lived there all our lives. Graynard is not a grand house, nor particularly large, but it is very dear to our family. There is a small formal garden, which I hope Mr Porth will have looked after in our absence, and then a large lawn where we play boules. The rest of the estate is productive farmland."

"Are there good views from the house? Do you have any neighbours nearby?"

This time Frederica replied. "There are views in several directions from the property. The nearest house is about half a mile away, on the road towards Ross on Wye. The members of the family that owns that estate are good friends of ours. They have been writing to me every month since we left Graynard for London."

As she spoke, the carriage began to slow, and Curry called down to them from the box to say that he was just about to turn into the drive for the estate. Frederica began to feel quite emotional as they approached the family home. Their conversation ceased, and Alver observed the views on each side of the carriage as they passed through the gates. When they arrived at the end of the drive, he was rather surprised to see that the property had been built not of brick as he had expected, but of well-weathered cream-coloured stone, with ivy growing up some of the walls.

The front door opened and there was the Merrivilles' butler, Buddle, to welcome them. Standing a few steps behind him was the elderly housekeeper, Mrs Hurley, her face wreathed in smiles.

Jessamy left the carriage first, keen to see familiar sights and the buildings of the home farm and, pausing only to greet the butler and Mrs Hurley, he went to the stables. The Marquis helped his wife down from the carriage and stood beside her to look around at the property that he had heard so much about.

"Everything appears to be very well kept outside, my love. Mr Porth seems to have been a conscientious tenant."

Once inside the house, Alver and Frederica were met with the enticing aroma of the meal being prepared for the family.

"Mrs Hurley, it is so good to see both of you again after so long. Could you please take Mr Knapp and my abigail, Emily Leonard, to where each of them will be sleeping, and then show them round the house. I will take the Marquis upstairs, and then we can explore the house from there."

An hour later, with the luggage unloaded, the coaches taken by Curry and his assistant to the stables, and Frederica and the Marquis comfortably seated in the drawing-room, Jessamy came inside to join them as Mrs Hurley brought a tray of tea and biscuits.

"Cousin Alverstoke, Frederica, I am very happy that you occupy my parents' room while we are here. I will be content to sleep in the bedroom that I have always used, at the far end of the first-floor corridor. I shall have plenty of time to get used to being the owner of the property when I'm older."

"That is very civil of you, young man. There will come a day, perhaps whilst you are studying at Oxford, when you decide to use your parents' bedroom. But, for now, Frederica and I are pleased to do as you suggest."

After they had finished their tea and biscuits, Frederica took Alver on a tour of the house. She had warned him not to expect the stylish decor and immaculate condition of his house in Berkeley Square, but the property was pleasantly furnished, seemed to be well-kept, and had been left very clean by the tenant Mr Porth.

The house had a small library near the entrance hall, which Frederica had used as her study and office when Mr Salcombe, their lawyer, came to visit. On the first floor, there were six main bedrooms, with more on the level above, including one that had been used as a nursery - most recently by Felix.

The house did not have a ballroom, but Frederica told Alver that the family had used the very spacious entrance hall for dancing at Christmas time. They found Mrs Hurley busy in the kitchen preparing the evening meal assisted by two girls from the village.

Then Frederica and Alver walked out into the grounds. The small formal garden near the house had been well-tended by their tenants, and the grass on the large lawn beyond had been recently cut. The stables, with the grooms' accommodation above, were set a short distance from the house, accessed across a yard outside the kitchen door.

Jessamy was already back in the stables, talking to the horses that they had left behind them when the family went to London.

"I suspect that you will have noticed, sir, that our horses are not as well-bred as yours?"

"They seem fine to me and to have been very well looked after in your absence, Jessamy. I shall enjoy riding out with you in the estate, perhaps tomorrow morning?"

Alver was pleasantly surprised at the meal which Mrs Hurley provided them with that evening. It might be very different from the more elaborate dishes that his chef in London would produce, but Frederica said that all the vegetables came from their own kitchen garden, and that the tender meat would be from local farms.

"Charles has arranged for Harry's coffin to be delivered here tomorrow, and Salcombe and your uncle will be coming to lunch with us on Friday. Charis and Endymion should arrive here later that day."

They had arranged for the executors, Mr Salcombe and Richard Winsham, to visit so that they could discuss with Jessamy any plans he might have for the property. When they arrived, Frederica and Alver joined the conversations, suggesting some ideas that Jessamy could consider.

Endymion and Charis Dauntry were expected to arrive at Graynard in time to join the family for supper that evening. The weather had been deteriorating, and it was almost dark by the time the travellers arrived. Once inside the house, Charis became rather tearful as she passed the doorway to her brother Harry's bedroom. Endymion consoled his wife, reminding her that Harry had died on Hounslow Heath driving his curricle - something that he had always loved doing.

Later, during the meal, Jessamy remarked, "I am very glad to be back in Herefordshire, although that is for the worst of reasons."

"There is no urgent need to make any changes yet, Jessamy. You have had a long discussion with Mr Salcombe, and he will be able to tell you if there are any outstanding issues arising in the future. I suggest that we all have a quiet day tomorrow, although you may like to go out for another ride with me around your estate. I hope to persuade Frederica not to do very much for the next few days!"

When he met Richard Winsham, the Marquis had been impressed by his quiet good sense. The doctor seemed to be a very suitable person to act on his nephew's behalf until Jessamy reached his majority. Mr Salcombe had brought them up to date about Mr

Porth's tenancy, and he had also confirmed that the arrangements had been made for the funeral in the village church. Local friends of the family had been informed of the date and were hoping to be present.

As was the convention on such occasions, ladies did not attend the funeral, so Endymion and the Marquis waited in the hall for Jessamy to join them. When he came down the stairs wearing a dark jacket, with his neatly tied white cravat arranged to perfection by Lord Alverstoke's valet, he suddenly looked several years older than his years, and Jessamy was very quiet as they travelled together in the carriage to the nearby village. The church was quite small, and the pews were filled with local people wishing to pay their respects to his elder brother.

Frederica had arranged for a generous meal to be provided for the congregation afterwards at Graynard, and this occasion gave the Marquis the opportunity to meet some of the family's neighbours.

The day after the funeral, Jessamy invited Endymion to go riding around the Graynard estate with him for a couple of hours. Meanwhile, Curry drove the Marquis and Frederica into Ross-on-Wye to visit Mr Salcombe at his office which was in the centre of the town.

"Were you happy, Frederica, that many of your neighbours went back to the house yesterday after the funeral?"

"Yes, I was very pleased to see many familiar faces at Graynard, as was Jessamy. Once he has finished his university studies, I am confident that the neighbours will welcome him back to Herefordshire, and some of the younger ones will probably become some of his closest friends."

"Do you foresee any problems in managing the estate, Salcombe, especially until Frederica's brother reaches his majority?"

"No, I don't. To be frank with you, sir, once he has completed the course at Oxford, Jessamy will be much more successful than his brother could ever have been in managing the estate. Harry's interests were very like his father's, except mercifully for gambling.

Fred Merriville was very close to bankrupting Graynard until he fell ill with his stroke five years ago. That illness was a blessing in disguise."

"We shall be very grateful if you can keep in touch with my uncle Winsham. It is very helpful that you both live and work in Ross-on-Wye. Lord Alverstoke and I will try to visit Herefordshire every few months, when our other commitments permit, but we will have to rely on you to keep us informed about anything that needs our attention."

After they left the lawyer's office, Frederica took Alver on a walk around the town, to see the local shops and to find a light meal in one of the inns. When they returned to Graynard, Jessamy came to find Frederica with a hopeful request.

"Charis and Endymion have asked me if I would like to travel back in their carriage to make a visit for a few days to their property in Buckinghamshire. Would you be happy about that idea, Frederica? I know that you and the Marquis have already seen their house, but I would really like to visit the estate, and to see the land that you gave to them as a wedding present."

"I cannot see anything wrong with that suggestion, Jessamy. Please don't tell them that I have told you this, but Alver and I both thought that their home needed a great deal of money spent to update it. If you go with Charis and Endymion to view the new land, there is a location with a lovely outlook over the village below that I thought might make a good location for a new house."

"But how could they get a good water supply for a house on top of a hill?"

"Perhaps you can find some hazel twigs here before you leave, take them with you, and do some dowsing!"

"And how could they afford to pay for building a new home, Frederica?"

"By selling the existing house, of course, together with a small area of land!" replied his sister.

Later that day, she told the Marquis about this conversation.

"Does your brother realise that he is going to be a spy on your behalf?"

"Jessamy is a very accurate observer, as you know, and he will enjoy looking all over the Dauntrys' estate and making suggestions for the future. Apart from Caroline's come-out ball, he has nothing much to look forward to, once he is back in town."

Alver smiled at her with a rather wicked look in his eyes, but he did not comment any further.

So, when Charis and Endymion left Graynard together on the following day, there was a third passenger travelling with them in their carriage.

Three days later, Frederica was thinking about Harry's death as she began to get ready with the Marquis to leave the Graynard estate. Mr Salcombe had confirmed that he would continue to oversee the management of the property and would pay the staff on Jessamy's behalf. Frederica and Alver walked around the house for the last time, before saying farewell to Buddle and Mrs Hurley and, with Emily Leonard and Knapp in the second carriage, set off on the long journey back to London.

Inevitably, their task on the first morning in Town was to spend some time with Charles Trevor. There was a pile of correspondence to be dealt with, but Alver's secretary had discovered a new tactic for ensuring Lord Alverstoke's interest. If he handed all the social invitations to Frederica, she would write a note on each one saying whether she would like to accept, or not. Meanwhile, the rather smaller number of letters relating to the family properties were passed to the Marquis to determine their fate.

"There is a rather pleasing note here from our neighbours the Jerseys, suggesting that we could go with them to Vauxhall Gardens. I have never been there, so I would love to accept, Alver!"

Sally Jersey, born as Sarah Fane, was a very good friend of Lady Eliza Kentmere, and was twelve years younger than her husband George. The Countess was very wealthy, having inherited the control of Child's Bank in Fleet Street, the ownership of the handsome mansion Osterley Park to the west of London, and other estates, from her grandfather Robert Child.

"Yes, that could be an enjoyable outing, my dear. We could travel by road, using the new Vauxhall Bridge to get there, Frederica, but you might prefer to take the ferry instead?"

His wife decided that it would be more interesting to cross the Thames by boat, so they set out a few days later in the Jerseys' opulent carriage for the pier at Westminster, ready to be taken across to the southern bank of the river in the ferry.

Alver had explained to her that one of the major features of the extensive gardens was the thousands of lamps that illuminated the area. The company would be mixed, with the nobility rubbing shoulders with shopkeepers and merchants, but everyone was welcome who could afford the entry fee of three shillings and sixpence.

"It is just as well that Felix is not going with us, my darling. There are said to be more than fifteen thousand lamps in the Vauxhall Gardens. So that most of them can be illuminated at the same time, the proprietors have laid a system of linked fuses, using cotton and whale oil, so that the lamps can be lit at dusk every evening. That would give your brother ideas that could only end in complete disaster!"

The Earl had booked a box for them immediately opposite the Rotunda, which was seventy feet in diameter, and had a raised floor to protect the musicians from the visitors, and a painted ceiling above that resembled an open lady's fan. The Rotunda was used by the large orchestra, as well as by several singers during the evening, with the very fine organ being situated at the back behind the musicians.

There was dancing for those who enjoyed the melodies played by the orchestra, before the guests sat down for the waiters to serve them food and drink. Other visitors were using small pavilions that had been built throughout the gardens, each displaying a transparent painting of a character from the works of Shakespeare. The Earl's party went to see the marble statue of Handel, said to be a good likeness of the great composer, who had been depicted by the sculptor in the character of Orpheus playing on his lyre.

More groups of musicians were seated in several locations to serenade the guests as they walked around the gardens, admiring the fountains, and mechanical attractions including The Cascade could be viewed. Some of the walks were well lit with the many coloured light bulbs, and others were more secluded for couples who sought more privacy. The overall effect was a fairytale atmosphere, with more lamps scattered around the trees and lamp posts, arches and obelisks.

Sally Jersey was well known for her rapid-fire conversation, and she chatted away to Frederica about her children, the youngest of whom was three years old, as they promenaded around the gardens.

Walking some distance behind them, George Villiers talked to the Marquis with the ease of an old friend.

"I admire your Frederica's calm commonsense, and her air of quiet elegance, Vernon. You are a very lucky man. Sally is a devoted mother to our children, but she has been a wealthy heiress since the day that she was born. Perhaps it is that, rather than the age difference between us, that has caused her to make her favours available elsewhere."

Lord Alverstoke was not sure how to reply to these remarks. Lord Jersey, once asked why he had never fought a duel to preserve his wife's reputation, was said to have drily replied that this would require him to fight every man in London!

"All three of your children have a strong resemblance to you, George, especially the youngest boy."

"That is true," his friend replied. "Perhaps my wife makes timely use of Pennyroyal Tea!"

The Marquis and Lord Jersey were both close friends of Richard Tattersall, who knew all the best sporting men of his time and was the third generation to run the auction house at Hyde Park Corner. It was said that he had inherited his grandfather's ability and his tact, both useful traits when dealing with wealthy members of the aristocracy.

"Have you any new horses in training, Vernon? I have a few promising young colts that I bought at Richard's auction house. Sally told me that Frederica has enjoyed visits with you to Newmarket and to Newbury."

"No, I have not made any purchases at Hyde Park recently, but I may go to an auction soon to buy two or three more racehorses."

They all returned to their box, where thin slices of ham and beef were served to them by the waiters, together with glasses of arrack punch and champagne, with a choice of other drinks to accompany the desserts. Then there were displays by acrobats and tightrope walkers to entertain the visitors, including the famous Madame Saqui, and the evening ended with a dramatic fireworks show. By the time they crossed the river on the ferry back to Westminster Pier, and returned home to Berkeley Square, Frederica was more than ready to go to bed.

Another interesting invitation was delivered to Berkeley Square. Alver's friend, Lord Petersham, was a Gentleman of the Bedchamber to the Prince of Wales, and Charles had invited the Marquis and Frederica to attend a ball at his family's London property, Harrington House. His father, the third Earl of Harrington, spent most of his time on his country property, Elvaston Castle in Derbyshire, and would not be attending.

"The Earl's absence means that Maria Foote will be at the event with Charles. I suspect that Prinny may be invited."

Frederica knew that the Prince Regent, who lived in London at Carlton House, was not popular with his subjects, and asked her husband about him.

"Prince George is, if you will excuse my choice of words, overweight, overdressed, and oversexed," said Alver.

"Despite all that, I should like to accept Lord Petersham's invitation, and I would be very interested to meet the Prince of Wales.

I have heard it said that no other member of the Royal Family has been such a staunch supporter of art, architecture, music, and science."

They duly presented themselves at Harrington House in Kensington Palace Gardens, suitably attired and with Frederica wearing all her emerald jewellery including her tiara. Maria Foote was not standing beside her lover as he welcomed his guests in the ballroom, but later Alver quietly took his wife to meet the lady. The Marquis was talking to Lady Jersey on the other side of the room when Frederica was very briefly introduced to Lord Petersham's younger sister, Sophia Stanton, but then there was a hush in the room as the arrival of the Prince of Wales was announced.

He was, she noticed, just as large as his reputation for personal excess, and she had not expected to be introduced to the heir to the throne. However, after Alver had returned to her side, Charles Petersham crossed the ballroom with his royal guest.

The Prince Regent greeted her with the words, "So you are the former Miss Merriville! I had been told that Alverstoke has finally succumbed to the charms of a beautiful and intelligent lady! I hope to see you both at Carlton House quite soon, Lady Alverstoke."

With that remark, he walked away from them to speak to other guests.

"Goodness, is he normally that abrupt, Alver?"

"That depends, my love, on how many glasses of wine he may have consumed during the evening! In case you wondered, his comment means that we shall soon be receiving a formal invitation!"

The Marquis was correct, as a few days later they received a summons to a soirée at Carlton House.

"Yet another occasion to give one of your tiaras an airing, my darling," said Alver.

Frederica promised Charis that she would write to her with all the details about their forthcoming visit to Carlton House. She would be assisted with her task because Alver had once been given an extended private tour of the property by Charles Petersham, in his capacity as a Gentleman of the Bedchamber to the Prince.

The Marquis told her that the building was about two hundred feet long and one hundred and thirty feet deep – more a palace than a house. Their carriage entered through the drive-through portico with Corinthian columns, and Alver and Frederica walked into a foyer flanked by anterooms on each side. The two-storey entrance hall had been decorated with Ionic columns of yellow marble, beyond which was an octagonal room, and both spaces were top-lit.

The grand oval staircase was on the right-hand side of the octagonal room, flanked by an open courtyard. The main anteroom then led to the formal reception rooms on the right – the throne room, the crimson drawing room where Alver said that the Prince Regent's daughter Princess Charlotte had been married to Prince Leopold in 1816, the music room and the dining room. Frederica's immediate impression was of gold everywhere, on columns, clocks, furniture and sculptures. All the main rooms directly faced The Mall, with views across the Prince's private gardens which had been designed by Mr Repton.

Frederica had heard that there were many paintings in the house and, as she and Alver walked through to meet the Prince of Wales, her husband showed her the pictures by Reynolds, Gainsborough and Stubbs, as well as by foreign artists such as Rembrandt, Rubens and Van Dyck.

They were greeted very affably by their host, Frederica performing a deep curtsy as was the custom to a member of the Royal Family. Then they both circulated through the rooms to meet other guests, and they were served refreshments before the recital by the musicians began.

After the music had ended, the Marquis said quietly to Frederica, "You will be interested to meet the man who is coming across the room to speak to us."

"Who is he, Alver?"

"Prince Frederick, Duke of York. He became Commander-in-Chief of the Army at the age of 30 before the Napoleonic Wars."

The Prince bore a strong resemblance to his elder brother, although he appeared to be in rather better health.

"Alverstoke, I am very pleased to see you here tonight. Is this your new wife? I have been told a great deal about the former Miss Merriville – all of it favourable."

"Yes, your Royal Highness. May I introduce Frederica, who has already transformed my life in a few short months!"

She dropped a deep curtsey to the Duke.

"The Marquis may not have told you, Lady Alverstoke, how fashionable you both are in marrying this year. Three of my brothers, William, Edward and Adolphus, had already reached the altar before you since January.

On a quite different topic, were you aware that Lord Alverstoke and I share an interest in the vaccinations against smallpox?"

"No, he has not said anything to me about that subject, Your Highness. Have you seen very beneficial effects in people who have had the treatment?"

"Yes, Lady Alverstoke, indeed I have, including for many soldiers in the Army. Now, may I suggest that, if your husband has not already taken you into the gardens, they are well worth a visit."

After the Duke had moved on to speak with other guests, Frederica asked her husband why three Royal Princes should have been married in the one year.

"The reason is the sad demise of Princess Charlotte in childbirth last year. Because of her death her father, the Prince of Wales, has no heir, so there is a rush for the King's other sons to procreate! The King and Queen have had fifteen children, including nine sons of whom seven grew to become adults. It is extraordinary that, despite that, at present there is no heir in the next generation."

The Marquis had told her that the Duke of York, who was a year younger than the Prince Regent, was said by many people to be the King's favourite son. The Duke had been an officer from a young age and had transformed the recruitment methods and administrative practices used in the Army.

"The Duke of York's interest in vaccination is inherited from his mother, as his baby brother Alfred died of the disease. Unfortunately, Queen Charlotte is now said to be suffering from dropsy and may be close to death in the palace at Kew."

"My interest in vaccination arose from a tragedy in our own family, as the Jevingtons lost their two eldest children to smallpox. That is the only occasion that I can remember when I have seen my sister Augusta cry. After that happened, Humphrey and Augusta decided to have Anna and Gregory, as well as themselves, protected from the disease. I had a long discussion at that time with my father about being protected. He was very wary of having the procedure done, but I was vaccinated a few months later after having discussed the options with John Kentmere. He, my sister Eliza and all four of their children have been protected."

"My father never discussed vaccination with me, Alver. However, after his death last year from the delayed effects of his stroke four years earlier, my uncle Richard suggested that all of us, including my Aunt Seraphina, should be inoculated, and so we followed his advice. As a doctor, he had often seen the dreadful scarring endured by patients who had survived the disease."

"Let us walk in the gardens now, Frederica, as the Duke of York has suggested."

So they spent a quarter of an hour walking along the paths and admiring the statues and plants in the formal garden beside The Mall.

"One more social hurdle surmounted, my darling," Alver told her at the end of the evening, as Curry drove them in the carriage for the short distance back to Berkeley Square. "You will be writing a very long letter to your sister in the morning. Now, what will your verdict be about Carlton House?"

"The rooms in the house that we saw during our visit were all wonderful; they were so spacious and each one was so handsomely decorated! The furniture had been chosen with taste and discretion – with many items in the French style - and the ornaments seemed to be of the highest quality. The marble fireplaces were particularly impressive, and I loved those wonderful chandeliers! The Duke of York did not exaggerate, as the gardens designed by Mr Repton were really delightful."

.

Chapter 11

Meanwhile, away from town at the Dauntry's house in Buckinghamshire, Jessamy had been visiting all parts of the estate owned by his new brother-in-law Endymion. Since Lucretia Dauntry had preferred to live in the town house in Green Street left to her by her mother, very little money seemed to have been spent on the property in the country.

"I don't want to worry Charis, Jessamy, but the building does seem to need quite a lot of attention. There are some leaks from holes in the roof, and the windows are in a bad way. The new steward who was found by your family's lawyer is due to arrive next week. He comes well recommended by Mr Salcombe, as well as by his previous employer."

"Perhaps he will be familiar with renovating buildings, Endymion?"

"All I know is that Cousin Alverstoke was quite happy about his previous experience, and told me that I should ask the steward's advice as soon as he has settled in."

Jessamy had noticed that his bedroom was rather draughty, and that the curtains at the windows were very worn. However, there was quite a handsome oak staircase in the entrance hall. There were 5 bedrooms on the first floor and, on the ground floor level, there were three main reception rooms, with the kitchen and staff quarters in an extension at the rear.

Endymion had told him that the previous steward, Mr Taylor, had moved out of his cottage on the estate to a house in the nearby village, but that his daughter, Annie Taylor, was the housekeeper at the main house. Annie Taylor told Jessamy an interesting story about a hostelry in the local town of Amersham that had been sold twice last year.

The new landlord of The Swan had refused to stock the beer produced by the brewery in Amersham, founded in 1775 and, for that reason, the town's people decided not to patronise the inn, but to go to The Crown or The White Hart in the town instead. After six months without any customers, the new landlord decided to sell the property, and the next owner reverted to stocking the local beer brewed in Amersham!

Frederica had suggested to Jessamy that he should ask to be taken to the land that they had given to the newly-weds as their wedding gift, at a location called Meadowsweet Lane. She had told her brother that there was a lovely view from there if the carriage could halt in a particular spot. So, when Jessamy suggested this outing to his hosts, they were happy to agree. However, Charis and Endymion were mystified when he produced some hazel twigs and put them in the carriage before they started their journey.

"Whatever are those to be used for, Jessamy?"

"Our sister recommended that we look for water in a particular location, Charis."

"With a twig?" asked Endymion.

"Yes. I will explain when we reach Meadowsweet Lane, where there is a good view over the village below."

When they reached their destination and had alighted from the carriage, both Charis and Endymion admired the outlook to the south. His brother-in-law asked, "Now, what do we do with those twigs, Jessamy?"

"Let's walk into this field, and I will show you."

He advanced about 150 feet, and then he grasped the twig as Caroline Kentmere had shown him in the garden at Berkeley Square, with one short arm of the twig in each hand, and the long arm pointing away from him. Then Jessamy began to walk methodically up and down, parallel to Meadowsweet Lane, getting closer and closer to where his hosts were standing by the field boundary.

Suddenly, when he was about 30 feet away from them, the twig twisted violently in his hands, and he shouted in triumph.

"There, just there, the water should be just below where I have stopped!"

Charis and Endymion came quickly across the grass to join him. His sister asked, "Does that mean water?"

"Yes. There must be a spring somewhere underneath this location, as we are much too high on the side of the hill for there to be an underground stream. But I will continue walking until I have covered the rest of this part of the field. Then I will walk the southern part, to complete my task."

The only other location where the twig twisted in his hand was down in the far corner of the field, and this time the movement was much weaker, which Jessamy guessed meant that the water source was rather deeper underground.

"Why do you want to find water here in this particular field, Jessamy?"

"I will explain but, before that, you may each like to try holding the twig."

First Endymion and then Charis took turns, and both were able to replicate the movement in their hands in the same location, about 30 feet from the boundary. Then they all sat down on a large log nearby, and Jessamy told them what Frederica had said to him in Herefordshire.

Endymion Dauntry was a handsome and very pleasant man, but he was rather slow to grasp a new idea. So, it was Charis who spoke to her brother.

"Build a house for us here, overlooking the view? But how could we possibly afford to do that, Jessamy?"

"Frederica told me that there are some people who prefer to buy an existing property that is badly in need of attention, as your home certainly is. But the location of that house is good, quite close to the main route to London, so it should not be difficult when you are ready to sell to find a purchaser who only wants an acre or two of garden.

But the one essential for a new house is a water supply and, of course, a road access nearby like Meadowsweet Lane. There is a delightful southerly outlook from this field, and you can see that the village is not far away. Would you like to have a new home in this location?"

Charis turned to look at Endymion before she replied. "Oh yes! I would – I would like that very much! But who would design a house for us?"

"Perhaps your new steward will have some talents of that kind. You can find out when he arrives from Herefordshire later this week."

Back at their home on the Dauntry estate later that day, there were lively discussions about what type and size of new home Charis and Endymion would like, or could afford, but Jessamy could see that they were both very attracted by the idea that he had suggested.

The new steward David Preece arrived in Buckinghamshire later in the week, and he spent the first three days settling into his cottage, and riding around the estate, including the recently purchased land, to acquaint himself with his new responsibilities. He seemed to Jessamy to be a level-headed young man, who asked sensible questions and made detailed notes of the answers in a large notebook. On the fourth day, Jessamy asked if they could ride together to Meadowsweet Lane, so that he could show Mr Preece the field with a view. On the way, he explained about the dowsing that had been done, and the possibility of building a new house there.

"Do you have any knowledge, Mr Preece, of how large a water supply might be required?"

"I am aware, Mr Merriville, of how strong the water supply was at the property where I was employed near Hereford. We would need to dig to find the spring, and then measure the flow. That excavation should only take a few days to complete, with two of the farmhands doing the work. Should I discuss that with Mr Dauntry when we return?"

"Yes, please do. I do not want to raise my sister's hopes if the water supply proves to be insufficient."

Jessamy had been staying in the Dauntry's home for nearly 10 days when this conversation took place, and he had received a letter yesterday from his sister Frederica.

She had reminded him that the date for the come-out ball in Mayfair for Caroline Kentmere was fast approaching, and that he should make sure that he returned to Berkeley Square in good time for the event. Charis and Endymion had been invited to the ball, but they had decided to stay in Buckinghamshire.

During his first evening back in town, Frederica said to Jessamy, "Lady Eliza has asked me to remind you that Caroline has two sessions with the dancing master this week."

Jessamy was beginning to feel rather apprehensive about going to the come-out ball, when so many of those attending will have had previous experience of such occasions. However, his sister would have none of that, saying that everyone must have a first time, and this would be his.

"I fear that my dancing skills will be very poor compared to Caroline's, for I have missed several weeks' tuition by going to Herefordshire and then staying with Charis and Endymion."

"Perhaps, but I'm sure that Caroline will be delighted to have her dancing partner back in London, Jessamy. Eliza has told me that they are expecting about 100 people to attend the occasion. John Kentmere arrived in town last weekend, and Jack has permission to miss school for a couple of days so that he can attend."

"Do you know whether Jack has been having any dancing lessons in Windsor?"

"Well, we must hope so for his sake, as otherwise he will be at quite a disadvantage. Alver has said that he must check what you are planning to wear that evening, in case you have grown any taller!"

As Frederica had foreseen, Caroline was delighted that Jessamy was able to be at the last two lessons. Her dancing was now very impressive, but the instructor gave him extra attention, and remarked that his skills were very creditable for such a young man.

When the evening for the ball finally arrived, Jessamy accompanied his sister and the Marquis in their carriage, Frederica wearing a very stylish cream silk dress, with her emerald jewels and tiara matching her handsome engagement ring. Soon Jessamy was in the ballroom, where the walls had been decorated with intricate flower arrangements, and the musicians were already playing quietly in the background.

Caroline was wearing one of Mlle Franchot's more expensive creations in a shade of pale blue that flattered her complexion. Standing next to her was Diana Dauntry, dressed in one of the carefully chosen satin gowns favoured by her mother Lucretia. At Alver's prompting, Jessamy was granted a waltz with Caroline, and a gavotte by Diana, for later in the evening. Soon the dance cards for both the young ladies were full.

When the time came, Jessamy was about to ask Caroline to dance their waltz when they were interrupted by a very tall young gentleman dressed in a colourful and extravagant style.

"Miss Kentmere, will you do me the honour of dancing this waltz with me?"

"I do not believe that we have been introduced, sir?"

"My name is Algernon Tweedie-Briggs. My aunt is a close friend of your mother Lady Eliza."

"Thank you for telling me your name, sir. However, I regret that my card is full for the whole evening, and I am about to dance this waltz with Mr Merriville," and she turned to smile at Jessamy.

The young man looked very taken aback, then he blushed bright red, and turned away from them. Jessamy lost no time in asking Caroline to take to the floor.

"Miss Kentmere, Caroline, will you please dance the next waltz with me?"

"Of course, Mr Merriville, Jessamy, I should be delighted!"

Once they had begun to circle the floor, Jessamy exclaimed, "What a stupid young popinjay, Caroline!"

"I was going to say that he is a real ninny, a coxcomb! There are times when I wish that I could be back home on our estate in the Shires, not having to endure fools in town like Mr Tweedie-Briggs!"

She laughed at him, and he smiled back. "Either description would do, Caroline! I must admit that I prefer country people, rather than a city coxcomb, any day!"

Jessamy managed a very creditable waltz, and he said to her as the music came to an end, "Thank you. Your gown is beautiful, Caroline, and you are the belle of the ball!"

"Except for Diana; she looks wonderful in that very stylish dress."

Later in the evening, Jessamy was standing at the side of the ballroom when he was approached by the young popinjay.

"Forgive my earlier discourtesy, Mr Merriville. Do you live in London?"

"I do at present, but our family estate is in Herefordshire."

"Is that where your father resides?"

"No, sir, my father died nearly two years ago. I am now the owner of the estate."

"Please accept my condolences on your loss, Mr Merriville. Do you know Miss Kentmere and Lady Eliza well?"

"Yes, I do, Mr Tweedie-Briggs. Lady Eliza is related to the Marquis of Alverstoke, who is married to my elder sister. That is the Marchioness over there, talking to Lady Eliza."

Mr Tweedie-Briggs seemed very impressed indeed with this information, and he hesitated before asking, "Would it be possible for you to introduce me to the Marquis? I should very much like to meet him. I assume that he is here this evening?"

In a spirit of mischief, and knowing well Lady Eliza's forthright manner of speaking, Jessamy decided to deflect the task.

"I suggest that it would be best if you ask Lady Eliza that question, sir. She might be willing to introduce her brother to you."

Mr Tweedie-Briggs thanked him for his suggestion, and he made his way across the ballroom towards her.

By the time the ball was over, Jessamy had danced with many of the young ladies present, as well as with Diana Dauntry, and he was becoming more confident about his dancing skills. He also took the opportunity to have a long conversation with Caroline's brother Jack, who had not had any dancing lessons at Eton, and was therefore very pleased to find someone he knew to talk to during the evening.

Later, on the way back to Berkeley Square in the carriage with his sister and her husband, Jessamy recounted his two encounters during the evening with Mr Tweedie-Briggs, to the considerable amusement of his companions.

"He sounds entertaining company, Jessamy, if for all the wrong reasons. I must ask Eliza what she said when he approached her."

"Indeed, I agree, love. She did not introduce the young man to me, probably deciding that I might be rather severe with him! May I congratulate you, Jessamy, on dancing a very competent waltz with my niece? I doubt that I would have done as well at the same age."

"All the credit must go to Caroline, not to me, for she is very easy to dance with."

"Did you enjoy the ball, Jessamy?"

"Yes, I did. Now that I have been to one occasion like that, I hope that I will not be so anxious next time."

Later that night, when the Marquis and Frederica were ready to go to bed, she said, "I may be wrong, and Caroline is not someone who wears 'her heart on her sleeve', but I have wondered if she is developing a tendre for my brother?"

"She is very young to do so – only just 17 – and there are many young men who are wealthier than Jessamy, who she will be meeting over the next few months."

"Yes, I agree with that. We shall see, no doubt, in due course, but they do have interests in common, including a preference for living in the country, and Caroline can be just as single-minded as her mother. I doubt whether money would be the deciding factor for her."

A few days later, Charis wrote to her brother from Buckinghamshire about the field adjoining Meadowsweet Lane.

'The farmhands working with Mr Preece took nearly three days to reach the level of the spring below surface of the field. He has asked me to tell you that there seems every prospect of the supply being sufficient for a new house. Perhaps you could persuade Cousin Alverstoke and Frederica to visit us here quite soon, to discuss the possibilities.'

When this letter arrived, Jessamy had begun to get rather bored with life in London, as he was not old enough to be invited to any other balls, and Jack Kentmere had returned to school at Eton. So he decided to persuade Frederica and the Marquis that now would be a good time for them all to travel to meet the new steward, Mr Preece, and to discuss with Endymion and Charis whether they would be interested in proceeding with the idea of building a new house. Charis and Endymion wrote to encourage them all to come to Buckinghamshire as soon as possible.

When the party from town arrived, he discovered that his elder sister and her husband had not previously stayed overnight in the old house on the Dauntry's estate, and they were not impressed with the run-down condition of the building, and the lack of normal domestic comforts.

However, the Marquis soon met Mr Preece and Endymion for a thorough discussion of the options for the estate, as well as for a possible new house. Lord Alverstoke told Jessamy afterwards that he was pleased with the knowledge displayed by the new steward, and his readiness to consider a wide range of ideas.

Meanwhile, Charis and her sister took the opportunity to catch up with each other's news, including the ball that Lady Eliza had held for Caroline and Diana.

"The ball sounds wonderful, Frederica, and you must be pleased that Jessamy did so well with his dancing at his first grown-up occasion? I suppose that, when he goes to university, he will be too busy studying to be distracted by such frivolities. I remember that our brother Harry had no interest in going to balls, and that he said that he was a very bad dancer. He had no enthusiasm for the fashionable life in London."

"I am not surprised that you are disappointed about the neglected state of this house, Charis, but I guess that Lucretia had little incentive to spend any money when she had no intention of living here. I suppose that, if her husband had not died prematurely, the situation might have been different. Alver told me that you have been discussing your plans for a new home with Mr Preece."

"I suspect that Jessamy might welcome being involved with that possibility. He told me that he is at rather a loose end, and he will not be going to start his studies at Oxford for several months yet."

"He could travel to Graynard for a few days, I suppose, but I would not want him to go there on his own, and Alver and I don't want to be away from town for too long at present. It will be several weeks before the horse racing season begins, but that will be a useful distraction for Jessamy when it starts."

Chapter 12

After several months, Alver and Frederica had settled happily into married life together, including their habit of drinking hot chocolate in bed, but not during the week - only on Saturday and Sunday mornings, although they left it to Cook to make the drink for them.

Frederica was surprised to see, when waking early one Sunday morning, that Alver had left their bed, although his side of the sheets was still warm. After a few minutes, he entered the bedroom from the side door leading to their private sitting room, and she could smell a faint aroma of hot chocolate.

When he saw that she was awake, he came across the room and gave her an affectionate kiss before saying, "I will fetch your wrapper, Frederica. Then come into the sitting room to drink the chocolate that I have made for you."

"Cook was not in the kitchen this morning?"

"I was rather too early for her, and I needed to revive my chocolate-making skills for you, my love!"

After finishing her drink, Frederica rose from her chair to put the cup and saucer on the tray. When she turned round, Alver had moved and was sitting in his father's favourite old armchair.

"Come and sit here on my lap, love. There is something that I want to discuss with you."

When she had settled in his arms, he said slowly, "When are you going to tell me, Frederica?"

She knew exactly what he was talking about.

"It is more than 9 weeks now since I last had my courses, Alver. When I had lunch with Marietta Ormond recently, she told me that both of her children had been born in London, and that she had been attended on each occasion by Sir William Knighton.

Although he practises also as a general physician, Sir William's particular reputation is as a well-respected accoucheur. Marietta suggested that I should wait another 3 weeks and, if my courses have not happened by then, I should go and ask for his advice."

"I will, of course, accompany you," Alver said firmly.

"No, you will not do that, Alver. Marietta has told me that Sir William is strongly of the view that aristocratic husbands always try to take over and to try to dictate to their wives what they should and should not do while they are increasing. Sir William prefers that all his clients avoid unnecessary stress, and that they only follow his advice."

Frederica was quietly amused as her husband struggled with this concept. Several times, he seemed to be about to speak, but then he thought better of it. Finally, he realised that his wife was trying very hard not to laugh at him, and he slowly began to smile.

"Minx! Frederica, please stop teasing me. It is surely quite natural for me to be concerned about your health?"

"I shall be grateful for your interest, Alver, but pregnancy and birth are very common occurrences, as you well know, and I am not going to allow you to tell me what I should do in my daily life! I promise that I will explain to you everything about my visit to Sir William, if and when it takes place."

And with that, Alver had to be content.

Frederica decided that it would be a good idea to change the subject. "Tell me, Alver, what should we do for the Christmas holidays? Where have you been for the festive season in the past?"

"Well, there are several answers to that, my darling. While my mother was alive, we always had our Christmas in London, here at Berkeley Square. After her death, and with all three of my sisters married by then, I used to accompany my father to Alver Park, and we had our Christmas festivities in Wiltshire with my widowed grandmother, Caroline. Then my grandmother died and later, after my father's death about 10 years ago, I was invited to spend each

Christmas with my friend Darcy Moreton and his family on their estate in Hertfordshire.

One year, when Darcy's mother became seriously unwell just before the holiday and I could not stay with their family, my eldest sister Augusta and her husband Humphrey Jevington took pity on me, and invited me to join them and their children, Anna and Gregory, at their country house for the festive season. What did your family do last Christmas, Frederica? You might like to continue with your family traditions, perhaps?"

"My father had died early last year, so the five of us together with my aunt Seraphina had our Christmas Day at Graynard. Then, on Boxing Day, we went to visit my uncle Richard Winsham for lunch. Before that year, because of my father's dislike of his brother-in-law, we had never been able to see him and his family in Ross on Wye, although Aunt Seraphina used to take the gig quite often to visit her brother in the town. What would you like to do this year, Alver?"

"My preference would be to have our Christmas holiday at Alver Park, and I should be very happy if you, Jessamy and Felix would introduce me to your Christmas customs. That is something that I have never had in my life up till now."

"Would it be possible for us to make a visit to the spectacle at Sadler's Wells before Christmas, Alver? I have heard that the naval melodrama of The Siege of Gibraltar is well worth seeing. Jessamy would probably like to go with us."

"Certainly, I have heard at White's that the diversion of the river to fill an enormous water tank covering the entire stage has been very successful. Darcy told me that the many miniature ships created by the shipwrights at the Woolwich Dockyard are very realistic, not to mention the acting by the young children employed to 'struggle in the waves' as the drowning Spanish sailors, and the theatre uses miniature cannon during the 'battle'. Why don't we take Charles Trevor with us, Frederica?"

Several days later, when they had taken their seats in the theatre before the performance was due to begin, they admired the colourful backcloth showing the English fleet drawn up in battle against France and Spain. They had been warned that the audience could be quite rowdy between the scenes, not to mention rather drunk, with a constant shower of orange peel being thrown across the auditorium. At the end of the performance, several young men jumped into the tank to assure themselves that the water was real! However, as Lord Alverstoke's seats were at the first balcony level, fortunately they were above the fray, and the Marquis, Jessamy and Charles were ready to protect Frederica if necessary.

Alver had invited Darcy Moreton to lunch with them a few days later at Berkeley Square, because his friend had an idea that Frederica might like to consider for a charitable venture. After they had enjoyed a pleasant meal, they moved with their guest to the drawing room. Frederica had poured the coffee for the three of them, and then she turned to their friend.

"Now, Darcy, what is this idea that you would like to suggest to me?"

"Some months ago, in the house in Upper Wimpole Street, I had a conversation with your sister, Charis. She told me that Harriet, your mother, had been a talented artist, and that there are several paintings by her on the walls in your family's home at Graynard.

I am a supporter of the Foundling Hospital at Bloomsbury, which was created by Thomas Coram nearly 80 years ago now. He was a retired sea captain, who was concerned about the babies being abandoned on the streets of London by unmarried girls. The children are admitted to the Hospital because their mothers are unable to care for them. To begin with, the babies are sent to 'wet nurses' in the countryside until they are four or five years old. Then they return to live at the Hospital in Hatton Garden, where they are educated until they are old enough to seek employment. There are separate wings at the premises for the boys and for the girls.

At present, their education does not include music or art, although there are moves afoot to introduce music for the boys so that some are able to consider careers as musicians in the bands of His Majesty's Household Troops.

I wondered, Frederica, whether you might be interested in joining a small committee to oversee and to pay for introducing art lessons for the girls. There may be some of them who have sufficient talents to produce artworks that could be sold to produce income for the Hospital. At present, the girls only learn embroidery and hat-making."

Alver watched his dear wife slowly turn this idea over in her mind.

"Darcy, does this committee already exist and, if so, who are the members?"

"Lord Petersham's younger sister Sophia Stanton has agreed to help. Her sister is married to the Duke of Bedford; perhaps you have already met Sophia? She was widowed in the Spring of last year when her husband had a fatal heart attack, leaving her with two small daughters to raise. Fortunately, she has no financial difficulties. But her brother, who as you know is a member of White's, has suggested that she might benefit by getting involved with a new interest. I have already persuaded Henry Cooke, who lives here in Berkeley Square with his wife Katherine, to join the committee. He is good friends with the Duke of York, which might be a useful connection."

Frederica had already heard about Henry Cooke from her husband – Alver had told her that he must be the ugliest man in England! But he was also a public-spirited philanthropist?

Frederica looked across the room at Alver, who gave her a supportive smile.

"I am no artist, Darcy – it was my mother who had considerable talents in that direction. But it would be good to support something in memory of Mama so, yes, I should be delighted to help you. Are you planning to be on the committee yourself?"

"Yes, I am, Frederica."

A week later, she went in his carriage with Darcy to visit the Foundling Hospital, and to meet some of the girls who had expressed an interest in learning to draw and to paint. They were between eleven and fourteen years of age and they were accompanied by the matron who supervised their studies. Afterwards, Darcy and Frederica met Sophia Stanton and Henry Cooke in the matron's office.

Sophia seemed to be a pleasant and lively young woman, perhaps a few years older than Frederica, and she said that she enjoyed drawing and painting. Her brother Lord Petersham had been at Frederica and Alver's wedding and at the reception at Alver Park, and the siblings had the same dark brown wavy hair.

Henry Cooke was, as Alver had told her, not a handsome man, but he seemed interested in the project, and was happy to assist.

The benefactors of the Hospital over the years had included several renowned artists who had donated some of their pictures, and Frederica was told that a young curator was in post to arrange regular exhibitions of their paintings. Many pictures had been given to the Hospital by artists such as Hogarth, Reynolds, Gainsborough, and the Italian artist Casali. Most of the visitors who came each week to see the paintings also made donations to the Hospital. They agreed that the curator should be asked to find an art teacher for the girls as soon as possible.

Darcy Moreton suggested that each member of the new committee should subscribe enough money to pay their share of the fee for a teacher to teach a weekly lesson, plus the cost of materials such as paper and paints. He also proposed that the committee should meet every second week in Henry Cooke's mansion in Berkeley Square. Frederica soon received a message that the curator had found a suitable artist, who would be introduced to the committee at their meeting on the following Tuesday.

They all seated themselves in the library of Mr Cooke's house in Berkeley Square, where a Mr Francis was waiting for them. Henry Cooke explained that the artist already gave private lessons to members of the aristocracy, and that he came with favourable recommendations from them about his technical skills, pleasant manners, and his patient approach to teaching his clients.

Mr Francis was quite a young man with a suitably artistic hairstyle. He said that he had already met the girls for an introductory art lesson. He had given them each of them a task to reveal what abilities they might have, although he did not intend to exclude those who were interested, but who did not have any special artistic talents.

"Members of your committee, Mr Cooke, will of course be very welcome to observe the weekly lessons. However, may I suggest that no more than two of you should attend at a time, to avoid being too much of a distraction for the girls."

"Since we both live in Berkeley Square, Frederica, I suggest that you pair with me. Sophia, are you willing to pair with Darcy?"

"Yes, of course, I should be very happy to do so, Henry."

The following week, Darcy Moreton and Sophia Stanton attended the art lesson, and reported that the girls seemed to be really enjoying their new opportunities.

The next week, it was Frederica and Henry Cooke's turn to go to the Foundling Hospital, and she told Alver afterwards that she had enjoyed the experience, and hoped to see the girls improve their skills over time. The committee members met at Henry Cooke's home later that week, to discuss various suggestions that they had developed for improvements to the classes.

Several weeks later, Alver had taken Jessamy Merriville on an outing in his carriage to Richmond Park and, as it was a very sunny morning, Frederica decided to walk to Bond Street to do some shopping, accompanied by her abigail, Emily Leonard.

As they turned east out of Berkeley Square into Bruton Street, Frederica saw Sophia Stanton on the opposite side of the road, walking towards the Square, and accompanied by two young girls aged about eight and six years. But it was not the children that caught her attention, but the man walking beside Sophia – Alver's friend Darcy Moreton. He was deep in conversation with the older child, and neither he nor Sophia noticed Frederica.

She guessed that their destination might be Gunter's café in the Square – just the place for a young child to enjoy a delicious pastry or an ice cream. Gunter's also sold syrups, candied fruits, cakes, biscuits, delicate sugar spun fantasies, and elaborate table decorations. It was said to be the only establishment in London where a lady could be seen eating alone with a gentleman who was not her relative without it harming her reputation.

As she walked home with Emily carrying the parcels after completing her shopping, Frederica debated with herself whether to tell Alver what she had seen, but she decided not to. If Darcy and Sophia were seeing more of each other than she had been aware of, that was excellent news. After all, she had once suggested to her husband that Darcy might be well suited to marrying a widow with young children!

Alver had continued his habit of lunching at White's, if now only from time to time, on a Friday so that he could meet friends who were fellow club members. He returned to Berkeley Square one Friday afternoon to tell Frederica that Darcy Moreton had not been at the club for lunch that day. Another member of the aristocracy had told Alver that Darcy's mother, who had been suffering from a heart complaint for several years, had taken a serious turn for the worse. His friend had left London in a hurry on the previous day for Hertfordshire to be with her.

The members of the committee supporting the art class at the Foundling Hospital were due to meet at Henry Cooke's house the following week, but Frederica received a note from Henry to say that, as neither Darcy nor Sophia Stanton would be in London, the meeting should be postponed until they were both available.

Alver wrote a letter to Darcy Moreton at his family's estate, but it was a week before he received a reply from his friend. Having read the letter, he passed the message across the breakfast table for Frederica to see what it contained.

"As you will see, Darcy's mother died a few days' ago, and he has been busy consoling his father, and making the arrangements for the funeral. I shall attend and, although it is not thought appropriate for ladies to be at the church, I should like you to go to Hertfordshire with me. Darcy's mother, Mrs Moreton, was always kind to me, and very supportive after my mother, and later my father, passed away."

Having read the letter through, Frederica noted that Darcy asked them to stay with him in the family home.

During their journey to Hertfordshire, Frederica decided to tell Alver about the occasion when she had seen Darcy Moreton walking with Sophia Stanton and her children towards Gunter's café in Berkeley Square.

"Why didn't you tell about that before now, Frederica?"

"I suppose that I did not want you to tease him about Sophia. Sometimes, matters of the heart can be quite fragile early on in a relationship. I knew that, if everything went well, Darcy would tell you in his own good time. When Henry Cooke said, a couple of weeks ago, that neither of them were in London, I guessed that Sophia might have gone with him to visit Mrs Moreton. So don't be too surprised if we find that she is already in Hertfordshire with Darcy and his father."

Frederica's guess proved to be correct, and she watched with interest to see what Alver made of Lord Petersham's sister on meeting her for the first time. Although the Marquis could be quite severe sometimes when meeting someone new, he went out of his way to engage Sophia in friendly conversation.

"How did you know," said Darcy to Frederica, "about our relationship? Ver was obviously aware that Sophia might be here."

Frederica explained where and when she had seen Darcy and Sophia together in Bruton Street with her children.

"I am so happy that my mother lived long enough to meet Sophia. Mama always wanted me to marry, and finally settle down. Sophia has been very helpful towards the end of my mother's life. Frederica, will you look after her for me here during the funeral at the village church? She has been assisting my staff with plans for the meal when everyone returns here after the funeral."

"Of course, Darcy. And I am very delighted to know that you have finally succumbed to Cupid's arrow!"

Alver and Frederica stayed in Hertfordshire for a couple of days after the funeral, and then returned to London so that they could be with her brother Jessamy in Berkeley Square. They resumed their normal pattern of life, including Frederica attending the fortnightly committee meetings at Henry Cooke's house.

She waited a little longer to make the appointment to visit Sir William Knighton at his consulting rooms in Stratford Place, near Bond Street. She told her husband about the day for the appointment, and he quietly wished her well as she left the house with Emily in attendance.

On entering the consulting room, Sir William immediately recognised her. "Ah," he said with the easy smile that she remembered, "I recall meeting you a few months' ago when I examined your brother Felix at the house in Upper Wimpole Street. How is the young man doing now? He was quite a lively character if I recall correctly!"

"Yes, indeed, Sir William. He is quite recovered, and Felix is in his first term at Eton. No doubt he is causing the school no end of trouble. Certainly, life at home in Berkeley Square is very much quieter without him in the house! Your services have been recommended to me by Marietta Ormond, the daughter-in-law of Lord and Lady Ormond, who was very happy with your advice and care when both of her children were born. It is now 12 weeks since I last had my courses, so I suspect that I may be increasing."

"Well, let's have a good look, and I will tell you what I find."

It only took him a few minutes before Sir William was able to confirm what Frederica had suspected.

"What kind of man is your husband, the Marquis? I had heard of him several years before your marriage."

"Lord Alverstoke likes to be in control of everything in his world, but I have already told him that he is not to try to control mine during the next few months! We have a good relationship, I would say, and share a very lively sense of humour. In general, we respect each other's choices."

"Good – that is not always the case. Some husbands can be the very devil, in my experience! I should like to see you here at my consulting rooms please, every 4 or 5 weeks, from now on.

Once you reach 3 months before the likely birth date, you should bring the Marquis with you to the next appointment. In the meantime, continue to do everything that brings you pleasure in life, including conjugal relations. Should anything happen between our appointments to worry you, do not hesitate to contact me immediately."

Frederica's account of the discussion with Sir William at his rooms in Stratford Place was eagerly awaited by Alver when she returned home. He seemed to be satisfied with what his wife had told him, and especially pleased that he would be able to meet the doctor himself in the not too distant future.

Christmas was now fast approaching, and with it the date for Felix's return home at the end of the school term. He was not a frequent correspondent and, when he did write, the letters did not tell Alver or Frederica very much.

More informative was the news about his activities that they received from Alver's sister, Lady Eliza, whose second son Tom Kentmere was in the same year at Eton as Felix. Tom was a more helpful correspondent and gave his mother some details about Felix that Frederica guessed her brother might not want her to be aware of!

Tom's elder brother Jack was in his last year at Eton before moving on to Oxford University and, as a successful scholar, was a member of "Pop", the most senior group of prefects in the school. At his mother's request, he was also keeping a careful eye on Felix Merriville, and was aware of his interest in all matters scientific. He told her that Felix would not qualify to join the Scientific Society until he was in his third year at the school. But one of the senior masters had been asked to supervise Felix, and to guide his inquiring mind into matters that would maintain his interest in science but protect the other pupils from harm!

Once the end of the Michaelmas Term came, and Felix came back to Berkeley Square, the family began to prepare to leave town for their Christmas holiday in Wiltshire. Frederica was kept very busy shopping for gifts for Charis and Endymion Dauntry, as well for the Marquis and her younger brothers.

Two days before they were due to leave for Alver Park, Felix went to find Alver's secretary, Charles Trevor. Assuming his most persuasive expression, he said "I have a problem, Mr Trevor, which you might be able to help me with."

"What's that, Felix? Please explain."

"My sister has asked me what present I would like her – and Cousin Alverstoke of course – to give me on Christmas Day. My tutor at Eton has been telling us at school all about mediaeval battles, and how they were fought. The soldiers did not have any guns at that time, so they had to find other ways of defeating their enemies and fighting their way into other people's castles. The most popular ways were to use battering rams and trebuchets."

Charles was beginning to wonder what Felix was going to ask for as his Christmas gift. "What is a trebuchet, Felix?"

"It is a very tall wooden tower with a large catapult at the top, and a weighted arm, to throw stones at the castle – I could draw you a picture, if that would help?"

Charles was not sure what his employers were going to think about these suggestions. "No, that will not be necessary, thank you. Are you wanting to construct a battering ram, and a trebuchet, in your workshop at Alver Park? You would need quite a large quantity of wood, I assume?"

Felix gave him a very grateful smile. "Exactly. Although I would only want to build quite a small trebuchet, and a middle-sized battering ram."

"Well, you may know that there is a sawmill in the village near Alver Park, which is driven by the water from the river. No doubt they could cut whatever type of wood you might need. Why don't you leave the idea with me, and I will discuss your suggestion with the Marquis when I next see him."

Alver rolled his eyes at his secretary. "So Felix has decided to move backwards in history, from mechanical devices to mediaeval warfare, has he? Lord protect us! At least we should be grateful that he does not want to create battles here in Berkeley Square!"

"I could make that suggestion instead, if you like, sir?"

"No, I do not want you to do that, Charles! The last thing that I desire is for Felix to be scattering heavy projectiles from a trebuchet into my neighbours' gardens! Please do not tell my wife about Felix's suggestion until after we reach Wiltshire – she is supposed to be avoiding stress now that she is increasing."

Once they had travelled to Alver Park, Frederica kept her brothers busy searching the woods for mistletoe and for holly branches to decorate the house. As well as Knapp and Emily Leonard, Wicken and Cook had travelled with the family, and both Felix and Jessamy were sometimes to be found in the kitchen, when Cook was willing to let them 'assist her' in tasting some of her creations.

Alver enjoyed all the festive preparations, and he was particularly useful when much longer arms were needed to fix the decorations in the house at a level well above the boys' reach.

Frederica gave her husband "short shrift" when he tried to make her rest during the day, pointing out that she had had strict instructions from Sir William Knighton not to change her habits just because she was increasing. She knew that Alver was eagerly anticipating the day when he would be allowed to go with her to visit the doctor. Alver was aware that Frederica would tease him immediately if he showed any sign of becoming overbearing, or at least more overbearing than usual, before then!

On Christmas Eve, Frederica could not find either of her brothers when she went to look for them in mid-morning. She had searched everywhere, and she ended by going to the drawing room, which was the least likely location for them to be. She opened the door quietly, but paused, for she saw that Alver was standing still in the centre of the room. She must have been waiting there for several minutes before her husband turned, and he saw her watching him.

"How long have you been there, Frederica?"

"Not for long, and I did not want to disturb you. What are you thinking about, love?"

"I was realising how very happy I am to be here with our family Christmas to look forward to tomorrow."

She smiled and went forward to embrace him. "Where is the mistletoe, Alver?"

"Look behind you, my love. The mistletoe is just above this side of the doorway."

"Ah, so it is. I remember that you said there should be some in every room in the ground floor of the house."

"You and I need to test all of them, to make sure that they have the real magic of Christmas! Are you willing to do that?"

"Why not? But first, I am looking for Jessamy and Felix. Do you know where they are?"

"As it happens, yes, I do. They have gone riding together in the park, and I asked Curry to go with them, as he knows where the new wide tracks are that I have asked to be constructed. Knowing that your brother Felix might do something stupid, Curry is there to restrain him, so that nothing untoward can happen to either of them before Christmas Day! I do not think that they will be back to the house until lunchtime, so there will be plenty of time for us to check all that mistletoe!"

Jessamy had told his sister in advance that he was now much too old to have a Christmas stocking tied to his bedroom doorknob overnight. But Felix, knowing that his stocking would at least include an orange and some chocolate to eat, as well as other small presents, was very happy (aged 13) not to be too old to continue the tradition!

The family had breakfast together on Christmas morning – a second breakfast for Felix, who had dressed himself very early, and been to see Cook in the kitchen, so that he could eat some mince pies to keep him going until his family appeared in the dining room. Then it was time to unwrap all the presents in the drawing room, where they had been piled up under the tall Christmas tree.

One of the presents for Felix was a large white envelope, which contained a piece of paper. As he opened the envelope, Alver spoke to him.

"Listen to me very carefully, Felix.

I am willing to pay the sawmill in the village to provide you with enough wood to build a very small trebuchet, and a battering ram as well, if you want that.

But there are several conditions, which Charles Trevor has listed for you on this piece of paper. These are –

the construction must only be done in your workshop, and with the assistance of the estate carpenter;

once constructed, the trebuchet and the battering ram may only be used on the further side of the stream and the lake, and facing away from the house. They are not to be 'discharged' towards the formal gardens; and you may only use the trebuchet, as well as the battering ram, if you always have an adult person with you at the time; either Mr Trevor or myself (not Jessamy). Frederica is to be kept well away from whatever you are doing.

Is that quite clear?"

"Yes, sir. May I go now and start to prepare my drawings, ready to order the wood?"

"That is a very good idea! Mr Trevor will be returning here in 2 days' time after having had Christmas with his family. He can help you to decide how much wood you will need."

Frederica, who had no idea about what a trebuchet was, and only a limited knowledge about battering rams, turned to Alver and said, "What is all that about? What is a trebuchet?"

"Your brother has a new enthusiasm for mediaeval warfare, inspired by his history tutor at Eton. I will explain more later on today."

Alver and Frederica had agreed in advance that their presents to each other should be a surprise. Having waited until her brothers had unwrapped all their gifts, she turned to Alver.

"I gave my present for you to Wicken for safekeeping earlier this morning, to conceal it in his room. I will go to find the present now."

When she returned, she was carrying a parcel about 24 inches by 18 inches.

Alver slowly unwrapped it, and then his face was overtaken by a big smile. "Frederica, what an absolutely wonderful gift – thank you so much, my darling!"

"What is it, sir?" said Jessamy.

Alver turned the painting to face Jessamy so that the boy could see a delightful 'head and shoulders' portrait of Frederica.

"That is a particularly good likeness of my sister, sir. The artist has caught the exact expression on her face when she is trying hard not to laugh!"

"I agree, Jessamy. Who painted the picture, love?"

"You know of him, although you have not met the artist – Mr Francis, who is teaching the girls at the Foundling Hospital. I asked him whether he ever painted a portrait as a private commission, and he told me that he had recently completed a picture of your friend Sally Jersey, our neighbour at 38 Berkeley Square. I went to visit her to view the picture, and her husband was there. George said to tell you that he is absolutely delighted with her portrait. However, I asked them not to say anything to you before Christmas, as I wanted the picture to be a surprise."

"I did overhear George during lunch at White's recently, telling another club member that he had an excellent new portrait of his wife, and recommending the artist to him. Now I know why."

"Where will you hang the picture, sir?"

"The best place would be in my library in London, Jessamy, where I would be able to see the picture whenever I am sitting at my desk.

Now it is my turn to surprise you, Frederica. Put on your warmest pelisse, my dear, as we must go out to the stables. Jessamy, you might like to come with us?"

"A new horse, Alver?"

"No, not a horse, my love. Come with me!"

They walked outside and across the stable yard to the large building that housed the carriages when they were not in use. Alver took a key out of his pocket, and then unlocked the door to a space at the further end of the structure. When Frederica looked through the doorway, there she could see a very smart new barouche, painted in blue and yellow, and with a dark blue folding hood over the rear seats of the carriage.

"One reason, Frederica, why I decided to have the paths widened, and to have more of them constructed, was so that we could use this new barouche to drive on the tracks, and to see the deer in the park. Do you like the colours, love?"

"Oh yes, I do – they are very stylish! What an absolutely lovely surprise, Alver! Thank you very much for my Christmas present!"

Felix had explained to Jessamy what the schoolmaster had said about how the components for a trebuchet were constructed in advance before a military campaign. All the parts were then taken by the invading force in wagons to an enemy castle or town, where an expert team of carpenters and labourers assembled them. This method made the trebuchets quicker to build, easier to transport, and available to be used again in multiple sieges.

Felix was kept very busy for several days cutting wood, and checking that he had all the parts needed for making the trebuchet, before asking Jessamy to tell everyone that he wanted to do a trial 'firing'.

"Felix has asked me to take you out onto the terrace," his brother said, "so that you can see him using his trebuchet on the far side of the stream."

"This could be very interesting!" remarked Alver, as he took his wife's arm, and they left the house by the front door.

In the distance, they could see Felix, with his wooden construction and its sling facing in the opposite direction, and with a pile of large stones next to his tower, ready for firing at the 'enemy'.

"Now!" shouted Jessamy, as he waved his arm at his brother.

Felix loaded a stone onto the sling and pulled the arm of the trebuchet back before firing the stone away from them. The stone hit a large tree in the distance, and a scatter of branches and leaves fell to the ground. Frederica had a fit of the giggles as Felix shouted in triumph, "It works! It works!"

"Indeed, it does," observed the Marquis. "Should we ask him to repeat the process?"

"You try stopping him, sir!" said Jessamy with a smile.

Chapter 13

Having lunched together at White's, Alver and his friend Darcy Moreton moved to the ground floor to have coffee in the bow window of the room overlooking St James' Street.

"Well, Ver, how is married life suiting you? You seem to me to be very content with your new status."

"I can recommend marriage wholeheartedly, Darcy. When I remember that, 12 months ago, I did not know that Frederica existed, not to mention her brothers and sister, my world has been totally transformed! Before I met her, I was attempting to fill my time with trivial matters, and transitory relationships that meant nothing to me. Now I wake up every morning with a smile on my face, my wife in my arms, and a future family in prospect.

I suppose that I was concerned about the possibility of having a sad marriage as my father did, with both my parents unhappy with their lives. But I am very fortunate – I have a passionate relationship with Frederica, and I have never been so content!"

"Yes, you certainly were a disillusioned rake for so many years! Your decision to marry at Alver Park rather than in London was very wise, even if it upset those members of the Ton who were expecting you to choose St George's Church in Hanover Square. We have decided to follow your example and marry in a country church."

"Now you are engaged to Sophia, when do you plan to marry?"

"We will probably wait until Midsummer. It is only two months since my mother died, and my father is still adjusting to that situation. Meanwhile, he is going soon to stay with my sister and her family for a couple of weeks, since our property holds too many memories of his married life."

"That timing seems sensible, for the weather should be better in June or July. Frederica will have given birth, and so she should be able to travel with me to Hertfordshire."

"My father's age and increasing infirmity would make it difficult for him to travel to town. Sophia's brother Petersham is happy to make the journey to give her away at the church near our estate. Sophia's daughters will be her attendants, and they are already very excited about the prospect of having lovely new dresses to wear for the occasion. Like you, I will have a ready-made family, although Sophia and I hope to add more children in due course. Are you very daunted by the fact that you will soon become a father?"

"I must admit, Darcy, that I am finding that prospect unexpectedly stressful. I don't worry about Frederica's health now, but I am only too aware that some women die in childbirth."

"Ver, surely you have no reason for concern? Sir William Knighton is a very well-respected physician. Frederica's mother had five children, as I understand it, without having had any problems. She did not die in childbirth, but from rheumatic fever."

"Am I easy to read? If so, Frederica might have noticed that I am concerned about her. Having at last found someone to love so much after many unhappy years alone, I cannot bear to think of her not being in my life!"

"Exactly, Ver, that is why you must stop worrying about something that is very unlikely to happen."

Time was passing, and the nearer Frederica came to the end of her pregnancy, the more tiresome Alver's efforts to protect his wife from any harm had become. He was treating her as though she was a fragile flower – the exact opposite to how she was feeling. She did not doubt his good intentions, but she knew that the fundamental problem was his increasing concern about the hazards of the birth process.

The day after he had seen Darcy, the Marquis was walking down the stairs to the entrance hall when he saw Jessamy Merriville standing there, apparently waiting for him. When the boy looked up, he said, "Cousin Alverstoke, may I speak to you privately, please?"

Jessamy sounded very serious, and so Alverstoke stopped immediately.

"Of course. Let's go into the library."

Jessamy closed the door behind them, and Alverstoke invited him to sit.

"No, thank you sir. I would prefer to stand."

The Marquis decided to remain upright himself and replied, "What is it, Jessamy?"

"You may not intend to, sir, but you are making my sister very unhappy by restricting what she is allowed to do."

"Jessamy, I am doing absolutely everything in my power to keep Frederica comfortable. What is wrong with that?"

"No, sir, you are terrified of losing her in childbirth, and so you are preventing her from leaving this house, making her bored and miserable!"

Alverstoke stared at the boy, and then sat down slowly in his chair, and put his head in his hands.

After a long pause, he lifted his head, and said, "Forgive me for being such an idiot, Jessamy! It has taken me so many years to find someone who I can love and trust. Now I have realised that Frederica might be taken away from me in childbirth. I have heard such dreadful stories at my club, where other members have become widowers by the death of their wives, due to the incompetence of doctors, or worse."

Jessamy almost shouted at his brother-in-law as he replied.

"Why are you putting your own worries ahead of my sister's peace of mind? She wants to have children with you. You are paying for the very best care for my sister's health – why should she be at any particular risk? Our mother gave birth to all her children safely in rural Herefordshire, without any help from a high-class expert in London."

Alverstoke admired the spirit of the young man in challenging him.

"Jessamy, you are a very good brother to be thinking about Frederica's comfort!"

"Now that my brother Harry is dead, I am the head of the Merriville family. Considering her needs is one of my responsibilities, as he would have done."

Alverstoke thought, but did not say, that it was very doubtful whether Harry Merriville would have spent too much time thinking about anyone apart from himself, if he had lived. Jessamy was already proving that he was a better person and had every ability that would be needed to help his siblings, and to manage the estate at Graynard, once he was old enough.

Jessamy hesitated, and then slowly walked forward, bent down, and put his arm around the shoulders of the Marquis.

"Shall I tell you what you should do, sir?"

Alverstoke raised his head and looked up into the boy's eyes.

Then he said slowly: "Yes, Jessamy, you need to advise me, if she is really as miserable as you say."

"Frederica told me that, on the morning after your wedding, how delighted she had been that you had taken the trouble to learn how to make hot chocolate to surprise her, because she had so enjoyed the drink at Gunter's when you took her there. Their shop is only just across the other side of Berkeley Square from here. Why can't you take Frederica out to have a cup of hot chocolate with you? And why don't you take her for a drive in Hyde Park in the barouche?

I know that you have been advised by Sir William to stay in town, so that she can be near the accoucheur when the time comes for the birth, but driving in the open air would be the next best thing to being able to enjoy the countryside at Alver Park."

"Jessamy, have you ever had hot chocolate yourself?"

"Frederica took me with Charis and Felix to Gunter's soon after we came to London, sir, but on that occasion we all chose to have their wonderful ices. No, I have never had a cup of hot chocolate there."

"Then perhaps we had better go now, and find my wife, and invite her to walk with us across the Square, so that we can introduce you to drinking hot chocolate?"

Jessamy, who often had the tendency to take life more seriously than was necessary, replied, "I was not seeking to have hot chocolate for myself, sir."

"Perhaps not, young man, but there is nothing wrong with anyone having an unexpected treat from time to time, is there?"

Jessamy gave Alverstoke one of his rare smiles, and then nodded his head in agreement.

As the Marquis crossed the hall towards the stairs, Wicken looked at him with surprise, for Lord Alverstoke seemed to be deep in thought and was moving much more slowly than usual. But then his speed increased as he went up the steps and, by the time he reached the door to the private sitting room, he was walking at his usual pace.

His wife was sitting at her desk, writing a letter. When she saw him, she put down her pen.

"What is it, my love? Were you looking for me?"

"Yes, Frederica. Is that a very important letter?"

"Not really, just my weekly message to my sister Charis."

"Then let me interrupt you. Jessamy would like to go to Gunter's this morning, to taste hot chocolate for the first time. Can you leave your letter for later, and come with us?"

His wife smiled and rose from her chair.

Some 30 minutes later, Frederica was crossing the Square towards Gunter's with her husband and Jessamy, wearing her pelisse and with a parasol in her hand. By 11 o'clock in the morning, the establishment would be getting busy with families buying the famous ices, as well as other treats.

Lord Alverstoke asked for a quiet table at the back of the shop, away from the hustle and bustle of the main area. Summoning a waitress, he placed their order for 3 cups of hot chocolate, plus some of the delectable pastries that young Felix Merriville would have been delighted to sample. But Felix was safely miles away at Eton, and their conversation was much more peaceful than it would have been if the boy had been with them.

After a few minutes sipping at her cup, Frederica said, "Oh, how delectable, Alver! I just love Gunter's hot chocolate! Don't tell Cook that I said so, but their chocolate drinks are really the best!"

Her brother, having finished his drink first, turned to Alverstoke and said, "Would it be very wrong of me, sir, to ask for a second cup?"

"Yes, Jessamy, it would really be very wrong! But, if you have a second cup, then Frederica and I can do the same!"

Frederica laughed at this exchange. She thought of suggesting that they could order some more pastries, as she was still quite hungry. But then she recalled that they would be having lunch soon, so perhaps that would not be such a good idea.

As they finished their second cup of chocolate, Jessamy asked them whether they had decided on any names for the new baby.

Frederica replied first. "We have not had that discussion yet, but perhaps we need to, quite soon. Do you have any preferences, Alver?"

"I suppose that it would be pleasant if we used some family names, like Harriet if the baby is a girl, in memory of your mother. My sister Louisa named her younger son after our grandfather George. Do you like that name, Frederica?"

"Yes, I would be very happy with that."

Later, once back in their house on the far side of Berkeley Square, Alverstoke turned quietly to Jessamy as he turned to walk up the stairs.

"I have not forgotten your other comments, about visiting Hyde Park. We could also drive to Richmond on another day if the sunny weather continues, and if Frederica likes that idea. You could take turns with Curry in driving the barouche, and perhaps we could take a picnic with us and make a day of it?"

Frederica, overhearing the end of the conversation, smiled at Alver and told him that she would love to go to Richmond Park, as soon as possible.

The next time that the Marquis met with Darcy Moreton, his friend had a question for him.

"Ver, I believe that Felix Merriville is in town, as the next term has not yet started at Eton?"

"Yes, that is true. Why do you ask?"

"Because I shall be taking Sophia's elder daughter Primrose, who is a very intelligent child, to see Master George Parker Bidder on Saturday. Perhaps you would like to bring Felix and join us?"

"Who is George Parker Bidder? I have never heard of him."

"The boy comes from Devon and seems to be some kind of mathematical genius. He is about the same age as Felix – 12 or 13 - and his father is taking him around the country exhibiting his skills. Master Bidder calculates numbers in his head in only a few seconds."

"What kind of numbers?"

"Well, the billboard said – 'Suppose that a city is illuminated with 9,999 lamps, each lamp to consume one pint of oil every four hours in succession; how many gallons will they consume in 40 years?' He answered, immediately, 109,489,050 gallons!"

"Good heavens, how extraordinary! I am sure that Felix would be very keen to go with you. But I would prefer not to join you, or Felix will decide that I have a new enthusiasm for matters scientific!"

Darcy laughed at his friend.

"Very well! I will purchase three tickets for tomorrow. Please make it clear to Felix that Sophia's daughter is to be treated with proper respect, or he will be in very serious trouble! Primrose has just as quick a mind as he has!"

Having returned from this outing on the following day, Felix was full of what he had heard and seen.

"You would not have believed it, Frederica! George Parker Bidder was asked how long it would take to build a rookery, with each rook's nest having 549 sticks, and each rook bringing 11 sticks a day. It took him only 90 seconds to answer – '24 days, 22 hours, 54 minutes and a fraction'!"

Lord Alverstoke was very impressed.

"You have a really excellent memory for the answers, Felix. How old did you say that the boy is now?"

"Master Bidder is nearly 13, Cousin Alverstoke, and he told us that he has been making these large computations in his head since he was 7 years of age. Mr Moreton said that his father must be making a great deal of money, since they are doing 3 or 4 events every week. George Bidder was presented to Queen Charlotte in 1815, to show her what he could accomplish."

"How sad for the boy!" said Frederica. "He must be missing his education and all the fun of his childhood, time that he will never get back!"

This idea had obviously not occurred to her brother, who looked rather thoughtful.

"And what did Miss Stanton say about the event, Felix?"

"She thought that George Bidder is really clever, and she was going home to practice doing similar sums in her head!"

His sister was very amused at this remark, since her young brother was usually very dismissive of girls being able to do anything useful.

"Are you planning to do large sums in your head, Felix?"

"No, I don't believe that I have that ability, Frederica. I am much more interested in how new mechanical inventions work."

Charles Trevor had taken Felix to Hatchards' bookshop before he had started school in Windsor, and the boy was now busy reading a book explaining how water pumps were designed and constructed. He was hoping to impress Lady Eliza's husband with his knowledge; Mr Kentmere was now living in the rented house in Mayfair with his family for the Season, after his daughter Caroline's come-out ball.

Having read the book that Mr Trevor had purchased on behalf of Lord Alverstoke, Felix had experimented with drawing several designs, before settling on the one that he liked best. Accompanied by his sister, Felix then went to see John Kentmere.

He waited anxiously with Lady Eliza as her husband took the drawing to his study to give the sketch a closer look, whilst Felix and Frederica had tea in the drawing room with their hostess.

"Felix, there is no need to consume all the biscuits on that plate! Eliza and I might like to have a second one!"

"Tell me, Felix, about that mathematical genius that you went to see with Darcy Moreton."

Felix had to finish eating the last biscuit before replying to his hostess.

"Mr Moreton told us that, when George Bidder was 9 years old, he was presented to Her Majesty the Queen. She asked Master Bidder to answer a question - 'From the Land's End, Cornwall, to Farrer's Head, in Scotland, is found by measurement to be 838 miles; how long would a snail be creeping that distance, at the rate of 8 feet per day?'

He took only 28 seconds to reply – 553,080 days."

"Good heavens! That is a truly impressive feat, Felix."

"Darcy Moreton told us that George Bidder has had almost no education, so he can hardly read or write," said Frederica. "Apparently, he started showing his skills at country fairs when he was only 7 years of age, and he went from being a local fairground attraction to being taken all over the country by his father to earn money for the family!"

Lady Eliza decided to use that comment to teach the boy a useful lesson.

"You do not realise how very fortunate you are, Felix, that you can go to school, and that your family will buy you whatever books you may need about any subject. But perhaps some wealthy man may sponsor Master Bidder to be properly educated, and then to go to university. How sad it would be if the boy's abilities are wasted! With such mathematical skills, he might become a talented engineer in the future?"

"I would like to be an engineer when I grow up," said Felix. "I do not want to own a country estate like my brother Harry. Oh! I should say Jessamy now. And, in any case, I do not much enjoy life in the country. I would prefer to live in a city, or a town. There are so many more interesting activities happening there!"

At this point in the conversation, John Kentmere returned to the drawing room, and Felix waited for his verdict on his design.

"I see that you have copied two different types of pump at the top of the page, Felix. I assume that they are from the book that was purchased in Piccadilly?"

"Yes, sir."

"The design of the pump that you suggest is lower down the page. That does seem to be an improvement on the other two designs. I shall need to return to my estate for several days soon, as I am due to sit as a magistrate in the local town. I could take you and my son Tom with me if you like. We could meet with a local metalworker and ask him to construct your pump design. Would you like to do that?"

For several seconds, Felix was speechless – a very rare occurrence! Then he turned to his sister.

"May I go, Frederica – please!"

There was a twinkle in her eyes that the Marquis would have enjoyed, as she hesitated, and then said, "I can see no reason why you should not, Felix."

For a second, he was suspended in time – then he crossed the drawing room and threw his arms around her in a rare embrace. Frederica turned to John Kentmere.

"Thank you for that very kind offer to my brother. I look forward to seeing the completed pump in due course."

"I must admit, Frederica, that I shall not be sorry to have a few days' respite from the Season. I am very much a countryman at heart!"

When she reported this conversation to the Marquis, he was highly amused.

"Felix must be beside himself at having the opportunity to have his invention fabricated. I wonder if the pump will actually work in practice? Anyway, we shall have a few peaceful days in Berkeley Square without him, and I must thank my brother-in-law for that!"

John Kentmere was as good as his word and, later in the week, his carriage arrived early in the morning to collect Felix. After two days' travelling, they reached the Kentmere estate in the Shires, and on the next day Felix and Tom accompanied Tom's father into the nearest town. Felix had redrawn his design to a larger size, and carefully explained to the metalworker what he wanted him to do.

"The hand pump has a lever used as a handle; then a piston rod connects the handle with a reciprocating piston. That piston is fitted with a non-return valve, and another non-return valve is fitted at the base of the cylinder. A pipe is connected to the cylinder which will be submerged in water, and an outlet is fitted through which water flows out of the pump.

When the handle is pushed downwards, the piston moves vertically upwards, and then the piston valve closes, and the foot valve opens. This forms a vacuum below the piston valve, and then water is drawn upwards to fill the vacuum. Next, the handle is pulled upwards, the piston valve opens, and the water is drawn above the piston. Simultaneously the foot valve closes and prevents water from returning to the pipe or to the well. In the next cycle, the piston displaces the water through the outlet as I have shown."

John Kentmere's head was buzzing with all these unfamiliar terms, but fortunately the metalworker seemed to understand what Felix wanted him to make. They left the man with enough money to purchase the materials needed and agreed to return after three days had passed.

Back at the Kentmeres' home, his host took Felix aside, and explained something that he wanted him to practice.

"I noticed when you were here previously that my daughter Mary, although she is rather younger than you, is a much better rider. You need to remedy that. I am not asking you to reach your brother Jessamy's competence, but riding a horse safely is a very necessary skill. You are to go out with Tom twice each day whilst you are here, in the morning and in the evening, and he will advise you on what you should be doing. Before we return to London, I want you to show me how much you have improved."

Felix assumed a rather rebellious expression, for he had never been interested in horses or in riding them. But he realised that John Kentmere would not be likely to relent, and in any case was doing everything he could to create the new invention for Felix.

"Very well, sir. Shall we go to the stables now, Tom?"

After three days, Felix was beginning to enjoy his daily outings with his friend, and Tom told his father that he had noticed a considerable improvement.

When they returned to see the metalworker, there on his wooden bench were all the parts for the pump, just as Felix had shown them in his drawing. The man screwed the parts together, and then they filled a large barrel with water to test the pump. The cylinder was lowered into the water, and the man began to use the handle – and the pump worked!

Felix was so delighted that he could not speak, and it was John Kentmere who thanked the man, and paid him for his time and trouble.

They took the pump home with them, and John Kentmere locked it away for safety until they left for London.

"Now, boys, I must sit as a magistrate in the court tomorrow for several hours, so you must amuse yourselves on the estate all day, without causing any trouble to anyone, until I return here in the late afternoon. We shall be leaving early on the next day for London, so you may ask Cook to prepare some food for us to eat on the journey."

When they all reached Berkeley Square, Tom and Felix left soon after their arrival to walk to the rented house to see Lady Eliza. This gave John Kentmere the opportunity to sit down with Frederica and Alver to update them on the visit.

"The pump actually worked first time, John? I had feared it would not, and that my brother would be disappointed."

"Yes, it did work first time, Frederica. When Felix described in words what all the parts would do, I did not understand what at least half of the terms that he used meant. But, fortunately the metalworker, who has made items for me previously, did know what Felix was talking about. I have the pump here – I did not allow Felix to use it by himself. I can have another made if I need to.

I insisted that the boys went out riding together twice a day, as it is high time that Felix became more competent. He wanted to refuse to do that, but I gave him what my children would call 'the look', and he decided not to argue!"

The Marquis thanked his brother-in-law for all the trouble that he had taken, and tried to pay him for the pump, without success.

A few days' later, Frederica met Lady Eliza at Gunter's for coffee and some cakes, and she asked her how she had met John Kentmere.

"I was introduced to the Ton at my come-out ball at Alverstoke House, and then the usual round of balls and other events began. My elder sisters had, of course, described to me what that would involve.

My mother intended that I should marry a member of the aristocracy, as both Augusta and Louisa had done, but I soon discovered that most of the young men that I met were – how shall I put it – too entitled and boring to interest me.

You may be surprised when I tell you that I have Lucretia Dauntry to thank for what happened. Her husband Henry was abroad, serving as an officer in the Army, when she was invited to visit relatives for a week or so who lived in the area near Melton Mowbray, where Endymion now hunts with The Quorn. Lucretia asked me if I would go with her to help with the children. My father encouraged me to accept the invitation; he knew how bored I was with the young men who I had met in town.

During our visit, her relatives invited several local friends who live in the Shires to dinner, and John was amongst them. He was such a refreshing change from anyone else who I had met, and we got on together famously from the start. I persuaded Lucretia to extend our stay into a second week, and the rest is history!

When I returned to London, I told my father that John Kentmere had asked me to marry him. We both knew that we would have a real fight on our hands against my mother's opposition to the match. However, she lost, as my father was adamant that I should be able to marry the man that I loved. I don't think that my mother ever forgave me for not marrying a peer.

It was only a few months after our wedding that my father wrote to tell me that my mother was gravely ill in London, and she died a few weeks' later. Vernon was 17 and still at school when she was buried, not at Alver Park, but in the churchyard in her family's home village, as she had requested."

When Frederica next visited Sir William Knighton, he surprised her with an unexpected question.

"Is there any history of twins in your family, ma'am? Sometimes such a tendency can be inherited."

She looked at him thoughtfully. She had met Marietta Ormond recently for coffee and cakes at Gunter's café in Berkeley Square, and her friend had commented that, for someone with another few months still to elapse before the anticipated birth, the baby seemed to be quite large.

"I am interested that you have asked that question. My maiden aunt Seraphina Winsham, who was my chaperone when we were living in Upper Wimpole Street, has a twin brother Richard who is a doctor. He practises in Ross-on-Wye, in Herefordshire."

"Well, you are either expecting a very good-sized baby or, rather more likely, you are carrying twins. What would your husband's reaction be to that news?"

"He is already quite stressed and anxious, Sir William, although he tries hard to conceal that from me. I would certainly not want to give him any more reason to worry."

"Well, he will be coming with you for your next visit, so I suggest that we do not mention anything about that possibility. He will find out soon enough when the time comes! I should warn you, however, that twins are often born early, before the due date – sometimes up to a month in advance. You should be prepared for that eventuality, and I will make sure that the monthly nurse is booked in good time. You have already told me that you are planning to use a wet nurse after the birth (or births), so I will arrange for two women instead of one to be available, in case we should need them."

As Frederica walked back with Emily to Berkeley Square, her mind was fully occupied with the possibility of having two babies, not one. Alver had been joking yesterday that, if they had a daughter, he would be very worried about her encountering a rake, as he knew what the hazards might be when she approached marriageable age. What would his reaction be if she produced two daughters?

When Felix returned home from school at the end of the Spring Term, he took a scientific interest in her increasing size, but remarked that he was very glad that he was a boy, since becoming a mother seemed to be accompanied by various problems that he would not want to have to deal with!

"What a typical comment for Felix to make!" said Jessamy when his younger brother had left the room.

Frederica laughed and said, "I shall make very sure to keep him well away from the baby, once it arrives. I don't want him performing any experiments of any kind!"

Alver, hearing the end of this conversation as he came into the drawing room, made it clear that Felix would have a very short life if he even thought of extending his scientific activities to the new child.

As the date for her next visit to Sir William Knighton came closer, Frederica became more certain that she was expecting two babies. Fortunately, Alver assumed that her increasing size was the normal progression for a lady who was expecting a baby. Sir William, well used to dealing with members of the aristocracy, dealt firmly but politely with all the questions that the Marquis asked him when they met, and the possibility of twins was never mentioned.

Before Felix returned to Eton for the next term, the family left London to spend a week at Alver Park. All the paths through the park had been completed, so they made good use of the new barouche. The sofa had arrived that they had ordered for the summerhouse, to replace the old one that had been a favourite with Alver's grandparents. The route to the summerhouse from the mansion had been widened to accommodate the new barouche.

On the most recent visit to Sir William Knighton, he had encouraged the Marquis to take Frederica out on regular outings in London. "The last few months can seem very long and tedious to new mothers," he said,

So, after they had returned to town, Alver took his wife for their visit to Hampton Court. They did not use the maze, but strolled through the knot garden and other parts of the spacious grounds before going to the Mitre Hotel nearby for an enjoyable lunch in the hotel's garden by the River Thames. "You can pretend, Frederica, that you are a guest of King Charles II, as he had this property built for exactly that very purpose!"

The Marquis also took his wife and Jessamy to Richmond Park for the day. As the weather was rather chilly, they did not take a picnic with them, but instead visited the hotel on Richmond Hill, the Star and Garter, where they had an enjoyable lunch in the dining room with a fine view from their table overlooking the River Thames.

Another outing they took was to Greenwich, where there was a great deal of interest to see. Alver had carefully researched the history of the site before their journey, and he told Frederica that Queen Elizabeth 1 had been born at Greenwich Palace, although that structure had been demolished after it fell into disuse.

Unlike Jessamy, who had travelled to Greenwich by boat on the Thames with Septimus Trevor, Alver and Frederica went by road. They saw the Royal Hospital School for children destined to join the navy, and the Royal Hospital for retired Sailors including the magnificent Painted Hall designed by Sir Christopher Wren, with a ceiling that had taken the artist James Thornhill 19 years to complete.

Originally intended as a grand dining room for the naval pensioners, Alver told her that the Painted Hall soon became a ceremonial space open to paying visitors and reserved for special functions. Perhaps the most significant event had been the lying-in-state of Lord Nelson in January 1806, which had attracted large crowds for 3 days to view the hero's body.

Frederica particularly enjoyed seeing The Queen's House, designed by the architect Inigo Jones, and built for Queen Anne of Denmark. "There is something about such a symmetrical building that appeals to me," she told the Marquis, "And I liked many of the paintings inside the property".

Frederica had avoided visiting her sister-in-law Louisa Buxted since her marriage, but she had invited Augusta Jevington to Berkeley Square after she had asked for some advice about her daughter Anna's approaching nuptials, which were to be held at St George's in Hanover Square.

"Marietta Ormond has recommended a book to me, Augusta. The author is Hannah Glasse, with an 'e' on the end of her surname, and the title is 'Art of Cookery'. Your daughter might find it useful once she has married Mr Redmure? The book includes some quite unusual recipes. For instance, there are several from France and Italy, and there are others from Turkey, India and the Middle Eastern countries. Not everyone wants to eat roast beef, and there are also recipes for jugged hare, pigs' brains and calf's head!"

Lord Jevington had accompanied his wife, and the Marquis took Humphrey to see some books that he had acquired recently for his library. "I hear that young Felix Merriville has ambitions to become an inventor, Vernon?"

"Yes, that's true, and he seems to have some abilities in that direction. John Kentmere indulged him and had the parts made for a water pump that he had designed. I must admit that I was very surprised when the design worked! Let me show you the book that Felix had consulted before completing his design."

Frederica continued to meet Lady Eliza once a week at Gunter's café. "How is Caroline finding the balls and other events during the Season? Is she enjoying herself?"

"Yes - although, like her father, she much prefers to be in the country. John and I do not want her to be married too young, as some girls are, so there is no hurry for that."

"Perhaps she would like to go riding in Hyde Park with Jessamy? I'm sure that Alver would agree to her using one of his horses. My sister and Endymion will be in town next week to visit Lucretia Dauntry, so I will hope to bring Charis with me to Gunter's the next time we meet."

Frederica had continued to attend the fortnightly meetings at Henry Cooke's house about the art classes for the girls at the Foundling Hospital. Together with Sophia, Darcy and Henry, they were pleased with the progress made with the tuition being provided by Mr Francis, and some new materials were being purchased for the girls. An exhibition of their work was now being considered for a couple of months' time.

Charis and her husband arrived in town during the next week to stay in Green Street with Lucretia Dauntry. Leaving Endymion with his mother, Charis came to see Frederica.

"How much longer have you to wait before the baby is due, Frederica?"

"Sir William told me, the last time that I went to his consulting rooms, that I probably have about 6 weeks to go before the due date."

"I had not realised how large the 'bump' can become when one is increasing!"

"Well, it isn't for ever, Charis, though I must admit that it is beginning to be quite tiresome to have to walk any distance."

"Is that the Sir William Knighton who came to Upper Wimpole Street when Felix was ill?"

"Yes, he is based in Stratford Place, near Bond Street, and he was recommended to me by Marietta Ormond. He attended her when both of the Ormond children were born. To change the subject, are you still hoping to build a house on the land that we gave you as a wedding present, Charis?"

"Yes, we have decided that we do not want to renovate the existing property. In truth, we do not have enough money to do so. Once we know what our house is worth in its current state, we can decide whether we can afford to proceed with our plans. The good news is that Endymion is very happy with his new steward, Mr Preece."

"That must be very helpful, Charis."

"How is Cousin Alverstoke, Frederica?"

"Alver is fine, although he is a rather anxious prospective father. I am trying to keep him busy thinking of other things, with limited success! Do you have any other news to tell me?"

Her sister looked rather embarrassed, and then spoke in her soft voice.

"I haven't told Endymion yet, but I suspect that I may be increasing. I will wait for another few weeks, and then consult Sir William. I want to delay telling anything to Lucretia for as long as possible, since she will make a fuss, and will drive me mad once she hears the news about the baby. Please do not pass on anything that I have told you, Frederica."

"Oh! Charis, that is wonderful news! I do hope that everything goes well for you in the next few weeks. I promise not to tell anything to anyone."

Chapter 14

Alver continued with his habit of occasionally going to his club on a Friday, and he usually had lunch with Darcy Moreton. About a month before Frederica's due date, his friend had praised Frederica's care for her family.

"Yes, Darcy, she was about the same age as her younger brother Felix is now when Harriet Merriville died. She took on the burden of replacing her mother and looking after the four siblings, the youngest only a few months old, and the eldest aged 9. I know that her aunt, Seraphina Winsham, moved into the house to provide some domestic support, but I rather doubt whether she was a very positive influence otherwise."

"Frederica has done remarkably well, Ver, in looking after them all, as their lawyer Mr Salcombe told me when we met during the few days before your wedding. Because Fred Merriville could not bear to be at Graynard after his wife's death, he fled to London, and did his best to squander his inheritance by gambling and other unfortunate activities. By the time Frederica reached her fifteenth birthday, she was managing the estate at Graynard with some help from Salcombe.

How is Jessamy– his brother Harry's sudden death must have come as a great shock?"

"Yes, indeed it did, but I have been impressed with his commonsense; and he has always been very supportive of Frederica. I asked him the other day where he thought young Felix gets his personality and interests from. He replied that both Harry and Felix took after their father – tending to put themselves first, and other people second. However, Felix may inherit his interest in scientific matters from their uncle Richard Winsham who, as you know, is a doctor practising in Ross-on-Wye."

"How is his school coping with Felix – they can't have too many pupils at Eton with his very persistent enthusiasm and inquiring mind?"

"No, indeed. It is certainly much more peaceful in Berkeley Square when he is away in Windsor! I must remember to make some inquiries in due course – he might be just the person to go into a manufacturing enterprise after he leaves university. Hopefully, he would make good contacts at Oxford for whatever he wants to do after that!"

"I have a feeling that your mother Esther would not have approved of that idea! I don't recall her having much of a sense of humour?"

The Marquis smiled quietly to himself. "Perhaps not, but my father would have taken a more pragmatic view."

"May I ask you to do me a favour, Ver?"

"Of course, what favour is that?"

"I should like to see the portrait that Frederica gave you for Christmas. She told me that you are delighted with the picture. I might be interested in asking Mr Francis to paint us together with Sophia's children, after we have been married in June. Did you know that Mr Francis is a distant cousin of Lord Petersham?"

"No, I was not aware of that. Why don't you come back to Berkeley Square with me today, and you can decide whether you like the picture and the artist's style of painting."

Darcy's reaction to the picture was the same as Jessamy's had been – that the portrait was a remarkable likeness of the sitter, and that Mr Francis had captured Frederica's personality as well as her physical appearance.

Frederica went on her own to visit her aunts, the widowed Amelia Scrabster and Miss Seraphina Winsham, at Amelia's home in Harley Street. They seemed to be settling in well together after the death last year of Amelia's husband. Frederica discussed all the family news, including the death of Harry, how Felix was faring at Eton, and

Jessamy's success in the entry exams for Oxford University. Her aunts had decided not to attend her wedding in Wiltshire, but they were interested in her description of Lord Alverstoke's estate at Alver Park.

"Your mother would have been very proud of you, Frederica," said Aunt Amelia. "You have done very well looking after your sister and brothers, and we enjoyed attending the wedding in London between Charis and Endymion Dauntry. We shall look forward to meeting your new baby in due course."

The Marquis had continued to attend the boxing academy of Gentleman Jackson at 13 Bond Street, which was only a few minutes' walk from the Square. He had done so on the afternoon of the day that Frederica was visiting her aunts in Harley Street. He had just started a bout with the proprietor himself when he lost his footing, and fell, bruising himself on one of the posts at the corner of the ring. Jackson, who found himself boxing into mid-air, also fell, so that they were both sprawled on the floor. After a few moments to recover his breath, Lord Alverstoke burst out laughing, quickly followed by John Jackson.

Frederica had returned from Harley Street about an hour before her husband came home, and she was crossing the entrance hall towards the back garden when Wicken answered a knock on the front door. She was very surprised to see his master enter the house, dressed only in his shirt sleeves, with Curry walking behind him carrying his lordship's jacket.

"Goodness! What has happened to you, Alver?"

"A mishap at Jackson's, Frederica. I fell and bruised my forearm. My tailor, Weston, makes his clothes such a close fit that I did not attempt to put on my jacket. I decided not to go on to the bookshop in Piccadilly, as I was not suitably dressed, so you will have to wait a few more days for me to purchase that book that you wanted to read."

Alver turned to speak to his butler.

"Wicken, has Knapp returned from his errand to Covent Garden?"

"No, milord, not yet," replied the butler.

Frederica intervened.

"No matter, Alver. I have had plenty of experience treating bruises on my brothers. I can look after you, with Emily to help me."

She turned to the footman, who was standing at the side of the hall.

"James, please take Lord Alverstoke's jacket upstairs to his dressing room and tell Miss Leonard that I need her to come down quickly to the garden to assist me.

Wicken, could you please ask Cook to put a second cup on the tea tray for the Marquis that is being brought to me in the garden. I will also need several cloths, and a basin with some ice, for treating Lord Alverstoke."

Alver soon found himself sitting on a bench in the garden, with Frederica and Emily busy creating a bandage for the damaged arm.

"We will alternate a cold poultice with a hot poultice, Alver, and it is a good idea to hold your arm above your heart for as long as you can, to drain away the fluid from the bruise. If I was at Graynard, I would have used some dried comfrey leaves boiled in water for 10 minutes to make a compress."

"A good country recipe, my dear?"

"Yes, indeed. I have heard that pineapple is also helpful for bruises, but that would have been too expensive for me to afford."

"There are some pineapples in the conservatory at Alver Park, Frederica, should Jessamy or Felix ever decide to have a mishap there!"

Once the poultice was in position, and the tea consumed, Alver asked his wife how her visit to her aunts had gone.

"They are both very excited about the new baby and expect it to arrive exactly on the due date! I warned them that Sir William has said that no one is able to predict when the actual event will occur.

Your sister Eliza told me, only the other day, that none of her four children arrived on their due date!"

A week after this conversation on a Friday morning, Jessamy had decided to walk to Hatchards in Piccadilly, so that he could buy two or three books that would be useful for his university course in September. Then he was to walk to the spacious house in Mayfair that Lady Eliza Kentmere had hired for the season for the 'come-out' of her elder daughter Caroline. After he had dined there, the family's coach would be returning him to Berkeley Square.

The legal formalities for purchasing more land for Endymion Dauntry to add to his estate had finally been completed, so Alver had arranged to visit his lawyer, Mr Muirhead, today to authorise the payment from his account at Child's Bank, and for his cousin Endymion to add his signature to the contract for the property.

Before leaving Berkeley Square, Alver had spent an hour with Charles Trevor, as his secretary had a pile of papers which needed his attention.

After that, he was about to cross the hall to go upstairs when Wicken spoke to him.

"Miss Leonard came downstairs about 30 minutes' ago, sir, to tell me that her mistress is fast asleep in her bedroom, and it would probably be best if you do not disturb her before you leave for your appointment with Mr Muirhead."

Alver had been about to do just that.

"Oh! Very well, Wicken. After my appointment in the City, I shall be lunching at White's with Mr Moreton and Lord Petersham, so don't expect me back here until just before four o'clock. My wife knows about both those appointments."

"Very well, milord."

Curry was already waiting outside with the carriage, so Alver put on his coat, took his hat and walking stick, and left the house.

Upstairs, Frederica was at her desk in the private sitting room, writing a note, whilst Emily was looking discreetly out of the window at Curry waiting on the street below.

"The Marquis has just left the house, milady, and he is getting into the carriage now. Yes, the carriage is now moving away towards the Square."

"I feel very guilty about asking you to deceive Lord Alverstoke, Emily."

Her abigail turned from the window, and said, "You made the correct choice, milady, if I may say so. If the Marquis had known that your contractions had begun, he would never have left the house. As it is, you will have several hours without him causing you any anxiety, and you can look forward to his support as soon as he returns to the house."

Frederica finished writing her note, then she folded and sealed the paper, and addressed her letter to Sir William Knighton.

"Please go down to the hall now, Emily, and ask Wicken to arrange for one of the footmen to take this letter to Stratford Place. Walter would be best, and he should not return here until he has been given a reply from Sir William."

After her abigail had left the room, Frederica went along the corridor to her bedroom and sat down. She leaned back in the comfortable armchair and waited for the next contraction to begin. The intervals between them were slowly decreasing. She was doing quite well with the shallow but frequent breaths that Sir William had suggested that she should use during each contraction.

After about an hour, Frederica asked Emily to go downstairs to ask Cook for two plates of ham with some buttered bread, together with a jug of lemonade and two glasses, to be delivered to the private sitting room.

Having passed on this message, Emily was just about to go upstairs again when Walter appeared from the service corridor.

"Miss Leonard, here is the reply from Sir William for Lady Alverstoke," he said, giving her the note in his hand.

She thanked him and went up to the room where her mistress was sitting.

"Oh, thank you, Emily! Let's see what the note says. Ah, Sir William is currently with another patient, but he should be able to arrive here at about two o'clock."

"The food tray should be brought up to you very soon, milady. I will come and tell you when it has arrived."

Time seemed to be passing very slowly, but Frederica tried to be patient. She sat with Emily in the private sitting room for the next couple of hours, with the contractions happening every few minutes. At last, just after two o'clock, she heard a carriage enter the drive and stop outside the front door.

"Do you think that is Sir William, Emily?"

Emily went to the window and looked out. "Yes, milady, I think so. He has a doctor's bag in his hand."

The abigail went out of the room and stood at the top of the stairs to greet the visitor. Then Sir William entered the sitting room and greeted Frederica.

"How are you, Lady Alverstoke? How often are the contractions coming at the moment?"

"Rather less than every 15 minutes now, Sir William. I am very happy to see you - thank you for coming."

"Are we going to stay in this room, or do you wish to move to your bedroom?"

"I suggest that we stay here for now. Would you like me to send for a tea tray for you?"

"That would be very welcome, Lady Alverstoke. Thank you."

"Emily, perhaps you should go to my dressing room and take my nightgown and my dressing gown to the bedroom, for when I need them."

Emily left the room to follow Frederica's instructions.

"I assume, milady, that your husband is not in the house at present?"

"No, sir, he went to an appointment in the City, and then on to have lunch with friends at his club. I am expecting him back in Berkeley Square just before four o'clock. I did not tell him before he left that my contractions had started."

"Very wise of you, if I may say so. Do you know if he intends to support you during the birth?"

"Yes, I believe so. He would leave the room if I asked him to, but I doubt if he would be very happy about that. He says that he helped create the child, and that therefore he should take his part in helping me during the birth."

"Well, let me take a look to see how you are progressing before your maid comes back."

Sir William put his hand on her stomach just as the next contraction came. When it was over, he smiled at her and said, "You are doing very well, and that was a good strong contraction. I would guess that it will be an hour or so before we need to move to your bedroom, so let's have some conversation in the meantime.

I have asked Mrs Murphy, the monthly nurse, to get here as soon as she can, so it is possible that she may arrive before your husband returns. She is a very experienced woman, and you will be safe in her hands. I intend to remain here with you unless I get an urgent message from any of my other patients."

Frederica felt reassured by this conversation.

"Do you still think that it may be twins, Sir William?"

"Well, all I can say is that it is a very large child if there is only one. I am almost certain that you are expecting to give birth to two babies. I assume that you have still not told Lord Alverstoke that news?"

"No, as I told you before, that would have caused my husband quite unnecessary worry, and he would have driven me mad with fussing about my health. Once he arrives home, I suggest that you are very clear about what you want him to do, and what not to!"

"Well, once we move to your bedroom, I will take off my jacket and roll up my sleeves. When your husband arrives, I will suggest that he does the same. That way, the dust from the street will be left in his dressing room, and he can sit next to you in a chair and help you as we get closer to the time of the births.

Now, perhaps you would like to tell me about your country home at Alver Park. I believe that the property is situated in Wiltshire. When were you last there?"

"Just after Easter, when my younger brother Felix was on holiday from Eton. We took him and his older brother Jessamy down to Alver Park for about a week. My husband has had the paths through the park widened and extended, as he had given me a handsome new barouche as a Christmas present, partly to save me having to walk too far during my pregnancy. There are deer grazing in one part of the park, and an extensive area of woodland on the slope up to a viewpoint on the hill.

My husband has given Felix the use of a building for a workshop at Alver Park, to carry out his experiments. He is very interested in scientific matters and, so far, has managed not to blow either himself or anybody else up! Do you have children, Sir William?"

"Yes, I have three children, two daughters and a son, Dorothea, William, and Mary. So far none of them has asked for a workshop. However, I shall bear the possibility in mind, having heard what you have said!"

"I assume that your family do not live in Stratford Place. Where is your home?"

"We leased a house in Hanover Square when we first came to London in 1807. Then, after we had spent some time in Spain where I was the personal physician to the English ambassador, after our return from Madrid our children were getting older and needed a larger garden, so I purchased Sherwood Lodge, a villa on the banks of the Thames with six acres of pleasure grounds. My dear wife enjoys the views there over the water; she is a very talented artist. We are happy living in Battersea, although we have been considering moving to a country property near Blendworth. My sister-in-law Jane Hawker is married to Sir Michael Seymour, and they live in that part of Hampshire.

Have you and the Marquis discussed any names for the new arrival, milady, or should I say arrivals?"

"Lord Alverstoke and I have decided on Harriet Caroline as the name if the baby is a girl, and George Edward if the child is a boy. Although I would have loved to discuss a second name for a boy and for a girl if I have twins, I could not do that without alerting my husband to the possibility that he might become a father twice over!"

Shortly afterwards, there came a knock at the door and Frederica invited the caller to enter the room. James, the younger footman, appeared.

"What is it, James?" said Frederica.

"There is a person below in the entrance hall, milady, asking to speak to Sir William. Her name is Mrs Murphy."

"Ah, that is the monthly nurse who I had mentioned to you. I will go down to the hall. James, please come with me, and you can show me Lady Alverstoke's bedroom. We may need you to bring a small table to the room, and perhaps some other items as well. Please excuse me for a few minutes, milady. I shall return to you very soon."

Frederica sat back on the sofa and tried to relax. It was quite welcome to be quiet and on her own for a short while, but she had become aware during her conversation with Sir William that the contractions were happening more frequently than before, and that they were becoming stronger.

When he returned, Sir William smiled at her, and said, "Perhaps it is about time that we moved to your bedroom? Your footman has been very helpful, and I should like you to come and meet Mrs Murphy."

Frederica smiled at him gratefully and was happy to agree to this suggestion.

About 20 minutes later, she was sitting in the comfortable armchair in her bedroom when she heard a carriage draw up outside. Perhaps that would be Alver, back from White's?

Having walked into the entrance hall, the Marquis handed over his coat, hat and walking stick to Wicken, and asked where his wife was.

"Lady Alverstoke is upstairs, milord."

Alver was about to walk to the staircase when his butler spoke.

"If I may make a suggestion, sir, you should not enter any rooms upstairs without knocking on the door first, and then standing back."

Surprised, he turned and looked at Wicken. "Is there someone upstairs with my wife?"

"Yes, Sir William Knighton is with her."

Alver, shocked at the news, paused.

"When did he arrive in Berkeley Square?"

Wicken turned his head and looked at the clock on the mantelpiece. "Nearly two hours ago now, sir."

Alver looked thoughtful, hesitated, and then turned and went slowly up the stairs to the first floor, and along the corridor to Frederica's bedroom. There he followed his butler's advice, knocked on the door, and then stood back.

After a short delay, the door opened and Sir William, in his shirt sleeves, came out and closed the door behind him.

"Good afternoon, Lord Alverstoke."

"Sir William - how is my wife? My butler has told me that you have been here for some time. I have not been expecting the baby to be arriving so soon."

"Babies arrive when they want to, sir, not when we choose. Lady Alverstoke is well, but I would not expect her to give birth for some hours yet. Shall we go to your dressing room first for a short discussion, and so that you can take off your jacket and waistcoat? I suggest that you roll up your shirt sleeves before you enter her bedroom."

Alver did as Sir William asked. When he rolled up the sleeves on his shirt, the doctor could see the colourful bruise on Lord Alverstoke's left arm, and he remarked, "That looks quite painful, milord."

"Not so much now, Knighton. My wife did an excellent job of making a poultice – she has had many years of practice with the bruises acquired by her younger brothers!"

The Marquis told Sir William the story of how he had acquired the bruise.

"You might be surprised, milord, if I told you how often I am asked to treat John Jackson's clients. However, I am in favour of physical exercise, in moderation!"

Then Sir William turned to a more immediate topic.

"It is always impossible to predict exactly how long a lady's labour will take before the birth, milord. Lady Alverstoke has been having contractions since about ten o'clock this morning, so some six hours ago. They are now more frequent, and she will no doubt be very pleased to have you here to support her. Forgive me if I remind you that it is very important that her wishes should be your only consideration. If she becomes stressed for any reason, that can prolong her labour and make it much more painful."

"I understand, Sir William. Thank you for your advice."

The doctor led the way as they walked together along the corridor to see Frederica. He knocked on the bedroom door and, when she invited them to come in, the doctor allowed the Marquis to enter first.

Her face immediately lit up with pleasure when Frederica saw him. She was sitting in the armchair, wearing a cotton nightdress.

Sir William introduced the nurse, Mrs Murphy, who was a middle-aged woman with a soft Irish accent.

"Just a few matters that I should mention to you, milord. That bowl on the side table will be for cold water. Each cloth in the pile next to the bowl will only be used once, and then disposed of in the bin on the floor. The damp cloths can have a welcome cooling effect if used to wipe Lady Alverstoke's face, or if they are wrung out and laid on her forehead. You may like to sit in the other chair next to her and, as I have already explained to you, you should carry out all her requests unless I have a very good reason to intervene."

Alver walked swiftly across the room, and gently kissed her hand. "How are you, my darling? May I put my arm around you?"

"That is just what I need, Alver! Sir William tells me that I am doing well enough, so I hope that he is telling me the truth! How was your lunch with Darcy and Charles Petersham?"

"They are both very well, and they asked me to pass on their good wishes to you. Darcy is busy with plans for his wedding to Sophia, and Petersham was wearing yet another new jacket – he really is quite the dandy!"

"Where is Jessamy, Frederica, do you know?"

"I sent him to spend the day with your sister and her family. He took a private note with him that I had written to Eliza, to explain what is happening here. I asked her to keep Jessamy there overnight, if she did not receive any more information from you."

"That was an excellent idea, love. He would only be worrying himself if he were to be here in Berkeley Square."

Whilst they were talking together, Mrs Murphy had been speaking quietly with Sir William on the far side of the room. She then came to join them and suggested that Frederica might like to move from her chair to the bed. The Marquis kept out of the way as Sir William and the nurse made his wife comfortable, adjusting several pillows behind her back. A chair was placed very close to the side of the bed for him to use.

Miss Leonard knocked and came into the room, to ask if anyone would like something to eat or drink.

"I would love some of my favourite biscuits, Emily, and a glass with a jug of lemonade," said Frederica. "But please remind Cook that I do not want her to add any orgeat to the mix – that would be far too sweet for my taste!"

Her husband opted for a glass of white wine, and Sir William suggested that two jugs of iced water and some glasses would also be a good idea, and Emily hastened away to the kitchen.

Ever since he had entered the room, the Marquis had been watching his wife carefully, and he had not missed how she was coping with the regular contractions by taking frequent shallow breaths. He knew that Frederica was aware of what he was doing and, once she was sitting on the bed, she took his hand in hers and squeezed it during the more difficult moments. He bent his head to whisper words of encouragement in her ear, and she smiled at him in return.

Then she said to him, very quietly, "The worst part is the tedious repetition, and the contractions are beginning to get rather stronger now."

From the far side of the bedroom, Sir William smiled at them as the refreshments arrived. Frederica was encouraged to eat a couple of biscuits, and to take a half glass of the cold lemonade.

After a while, the nurse suggested that the Marquis should sit behind his wife, supporting her back, as the contractions began to be more troublesome. Although he could not see Frederica's face clearly most of the time, he suspected that she might have tears in her eyes as each contraction came to a crescendo. However, she never cried out, and the only way that he could tell how much discomfort she was bearing was her very tight grip on his hand. Whenever she said that she felt too hot, he dipped a clean cloth in the basin of cold water and wiped his wife's brow.

A little later, the doctor asked Lord Alverstoke to stand aside, so that he could examine his patient.

Then, at last, Frederica called out to Sir William that she wanted to push, and Alver was asked to move away so that his wife could lie flat on the bed, with the doctor and nurse helping her. It seemed a very long time, but was perhaps no more than 40 minutes, as Frederica bore down as she had been instructed, and then suddenly the child was born, screaming loudly as she took her first breath.

The Marquis was somewhat concerned that the baby had such a red face, but Sir William told him that that was quite normal, and Frederica's delighted expression reassured Alver that she was well.

She laughed at him as she remarked, "What was it that I said to you - about wanting to have a feisty daughter?"

"She certainly seems to have a good pair of lungs, my darling! Thank you for our beautiful Harriet Caroline!"

The nurse had been busy clamping the cord, and then cleaning the baby with a wet cloth before swaddling her in a pink shawl and handing her to Frederica.

"Now, milord, we will need to attend to your wife for a few minutes, so we will put the baby in the bassinet. You may wish to take the opportunity to have a good wash, and to put on a clean shirt. Why don't you go to your dressing room now, and I will come and fetch you when we are ready for you to return?"

Lord Alverstoke did as he was told by Sir William, dropping a kiss on Frederica's head before he left the room.

As soon as he had shut the door behind him, the doctor moved to Frederica's side, to examine her carefully.

"Yes, there is a second baby there, Lady Alverstoke and, if I am not mistaken, it is going to arrive quite soon. Do you want to push again now, milady?"

When she nodded her assent, her attendants helped her deliver the second child a few minutes later and, to her delight, the baby was a boy.

"He seems to be quite a placid little fellow compared to his sister Harriet, Lady Alverstoke. I seem to recall that his name is to be George?"

"Yes, Sir William. He is to be named George Edward Dauntry."

The nurse had concealed a second bassinet under the bed and, after giving the baby to his mother to hold for a short while, he was placed in a bassinet next to his sister, with the two bassinets set side by side.

In his dressing room, the Marquis had washed his face and hands in the basin and put on a clean shirt. He sat down in the armchair and allowed himself to relax. He must have drifted off to sleep, for the next thing that he remembered was Sir William squeezing his shoulder to rouse him.

"We are ready for you now, milord, if you like to come with me."

"I must have been resting for a while. What is the time, Sir William?"

"About 30 minutes before midnight, milord, according to the clock behind you."

Chapter 15

When the Marquis was admitted to Frederica's bedroom, she was sitting up in bed, holding a baby wrapped in a blue shawl in her arms. Then he saw that there were two bassinets in the room, with one of them not in use, and a baby wrapped in a pink shawl lying asleep in the other.

"What ... what is this? Two babies! Frederica, did you know about this in advance?"

His wife, laughing at his consternation, replied, "Sir William suspected that there was more than one child - and he was right. The calm baby in my arms is your new son. Would you like to hold George?"

The Marquis was speechless at this news, and then, when he recovered his voice, delighted!

"What a very clever lady you are, Frederica – how wonderful! Yes, let me take the little boy from you for a short while. He seems to be rather quieter than his sister?"

Sir William was watching them from beside the door and he said, "May I congratulate you both on these very successful deliveries? I wish that all my clients were equally sensible."

"As you know, milady, I have two wet nurses on call, and they will arrive here in the morning. Meanwhile, Mrs Murphy will assist you with feeding the babies during the night. With two of them, you may not get much sleep!"

"I will return here tomorrow before midday, to make sure that all is well. If you will excuse me now, I must go and get some rest myself, after discovering whether any urgent messages await me."

The Marquis walked with the doctor down the main staircase to the entrance hall. Wicken, who had been dozing in his chair, looked expectantly at his master as he went to open the front door, but nothing was said until Sir William had left the house.

Then Lord Alverstoke turned to his butler and said, "I have a wonderful surprise for you, Wicken, indeed, two surprises. My wife has been safely delivered of not one but two children, first a girl and then a boy. They are to be named Harriet and George."

For a few moments, Wicken was quite speechless, but then he found his voice.

"Twins! I should like to offer you my most sincere congratulations, milord! I hope that I may be allowed to meet the new members of the family tomorrow?"

"Of course. But now we should both go to bed. It has been quite a long day, one way and another."

Early on the following morning, Wicken sent one of the footmen to Lady Eliza's rented house with a personal note from her brother. When Jessamy came down from their guest bedroom to join her family for breakfast, he was greeted with the news that he was an uncle – twice over!

"Harriet *and* George! Frederica never dropped any hint to me that there were to be two babies. And Cousin Alverstoke had no idea either?"

"Apparently not, Jessamy, and I am sure that I know the reason why he was not told. Vernon was so anxious about the whole process that Frederica would not have wanted to burden him any further.

Once you have finished your meal, I suggest that I walk with you to Berkeley Square to meet the new arrivals. It will probably be best if the rest of my family wait for an invitation, as your sister is probably quite tired after all her exertions yesterday."

When they reached the house, Lady Eliza told Jessamy to go and see his sister straightaway and said that she would join them in a few minutes' time. He went up the staircase alone and knocked on the door of Frederica's bedroom. His sister called for him to enter, and he found her sitting back in the bed against the pillows, with both babies apparently sleeping peacefully in their bassinets. After greeting her, he went to pick up one of the tiny hands in his own, and the baby opened his eyes to look at Jessamy.

"That is George. So far, he has been the quiet one, Jessamy, waking only to suckle, and then to return to more sleeping. Harriet is both hungry and noisy, with a very healthy pair of lungs!"

"They are so little, but just wonderful! I do hope that I shall become a father myself one day."

"Sir William told me that new babies cannot see very well, so you are probably just a blur to him."

"Where is Cousin Alverstoke, Frederica?"

"He is in the library, writing a note to tell Felix the news. I shall be very interested to read our brother's reply!"

At this point, Lady Eliza knocked on the door and was admitted to the bedroom, so Jessamy slipped away to talk to Charles Trevor.

In the next few days, Lord Alverstoke spent as much time as he could with his wife and the babies. When no one else was present, he held his wife close to him in his arms. "I do miss having you with me in my bed, Frederica."

"Not long now before we can sleep together again, my darling."

With the two wet nurses now taking most of the burden of feeding the babies, Frederica began to resume her normal habits as far as was sensible. They were both kept busy with visitors coming to the house to see the new additions to the family, as she began to recover her strength.

Charis and Endymion hastened to town as soon as the news reached them, and they stayed with Alver and Frederica for a few days. "We are about to break the news to Lucretia that she will become a grandmother in a few months' time."

"I suggest that you brace yourselves for her reaction!" said the Marquis. "Please do not let her try to control your lives until the happy event."

The Jevingtons arrived with a gift for each of the new arrivals, Lady Augusta looking unusually tearful as she met Harriet and George. Carlton Buxted brought his youngest sister Kitty with him to represent their family. Frederica and Alver were surprised to see that their brother George also came with his siblings.

"I thought that I would like to meet my namesake, Cousin Alverstoke. Am I really allowed to hold him? How very little his hands and feet are!"

"We all began our lives that small, George," replied the Marquis, after he took the child from the young man, and replaced the baby in his bassinet.

His sister ventured a rather shy comment to Frederica.

"After I told Carlton that I would like to buy gifts for Harriet and George, he took me in his carriage for a special visit to the Pantheon Bazaar just off Oxford Street, and he gave me the money so that I could buy a toy for each of your babies. Would you like to have the parcels, Aunt Frederica?"

"Of course I would, Kitty. That was very kind of your brother to help you. Come over here, and put the parcels on the table, so that you can undo the wrappings for me."

Inside the parcels, there was a soft toy for each baby, and Frederica gave the young girl a big hug for her kindness.

Marietta came on the next day with her mother-in-law Lady Ormond to meet the new arrivals.

"How clever of you, Frederica, to produce both a girl and a boy at the same time! Vernon must be delighted with his new family," said Susan. "Edward sends his best wishes to you all, and he hopes to visit you soon. He will be away from home for a week or two on Government business."

Sally Jersey came to see the babies, and for a quiet 'coze' with her neighbour, telling Frederica in confidence that she thought that she might herself be increasing again. "I am hoping for a daughter this time, after having had three sons."

On Friday, Darcy Moreton and Sophia Stanton came up the stairs with the Marquis to see his wife and their family.

"I haven't brought my daughters with me, Frederica, as they would never want to leave the babies behind after our visit! Oh! I had quite forgotten how very small new babies are!"

Darcy took one of the little hands in his. "Small but perfect, Ver, and I can already see how precious they are to you, my friend."

"Yes, they are only just over a week old, Darcy, and yet they already seem to have been here for ever."

"Are you still planning to go to Alver Park as soon as Frederica is well enough to travel?"

"No, and yes. She has her final appointment with Sir William Knighton soon. If he is happy with her health, we intend to travel to Herefordshire first with Jessamy, to introduce Harriet and George to their great uncle Richard, and to Mr Salcombe of course, as well as to Frederica's close friends in the locality. After a few days at Graynard, we shall travel back into Wiltshire, to Alver Park. If you and Sophia, with her daughters, would like to visit us there for a few days, you will be very welcome."

When Sophia heard this suggestion, she was delighted, and was sure that her two girls would be ecstatic at the news!

"You will know, much better than I would, Sophia, that we shall need three coaches for the journeys to accommodate not only the family, and Emily and Alver's valet Knapp, but also the two wet nurses."

"Yes, it is amazing how much extra baggage even one small child can require!"

The day before Frederica's appointment with Sir William Knighton, the Marquis had an unexpected visitor.

"Who is it, Wicken?"

"Lord Buxted, milord. He is waiting for you in the library."

His nephew appeared to be very tense and strained as he turned away from standing by the window.

"Carlton, this is an unexpected pleasure?"

"I apologise for arriving without any warning, Alverstoke, but I am at my wit's end. My mother's health has been declining for some months, but she is refusing to see a doctor. I believe that she may fear that she has a malignant tumour, which is why your mother Esther died whilst you were still at school."

"I am not at all sure that I am the best person to assist you, cousin. Your mother and I have never had a very friendly relationship, so why have you come to me? Have you asked your Aunt Augusta?"

"My mother would hate Augusta knowing anything whatsoever about her health, so that is not an option, and I could not rely on my aunt keeping silent about any enquiry. Apart from Frederica's recent confinement, I seem to remember that you consulted Sir William Knighton when her brother Felix was unwell last year. Do you have a good opinion of the man? If so, I shall go and see him at his consulting rooms in Stratford Place to ask for his assistance."

"I have heard that his services are often used by members of the Royal Family, so that must be a recommendation. Yes, I was very pleased with his care of Frederica, so I suggest that you describe your mother's symptoms to Sir William, and hope for good news."

Lord Buxted left the house as abruptly as he had arrived. His cousin was normally a stickler for good manners, as his late father had been, so the Marquis realised how worried her son must be about Lady Buxted. Lord Alverstoke spoke to Wicken and asked him not to mention anything to Frederica about the visit.

However, Emily Leonard had recognised the coat of arms on the side of Carlton's carriage when she had looked out of a window, and she had told her mistress.

When Frederica next saw her husband, she asked why his cousin had called at their house.

"Carlton has another problem that he wanted to consult me about, but he requested that I should not mention it to anyone."

"Not George this time, I hope?"

"No, my love, nothing to do with George."

The Marquis heard nothing more from his nephew until the day before the family was to leave town for their journey to Herefordshire. Then a short terse note from Carlton arrived at Berkeley Square.

'I made an appointment to see Sir William, and he has visited my mother. His verdict is not encouraging. Buxted.'

Once safely arrived at the Graynard estate, Frederica and Alver were inclined to agree with Sophia that travelling with their young children was going to be much more complicated than their journeys had been in the past.

"We just need to make several long lists each time, my love," observed Alver, after they had unpacked their baggage, settled the two wet nurses into their accommodation, fed both Harriet and George and put them into their bassinets, and collapsed with Jessamy into chairs in the drawing room for a glass of wine before dinner.

"Nevertheless," said Jessamy, "I am really looking forward to becoming a parent one day. The babies are already changing so much as they grow bigger, and I am trying to get a smile from George. Harriet is rather harder work, as all that she seems to want to do is eat!"

Frederica's uncle Richard Winsham and his wife had been invited to visit Graynard on the first day after their arrival. With them they brought Jessamy's dog Lufra for a short visit. He had been with the Winshams since Alver had decided that the large, rather boisterous, dog should not live in the same house as the new arrivals.

Having studied both babies carefully, and with a twinkle in his eyes, he said, "Your Harriet does remind me a little of her namesake; there is a facial resemblance at least. I was about 6 years old when my youngest sister was born. What I don't remember was your mother as a baby being so very noisy, Frederica!"

"We have found that there is an easy cure for that, uncle – milk and more milk. She is just hungry all the time, which explains why she is now heavier than her brother. Perhaps she takes after Felix, who always wants to eat. By contrast, we think that George is going to be the strong, silent type of fellow!"

"You may find a solution for Harriet by sitting her upright on your knee, Frederica, so that she can look around her for a while, even though she will not be able to see clearly for a few more weeks. I seem to recall that Felix from an early age always wanted to know what was happening. Perhaps she is bored already with lying in her bassinet! What is your opinion, Alverstoke?"

"All I care about is that Frederica, and both the babies, continue to be healthy, Richard."

"I shall be interested to see Mr Salcombe's reactions when he comes tomorrow," said Jessamy. "As a bachelor, and with no siblings of his own, he may not know very much about young children."

Having settled the lawyer on the sofa in the drawing room the next morning, Frederica was rather mischievous when she asked him to hold the babies, one on each arm. The expression on his face as he looked down at them was priceless; Alver thought that Salcombe might have tears in his eyes.

Eventually he said, "As neither of you has parents still alive, perhaps you would allow me to be an honorary grandfather, Frederica, Alverstoke, if that is not too presumptuous a suggestion?"

They told Mr Salcombe that they would be delighted to agree, and that his suggestion was a wonderful idea. He might have held the babies all morning if the wet nurses had not come to collect their charges.

On the next day, Jessamy rode into Ross-on-Wye for a discussion with Mr Salcombe about the Graynard estate, whilst Alver and

Frederica took the carriage to show their new family to neighbours who lived nearby.

Three days later, it was time to assemble all their baggage again and to set off for the journey to Alver Park.

After having made several visits to the Wiltshire estate, the mansion was much more familiar to Frederica. Jessamy went riding in the park with the Marquis each morning, whilst Frederica rested in a comfortable chair on the terrace, sometimes with Harriet and George in their cribs near her.

On other days, leaving their babies in the care of their nurses, they asked Curry to take them in the new barouche up to the summerhouse to see the view to the south. There they made good use of the new sofa for a delightful private interlude for an hour or so, before walking back down the hill to see their children.

Later that week, Charles Trevor arrived from town with some correspondence that needed their attention. One letter had been franked by Carlton Buxted's signature as a peer, and Frederica asked her husband what his nephew's message contained.

Unusually, he hesitated before replying to her.

"I did not tell you before now, Frederica, but my sister Louisa has been ill for some months. Having been to see me to ask my advice, Carlton insisted that she should be attended by Sir William Knighton, to establish what the problem was. Sadly, Sir William told him that she had the same fatal malady as our mother – a malignant tumour – with no useful treatment available. My nephew's letter is to tell me that Louisa died at her home in Grosvenor Place on Monday night."

"Oh! How sad, and very difficult for their family, especially for Kitty and her two elder sisters. Carlton will now have to be both mother and father to George and the three girls. He can be rather staid, but he is a very conscientious man, Alver."

"Yes, I agree with you. He may approach our sister Augusta and Humphrey Jevington for their support. I will travel to London without you to stay at Alverstoke House for several days, once I know the date for the funeral. Would you like to invite Charis to keep you company in my absence? I believe that Endymion is busy with the plans for the house on his new landholding."

A second letter arrived from Lord Buxted, to explain that there was to be a family discussion soon after the funeral, to decide what should happen to his sisters after their mother's death.

Charis arrived in Wiltshire to be with her sister, and they had a few days together, enjoying the chance to care for the babies in the afternoons, to give the wet nurses some leisure time to explore the park.

After Charis had returned to Buckinghamshire, the Marquis arrived at Alver Park from London to tell his wife what had been decided about the Buxted children.

"There was a long discussion after the funeral about the best arrangements to be made after Louisa's death, Frederica. Carlton, George Buxted, Humphrey Jevington and I sat around the dining table in her house in Grosvenor Place, and you may be surprised at what was decided.

My widowed cousin Mrs Osmington has agreed to move into Louisa's house to look after Jane and her brother. George had intended to join the Army as soon as he leaves Harrow later this year, but it was his own suggestion that he should wait 12 months before doing so, to keep his eldest sister company. Jane is the family member who will be most affected by her mother's death, but Mrs Osmington is a motherly woman who has grown-up children of her own. She is a very different person to Louisa, but that may be a very good idea. Jane cannot change her red hair and rather freckled complexion, but she would benefit from developing a more forgiving personality.

Augusta and Humphrey Jevington will take over the care for the two younger Buxted girls in their home, as part of their family. Perhaps that will be some consolation to them for their children who died of smallpox many years ago. Their daughter Anna is to be married to Mr Redmure later this year, so that event will be an excellent distraction for Maria and Kitty. Augusta and Humphrey's son Gregory Sandridge is a kind boy, very like his father in personality, so he should be helpful to the girls."

"Are you planning to do anything to assist Carlton, Alver?"

"Yes. I have agreed to keep in very regular contact with George Buxted, and hopefully to provide some guidance for him as he accompanies Jane during her next Season. Being so young, he might get into bad company, so I will keep a careful eye on what he gets up to. I have also said that Maria and Kitty will be welcome to accompany us to Alver Park from time to time, to give Humphrey and Augusta some rest from their responsibilities for caring for the girls. I hope that you don't mind my having made that suggestion?"

"Of course I don't mind, Alver. Maria and Kitty will be very welcome – they can be 'nursemaids' to assist us with Harriet and George as they get older!"

"My sister Eliza has written to say that she will invite Jane to visit the Kentmere's estate. She believes that she could transform her by introducing her to country life, and to young men who are robust enough to stand up to her if she tries to pretend to be someone who she is not."

"That could be very interesting but, if anyone can change Jane for the better, it must be your youngest sister!"

"Despite what Louisa used to say to everyone, Frederica, there is no shortage of money, but Carlton will be managing the finances, as well as needing to keep in contact with his siblings. He, of course, has lived in his own house since he was 21, and he was understandably not at all enthusiastic about the idea of moving back into his mother's home in Grosvenor Place."

Darcy Moreton and Sophia Stanton, with her two daughters, had postponed their visit until the Marquis had returned to Wiltshire, but now they arrived at Alver Park for a short stay with their friends. Sophia's daughters were rather too keen to carry the babies around the house, but they were allowed to sing quiet lullabies when Harriet refused to go to sleep.

The elder daughter, Primrose, was interested in learning to ride, so Jessamy was deputed to give her some lessons in the stable yard on a small pony that he had borrowed from a neighbouring family.

All too soon, the four weeks that Alver and Frederica had planned to spend at their country estate came to an end, and they returned to London with Jessamy, Harriet and George. They all settled back into Alverstoke House, and gradually Frederica and Alver became accustomed to being the parents of a young family.

Alver particularly enjoyed soothing the babies when they were unhappy by holding them against his shoulder to comfort them, either sitting down, or walking backwards and forwards across the nursery.

Richard Winsham had shown the Marquis how to seat his daughter or his son upright on his knee, with his right hand supporting their back, and his left hand under their chin, so that they could be aware of their surroundings, and hear what was happening in the room.

"Both of them seem to like that position, Alverstoke, and it is a particularly effective solution for a baby like Harriet, who seems to get bored very easily."

Frederica encouraged Alver to talk to the babies whenever he could find the time, and it seemed that they now recognised his voice, as they would turn their heads towards him when he spoke.

She could see from her husband's expression how much holding his children meant to him, as it did for her to see them together.

As the first anniversary of their wedding came closer, Alver had been considering what present he might give to his wife to mark the occasion. But first, he asked Frederica whether she would like to have a party.

"No, Alver, my preference would be to have a quiet dinner at home for just the two of us, with our favourite foods and wines to be served in the private dining room."

"Very well, Frederica. That sounds a lovely idea, and much better than having to make polite conversation with other people on our anniversary day!"

They decided to wear their wedding finery for the dinner – with two special requirements. Alver asked Frederica to wear her hair down at the back, as she had done for him on the wedding day. She asked him not to wear his jacket, so that she could see the full glory of his handsome embroidered waistcoat!

As was their habit every evening before dinner when they were at home, they visited Harriet and George in the nursery to make sure that they were settled for the night. Their son was sleeping peacefully, but Harriet was fretting a little.

Alver lifted her from her bassinet, and held her against his shoulder, walking back and forth across the room until his daughter's eyes began to close and she fell asleep. Then he quietly laid her down, and tucked her blanket gently around the child.

"I wonder if she will continue to be hungry all the time, Frederica, perhaps like your brother Felix?"

"As long as she does not take after him in any other respect, I won't mind. I doubt if mediaeval warfare would be a suitable accomplishment for our daughter!"

The Marquis had wanted to have a special gift created for his wife and, after a private discussion with Garrards in their premises in Albemarle Street, he had asked Frederica's abigail Emily in confidence to lay out his wife's wedding dress on a bed in one of the guest rooms. Then one of Garrards' skilled craftsmen came secretly to the house to copy onto a piece of paper the green and white pattern that had been embroidered around the borders of the dress.

All this had been done without Frederica's knowledge so, when the day of the wedding anniversary came and they had enjoyed the special dinner that they had requested, Alver asked Wicken to bring in his carefully wrapped present to give to her.

"What is this, my darling? A special gift for me? May I open it?"

He smiled at her with a twinkle in his eyes. "Of course you may. I hope that the contents will be a welcome surprise!"

When the present was revealed, she was speechless with delight.

His gift was a beautiful oblong box in gold, about the length of her hand. The border around the hinged lid was a miniature copy of the embroidered lilies of the valley on her wedding dress, in emeralds and diamonds, and in the centre of the lid the initials 'H' and 'G' had been intertwined.

"I hope that this box will always remind you of our first year together, my darling Frederica. You have made me so happy during the past 12 months, including our children's births. This is a token of my transformation from a lonely rake to a very contented husband and father!"

Frederica rose from her chair, and went to embrace him, with tears in her eyes – tears of joy! Finally, she spoke.

"Dear Alver, we have had such an eventful year together with births as well as deaths, and we have enjoyed so many entertainments, not to mention living with Felix and his enthusiasms for mechanical devices and mediaeval warfare! I look forward to seeing what our future together will bring us!"

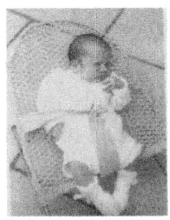

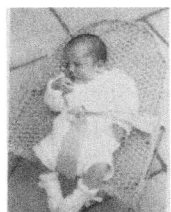

A few weeks earlier, a child named Alexandrina Victoria had been born in London. Her father, the Duke of Kent, died 8 months later. Perhaps, one day, the story about Harriet and George will be continued in 1837, when they will all be 18 years of age.

Postscript

Lord and Lady Jersey had 7 surviving children, born between 1808 and 1828, their 4 sons being followed by 3 daughters. Lord Jersey died in 1859, only 3 weeks before the death from tuberculosis of his eldest son and heir, also named George. Lady Jersey died at 38, Berkeley Square in 1867.

The building housing **Astley's Amphitheatre** was demolished in 1893, and the land is now occupied by the modern buildings of the world famous St Thomas' Hospital at the southern end of Westminster Bridge, opposite the Houses of Parliament and the River Thames.

George Parker Bidder was about 14 years of age when he was sponsored by Sir Henry Jardine to attend Edinburgh University After he left aged 18, George had a very successful career, and he was involved in many major engineering schemes both at home and abroad.

George Bidder worked with Thomas Telford, with George and Robert Stephenson, and with Isambard Kingdom Brunel. He designed and built the Royal Victoria Docks in London, and was known for completing his projects on time and within budget. He died at home in Dartmouth, Devon in 1878.

Burlington House, the home of Lord Burlington, is set well back from the north side of Piccadilly in central London. The building has been occupied since 1868 by the Royal Academy of Arts, which was founded by King George III a hundred years earlier, on 10 December 1768.

The Academy's Summer Exhibition, now held each year from June to August, is the longest continuously staged exhibition of contemporary art in the world.

The author **Georgette Heyer**, born in 1902, wrote more than 50 novels including 'Frederica' before she died in London in 1974. More than a million copies of her books were said to have been sold worldwide in that year.

Printed in Great Britain
by Amazon